*To fabulous friends and their fantastic beasts
who lent me their homes so I could write this*

HODDER CHILDREN'S BOOKS

First published in Great Britain in 2020 by Hodder and Stoughton

1 3 5 7 9 10 8 6 4 2

Text copyright © Patrice Lawrence, 2020

The moral rights of the author have been asserted.

A CIP catalogue record for this book is available from the British Library.

ISBN 978 1 444 95474 6

Typeset in Adobe Caslon by Avon DataSet Ltd, Arden Court, Alcester, Warwickshire

Printed and bound in Great Britain by Clays Ltd, Elcograf S.p.A.

The paper and board used in this book
are made from wood from responsible sources.

Hodder Children's Books
An imprint of Hachette Children's Group
Part of Hodder and Stoughton
Carmelite House
50 Victoria Embankment
London EC4Y 0DZ

An Hachette UK Company
www.hachette.co.uk

www.hachettechildrens.co.uk

1

Becks, Mum said, **fix up. Don't complain, just fix up. We've been clearing up after you for fifteen years**.

That ain't strictly true. Well, for Mum, it's true, but Justin's more recent. It's been seven years clearing up after me for him. Anyhow, I got home from school and found toast and Marmite balanced on the edge of the table. The cornflakes box knocked over like the cereal's trying to escape. Milk left out. It was like breakfast tried to commit suicide.

I'd sent a message to Mum straight away.

Silva didn't do the clearing up. She's in her room sulking.

That's when Mum told me to fix up. When I replied, she said the plane's taking off and the steward's walking towards her with a look on his face. I know Mum. She'll turn the phone off because she can never find flight mode and then shove it in the seat pocket in front. She won't turn it on again until her and Justin land in Japan. That's gonna be more than twelve hours.

I suppose I should leave them alone. It's the first few hours of their honeymoon. If it's still a honeymoon when you're heading out nearly two months after you got married. But Silva, though! I was a witness, standing right next to her when she promised our parents she'd make sure I was good while they're away. She even looked them in the eye when she promised. But what's she done instead? She's left dying breakfast all over the kitchen for me to find when I get home from school. I don't want her setting that as a mood for the next two weeks. Though, thinking about it, even mush-up cornflakes and bad milk is better than some of the moods she's been cracking recently.

Damn. It's gonna be a long two weeks if Silva keeps her sulk up all that time.

I knock on her bedroom door, not too hard, though. I hate the fact I got to knock at all. It's a recent thing. She says she don't want me to rush in and disturb her studying. *Studying*. Like I'm gonna believe that. The last few times I was allowed to walk in without knocking, my sister was lying on her bed studying the inside of her eyelids. The time before that she was studying her own sweet face in the mirror. Proper studying, like she'd seen a really small, but seriously deep blackhead that no tweezers forged on earth would ever shift. A few months ago, she tried to get Justin to put a bolt on her door, but he refused. (Though that's probably because Mum's better with a hand drill than he is.) Now Silva just pushes a chair against it. That's all the time now. Even Justin, her very own father, has to knock.

Silva don't answer. She could have gone out, but the front

door wasn't double-locked when I came in. I could knock harder. I *want* to knock harder. I stop myself. *Remember, Becks!* Mum and Justin have only just started their honeymoon. I mustn't topload my stress on to the first day. I need to stretch my grudges out over the next fortnight. And Silva having a mood ain't exactly news.

I clear up the breakfast, but I do it loud so I know Silva can hear me. She don't feel guilty enough to come out and help, though. I go into the sitting room and curl myself up in the armchair. It's weird being in here by myself. It's too quiet. I turn on the TV, but it's *Eggheads*. Those giant heads looking down at their quiz teammates freak me out. Too much face detail, man. I don't want to see no strangers' pores.

I turn off the TV and read Mum's messages again. Rome airport is boring and the staff haven't got manners. Her bra wire set off the alarm and the woman security guard gave her the roughest, most public handle she's ever had. I love my mother, but that's a bit too much information.

I wonder if Mum sent Silva her own message, or maybe Justin did instead. Mum to me. Justin to Silva. Even though me and Silva are sharing parents, it don't always feel that way.

Maybe Silva's doing exactly what I'm doing in her own room, reading her dad's texts, the same way I'm reading my mum's in here. She could be feeling down after saying goodbye to Justin at the airport. He always says I should give her space when she gets like that.

3

It's gonna take a while to get used to Mum and Justin being properly married. I don't know why. They've been together since I was seven and he's lived here since I was nine. A wedding shouldn't change things, though Mum did give me a hundred quid to get my hair braided and she's never done that before. I took some sharp snaps of my new style when it was fresh. Now it's all itching like hell, but I can't take it out yet. I've got to get Mum's money's worth. Silva didn't need nothing done to her hair so she got money for wedding clothes. She went up Fonthill Road and found a bargain on two dresses. So I wore a tux. Silva wore a cream bodycon number. It almost looked like we were the ones getting married. Tell you what, I almost did wear a dress to crumble them gay girl stereotypes, but when I saw Silva in her gear – yeah, she did look good – I decided there and then to stick with my suit. I want clothes that let me walk. And breathe.

The intercom in the hallway buzzes. It's the grocery shop delivery. I don't know why Mum thought she had to stock up even more. If I add one more tin of beans to the cupboard, the whole thing's gonna sink through the floor and squash Mr Bottler on his sofa below.

It's a short, white woman who's hoisting our bags out the crates today. It's never been a woman before. Her jacket looks a bit too big, like they only got sizes to fit men. Even so, I got a feeling she don't take crap from no one. She smiles at me and says, 'Good afternoon.' Her accent sounds Polish. She offers to bring the shopping into the kitchen, but as our kitchen's a) about three centimetres away from the front door and b) too small to fit me, the delivery woman and the groceries, I let her leave the bags in the hallway. It's tempting to stack them all up against Silva's door just in case she needs to get out. *Yeah, Silva, both of us can block up doorways.*

Instead, I put away the frozen stuff – vegan pretend fish fingers and soya mince for Silva and proper, full-fat chocolate ice cream for me – and have a rustle around in the fridge bags. Sausages, real and pretend. A pack of grated cheese. Olive oil spread. Basil. Peach yoghurt. It was like Mum plonked Azog on the keyboard when she was ordering and told her to jump around a bit.

That reminds me. Where is that cat? She should be keeping me company now everyone else has deserted me.

Is it mean to leave the store cupboard stuff for Silva to put away? I've done more than my bit and she's supposed to be the older sister here.

The thing is, I always sort of wanted a sister until I got one. I never wanted another dad, but when Justin came I got one anyway. Before that, my family was just Mum and me, even though I've actually got more parents than most people got cousins.

Starting with the dads, there's DNA-Dad, of course. He left my mum for another girlfriend when I was a baby, but boy that DNA came back to haunt him. Soon after Justin came to live with us, I dropped his new iPhone out the window. His camera was better at night shots and I wanted a decent picture of the moon. It was a genuine accident. It slipped through my fingers and hit the copper who was just coming out the Costcutter below. He was taking his first sip from his Coke can when he got clonked on the head. He wasn't happy. Neither was the phone. Or Justin.

I got taken to the police station as the copper wouldn't believe it was an accident. Mum was furious but agreed to them swabbing out my mouth. I didn't get charged, but DNA-Dad did. When the police database went 'ping', suddenly the feds knew who'd been wrestling cash boxes from security guards for the last four years.

Now I've got Justin. Justin's seen things. Maybe Justin still does. I reckon he necked a bucket-load of drugs when he set up illegal raves in the 80s. I asked Silva about it, but she said she doesn't know. She was born after Justin had settled down and started running media projects for kids who'd been thrown out of school. Silva's mum was a lawyer who came in to talk to the kids about their rights. She was. She's not a lawyer no more. She's not an alive person no more. It hurts when I think about it.

Because, my mum—

If anything ever happened to my mum—

Technically, I have other mums. DNA-Dad's been married twice, but I wasn't invited to none of them weddings. Me and them mums wouldn't recognise each other if we were standing side by side in a queue in Argos.

But my mum—

Yeah, she's DNA-Mum too, but DNA stands for Do Not Associate her with the wasteman who seeded me.

How can I explain what my mum means to me?

When I was five, I kept having nightmares about the apocalypse. I couldn't even pronounce the word, but I knew it was gonna come. Death rays, poison gas, nuclear fallout, the whole bag. Night after night, I'd wake up crying, sometimes even wet the bed, until Mum invented the Indestructible Duvet Cover. It was a massive, faded yellow thing we'd half-inched from Grandma. Every night after my bath, she'd dim down my night light, we'd wriggle inside the cover and she'd do up the poppers over our heads. That way, she said, no bad chemical voodoo would seep through and twist up our brains. Then she'd tell me a story. Not from a book. A brain and heart story. And in every story, I was the hero who made things right.

So when Mum said Silva was coming to live with us because Silva's mum had got ill, I wanted to make things right. Mum was really happy when Justin was around. I liked him and wanted Mum to stay happy. So it was my mission to make Silva happy too. You don't need to share blood to start hurting when your sister's ghosting you.

I stomp past the bags of baked beans and live-forever (as long as you don't open it) oat milk and stand outside Silva's door. I hold up my fist to give it the full knockdown. Then I think about it some more. Her parents were together for ages but never got round to getting married and then it was too late. But now Justin's married *my* mum instead of Silva's. How would I feel if that was me?

I let my hand drop down. I'll leave her alone until she's ready.

I go back into the kitchen and scrape the crispy lumps of old Sheba out the cat bowl. It's like Azog's too lazy to bother chewing and just licks the gravy off. Last year, Silva tried to turn my cat vegan with this special cat food. Azog crept into Silva's room and defiled her bed badly, I reckon on purpose. My cat got a lifetime ban from Silva's room but a happy return to her meaty chunks.

I return to the sitting room. Isn't that Mum's sandals and bra under the TV? She must have given up trying to jam them into her rucksack. Suddenly, I need to sit down. Mum's married. She's backpacking through east Asia, eight hours ahead of me. My sister's locked herself in her room and she don't want to talk to me.

I wish Mum was here with me now.

2

It's been two hours. Silva hasn't done sulking. I don't know what to do with myself. I'm getting kinda hungry. Mum's left some frozen bricks of stuff in old takeaway plastic in the freezer. It's from when she got that electric soup-maker. Most of it's greeny-yellow-brown and ALL of it's gonna stay right there until Mum gets back and then she and Justin can eat it. I remember there's four and a half kilos of pasta in the cupboard from Mum's three-for-two shops. All that pasta and tins, man, I could build a real-size model of Rivendell with enough penne left over to make Saruman's tower. I know that because Raych once took it all out and built a baby skate ramp across the kitchen with it. Then she used some wrinkled-up potatoes to knock it down.

Maybe I can boil up the pasta and mix it with some of the spicy tofu stuff that Silva made on Tuesday. Or maybe I can't. Maybe I definitely won't. Now McDonald's does delivery, it's damn rude if people like me don't use it.

If I was a better person, I'd slip a note under Silva's door and see if she wants anything. Their chips are vegan. I checked.

I should just relax. I've been looking forward to this moment for weeks. No, man, *years*. That moment when I get total control of the sitting room and I can invite round a guest. When I've imagined this before, I had a girl in my mind to snuggle down with on that empty sofa. It was Chen in Year 10, though she's head girl now and always was gonna be out of my league. Then there was that thing with me and Jocelyn at Cruz's party last month. I was kissed and dumped in an hour. The girl thought I should be flattered because she kissed a black girl and she liked it. I shoulda worn some Chapstick just for the occasion. Mango. Because that's exotic, right, Jocelyn?

But home feels so quiet I'd even have Jocelyn here right now, as long as she kept her black-curious self on the armchair over there.

The thing is, I could have hung out in central with the others this evening, but I came back because I was being the good sister. I wanted to send a selfie of me and Silva making our dinners to Mum so when she turned on her phone in Japan, she knew we were all right. Instead, I'm just sitting here feeling cross. I could still head out and meet the others but by now they'd be on their own vibe. I'd have to bust in halfway through their conversations. I don't feel like playing catch up.

So what now? Can I do the Middle Earth marathon again? Go to my room, dig out the old DVDs and give them a shine. (Last time I tried to watch *Fellowship of the Ring* it got stuck when Elrond raised his eyebrows and wouldn't move.) I could sit back and watch Gandalf doing his 'spin and stab' orc-killer move. And yeah, there's always Arwen. But then, is my mind set for fifteen hours of Orlando Bloom's elf expression? Elf sees the One Ring and he's perturbed. Elf gets charged by a warg and he's perturbed. Gandalf returns from the dead and Legolas? You feeling a bit perturbed, elf? Raych says he looks like he didn't have time to put on his pants then remembered he's got to kick his leg up high a few times.

Raych! Yeah, she'll come round and watch it with me. I call her. Her phone rings once and sounds like it's going to messages but then she picks up.

'You okay, Becks?'

'It's too quiet here.'

'Yeah, it must be with everyone gone. Not enjoying it?'

'Silva won't come out her room. It's like she don't want to talk to me.'

'Watching people go through the departure gates is pretty crap, Becks. Maybe it's triggered other stuff. She's got things on her mind.'

'Silva's always got things on her mind. Sometimes it's like her mind's the only one that's allowed to have things on it.'

I touch my lips. Those words just came out from my mouth? Two minutes ago, I felt sorry for Silva, but now I'm on the phone to Raych bad-mouthing her.

I wait for Raych to agree with me. Our awkward silence spreads like evil over Gondor.

She says, 'I know it's not always easy for you, Becks. But sometimes, you just have to be patient.'

11

'I am . . .' Then I laugh. 'I'm not, am I?'

'That's why I love you, Becks.'

'D'you love me enough to come round and watch Legolas stare a bit again?'

'Sorry, hun. Mum's got things planned for tonight.'

'Oh. Okay.'

'Call me later if you need me.'

She rings off. Of course she has things. Girls like Raych always have things. Her mum sent her to Mandarin lessons from Year 3 and made her go up to grade six on the flute *and* guitar. She don't do much music now but that's because she's busy winning all the medals for Bow Bridge swimming club.

So unless Silva shifts herself, it's gonna be me and my cat again, if I can find her. I stand by the window, scanning the block opposite. Sometimes I see Azog sitting on the wall or, when she's doing full cat facety, laying across Mr Phan's windowsill, her bum hanging over the edge like she's threatening his flower patch. Azog's not there tonight. No one's out. It's like an apocalypse really did sweep through the estate and no one told me. I look up at the sky. The clouds are low and Mum and Justin are somewhere above them.

I go back and stand outside Silva's room. She's been in there for more than three hours now. She hasn't been out for snacks or even a pee – not unless she installed her own chemical toilet next to her desk. I wouldn't put it past her these days.

Except something bad could have happened in there. What if she's fainted or done something to herself? I've seen all the memes and messages about being kind and listening if someone you love is struggling. I've even sent most of them on to my friends. But what *am* I doing? I'm just standing here.

Why?

Because that time I walked in on her last month, she was so damn vicious. How was I supposed to know she had a boy in there? I didn't even get a proper look at him because she screamed at me to get out so fast. I was shocked, man! It was the first time Silva's brought anyone home, boy or girl.

Or, she could have been murdered. Jesus! Why the hell did that come into my mind? The front door wasn't double-locked, though. A murderer could have got in if they knew how to work the lock. But you're more likely to be murdered by someone you know. That's what they say, yeah? It's not the strangers we've got to be scared of.

Right, that's it. I knock again. I knock hard. I call her name. Nothing. I press my ear against her door. Yes, there is a noise. *Is that?* It can't be . . .

I open the door and Azog saunters out. She stops, looks at me then does some more sauntering into the kitchen. I sniff. I can't help it. It's not my imagination, but cats can look guilty. If you know them well, you can tell what their face is doing under all that fur. Azog's face says GUILT in letters so big, they should have their own shop. I don't smell nothing, but Azog's chief of the stink surprise. Her full name ain't Azog the Defiler for nothing. She comes back out from the kitchen and winds herself round my feet. I pick her up and she puts her front paws on my shoulder. I kiss her head and whisper in her ear.

'You any idea what's going on? Like, how you ended up in there?'

Mum and Justin, they must have been all stressed out and in a hurry. Mum hadn't even finished packing before I left for school. No wonder they forgot to lock the front door properly. They were never gonna remember to check on Azog.

Silva's door's open. My brain nudges me. She's not in there. All the time I've been hanging around and trying not to disturb her, she wasn't here at all.

So what? She's eighteen. She's a grown woman. She can be wherever she wants, do whatever she wants.

But she was supposed to come back from the airport to be with me. She didn't. She didn't even warn me first.

I go and feed Azog. I pick her up and her whiskers tickle my cheek. She wiggles free from my arms and jumps down, turns to look up at me and meows. I know her meows like I know her expressions.

Open duck flesh pouch, human!

I feed Azog and then send Silva a text. I pour myself a pint of pineapple smoothie and go into my room. I'm not gonna latch the front door, in case Silva comes back. Man, I am tempted though. I want her to sleep on the stairs outside for making me feel so bad. When my McDonald's arrives, I eat it by myself in the kitchen. I'm not even that hungry no more. I go back to my room and put on the first Hobbit film. As I crawl under my duvet, Azog jumps up to watch it with me. She likes to see the pale orc astride a white warg.

3

Man, I don't like waking up in the flat alone. Don't take this as a dis, Azog. I'm really glad you stayed with me all night, but you don't exactly make great conversation. And you don't do much to help out neither. You don't check why the fridge is humming so loud. Maybe it's always been like that but we're all louder so usually I don't notice. You don't check to see if the window in the sitting room is shut, or if the tap in the bathroom sink has been closed tight so it don't drip all night. And you didn't even laugh, cat, when we saw Legolas's face in *The Desolation of Smaug* and he looks like his cheeks got ironed.

And you know what else you're not doing? You're not telling me how you ended up locked in my sister's room. And more important, Azog, did you hear Silva make plans for the weekend? Because she sure didn't tell me if she has.

And she still hasn't bothered messaging me to let me know where she is.

But it don't matter. Why should I care? If she's gonna do her thing, I'm gonna do mine. It's the first weekend of the Easter holidays. I made my promises too. Revision first, then fun. But thanks to Silva, I'm not doing neither. I'm in the kitchen putting away all the store cupboard items because

16

I got fed up stubbing my toe on chickpeas.

At least Mum's messaged me. They landed okay, but they've still got to find their apartment. She says she feels weird and out of place. *Yeah, Mum. I feel you on that one.* I bet Justin's getting a few looks, though. Even in London, a brown Vietnamese guy turns heads. They're gonna head out to Kyoto on Thursday. She sent me links to the places she's gonna visit and screen-grabbed her Japanese Duolingo score to show me how well she's doing. I want to tell her that Silva didn't come home. She broke her promise and left me alone. I wonder if Justin has heard from her. Instead I tell Mum to send me a snap of the apartment when they find it.

So, I'm not gonna think of Silva.

I'm not gonna think of Silva.

Hell, where are you, Silva?

I message her. I stare at my phone, but Silva can't be staring at hers because nothing comes back.

She's staying with friends, that's all. Though, I didn't even know she had friends. Great, now my mind's bouncing back to bad places. Like, she's been abducted and she's locked up in a cellar praying that I've called the police.

Calm down, Becks. I know them things happen, but it don't mean it's happened to Silva. Maybe it's more simple. She could have left me a secret note and she shut Azog in there knowing I'd look for her. She couldn't leave it anywhere else in the flat in case our parents saw it first.

Yeah! That's it! I just need to go into Silva's room and find it.

But one does not simply walk into Silva's room. Even if the door *is* open. It's like there's invisible police tape across it or a booby trap that's gonna fire arrows into my eyes as soon as my toe taps her carpet.

But I have to do it. I have no choice, because AZOG, YOU TROLL-SAC OF A CAT! I've just got the whiff. Why the hell am I feeding you good quality cat food if what comes out the other end stinks like that? And I bet you've done it right at the back near the wall. It's bad enough crossing into Silva's territory, but thanks to you, I got to dig through her secret places. Silva might have stuff under her bed that she wants to stay hidden.

I take a step into the room. I do have two reasons to be there now. To un-defile the carpet and to see if I can find out where Silva's gone. I still can't do it, though. It's like the invisible police tape has turned into the Wakanda force field and I can't push past it.

I need to talk to someone, maybe get them to make me cross through it. I scroll through my contacts. Savannah? Rianna? China? (Man, China.) I love them, but they don't really know Silva. She's not easy to explain.

I message Raych. I know it's only half eight, but she's gonna be up doing enrichment stuff.

Silva didn't come home.

18

Raych calls back a few minutes later. I'm still standing by Silva's door.

'Rudbeckia,' she says.

'Rafaella,' I say.

I smile because it's like we're ten again and we've just discovered I'm named after a flower and she's named after a turtle. (Her mum says it's after the artist, Raphael, but her dad reckons it's really the hero in a half-shell.) Our codewords for each other are our full names. No one else but our families know both of them.

She says, 'Sorry I couldn't come over last night. My aunt and uncle were round. I promised Mum I'd distract them while she got on with the cooking.'

'The racist uncle?'

'Yeah, him. He'd been for a walk down Whitechapel just so he could take photos of all the women in hijab and complain about it.'

'Families can be crap sometimes?'

'Yeah,' she sighs. 'He even goes on to Dad about it, like he expects Dad to agree.'

Raych can tell me this because she knows my family's had its own share of crapness. Grandparents from all over the world may look good in picture books, but them old people sometimes have views about the others who don't look like them. We got Trini-Indian, Bajan-African, my DNA dad's a mixed-race bloke from a children's home in Gloucester and when you throw Justin in the mix, there's Vietnamese.

Though that's just his dad. His mum's second-generation Ghanaian from Croydon. Sounds like we should be in an advert to make the world a better place, but, nah. If anyone wants a book about how folk from different places insult each other, I'm your girl.

Silva's mum, Marnie, was white and English. She would never insult anyone and according to Silva, her family welcomed Justin, though I don't think they knew much about him being a teenage wasteman. Luckily, he did his business before the internet happened. Silva said her mum's family traced themselves back five generations to a farm in East Anglia. None of them generations made an impact on the way Silva looks, though. She's a thinner, taller version of her dad.

Raych says, 'Have you heard from Silva yet?'

'No.'

'Do you have any idea where she is?'

'Maybe she's got some friends I don't know about.'

'So that's all right, then.'

'No, Raych! If she's got them, I don't know about them! She could be anywhere. It's just . . . it just don't feel right. She never stays out. If she's not coming back, she should say.'

I leave a gap for Raych to agree. I wait. The gap's getting deeper than the mines of Moria. I almost expect to see a load of orcs and a fiery hell creature crawling out my phone.

'You still there?' I ask.

'Yeah. Sorry. I was just thinking. Maybe, I don't know, Justin's a bit too over-protective? What if Silva's doing her own thing for the first time?'

'She can do her own thing and still tell me!'

'Yeah, but . . . Leave it a little bit. She's bound to get in touch. What are you up to tonight?'

'A few of us are hanging out at Savannah's. Hannah, Rianna, Sienna. Maybe China, too. Do you want to come?'

'I'm not sure.'

'D'you think you're gonna be the only straight girl?'

I touch my mouth again, but it's too late. The traitor words have already jumped out. Why does that happen with Raych?

'You being serious, Becks?'

'I . . . I . . . thought you might feel left out. But Hannah's into boys. And Sienna's not made up her mind yet.'

'Of course I'm gonna feel left out, Becks.' Raych laughs. 'You're going to be making a beeline for China.'

'Not really, I . . .'

'You've kind of mentioned her a lot recently. And it's the way you said, "Maybe China, too."'

'It's that obvious?'

'Only to me.' I wait for her to say something else about me and China, but, nah, she's done. 'Look, Becks, I know you're worried. I'm sure Silva's okay. I have to go but I'll have a think about where she could be. I'll phone again soon okay?'

I watch the green phone disappear and the red phone take its place. Call ended. I feel myself relax. Raych has my back, even though I'd forgotten to ask her about going into Silva's room. But I can't leave that poo there to fester. I just hope Silva stays away long enough for me to air it out. I go into the kitchen and assemble my cat crap kit. Gloves, plastic bags, kitchen towel, scrubby pad, washing-up liquid, Febreze and a bonus, the nose mask Mum used when she was sanding down that chair she found by the wheelie bin.

Sometimes I think it's weird that me and Raych are still mates. We're an unexpected friendship, a bit like Legolas and Gimli. (Guess which one is the tall, thin, elf-y one that's good at everything and which one would fall off the other side of a horse if they ever managed to get up in the first place.)

I take a deep breath and walk right into Silva's room. Then I let that breath out quick as I realise that it's a bad idea. I'm definitely gonna censor Azog's food flavours in the future. Maybe that vegan stuff wasn't so bad after all.

Silva's style is so different from mine. I've still got a full-size cardboard Shuri pinned on the door and a wall light that looks like Hulk's fist. I'd even drawn more cracks round Hulk's fingers to make it seem like the wall split. Silva's room looks like the inside of Muji. Everything is black, white and grey. I'm surprised her eyes didn't explode the first time she came to our flat. Me and Mum love bright. Our sitting room's got sky-blue walls, scarlet curtains and a rug that looks like a hyped-up kid had a bad Skittles accident across it. When we first moved in here, Mum painted enormous fluffy clouds across the walls. Then she added a little Mum and Becks flying kites because we loved the 'Fly a Kite' song at the end of *Mary Poppins*. She painted over the clouds and kites and the little me and her when Silva came. Mum thought they told too many stories that Silva might feel left out of.

Silva doesn't do colours, but she does do neat. I can't see no knickers poking out the top of her laundry basket and by some voodoo magic she keeps all her hangers on her rail facing the same way. There ain't no stacked-up books wobbling by the side of her bed, neither; they're all on the shelves. Her shoes are lined up side by side like they're waiting to march off to battle. The only thing out of place is the stink. I'm starting to think that Febreze ain't gonna do the job. Azog, serious, I hope I don't have to cut out that bit of carpet and burn it. If I do, you'll be staring at your own advert on Gumtree.

Silva's bed is up against the far wall under the window. When it was my room, I had curtains with rockets and puking space-girls on them. I moved to the small room when Silva came. I didn't mind because it made Mum happy. I've always had most of my things scattered over the whole flat anyway. My bedroom's just the place where I sleep.

How am I gonna do this? I wriggle under the bed with my torch and my kitchen roll. Pulling the bed right out would feel worse. I can see a box, nothing else. Azog comes in and nibbles my heel. I wriggle back out, pick her up and deposit her in the hallway.

'Go and think about your actions,' I say, and close Silva's door.

Then I say a silent 'sorry' to Silva, grab the bed and yank. It slides out easy. Silva always takes her clean clothes off the radiator and folds them away, straight off. They don't spend no time on the floor so don't jam up the bed wheels as I clamber on to her bed. Just rucking up her nice smooth duvet makes me feel bad. I peer over the other side. The first thing I see is the poo. Then I notice what Azog's done it on and I start laughing. It's on the chest of a pumped-up white bloke. Mr Buff-Man's body's on an Abercrombie and Fitch bag, one of them totes you have to pay the shop for so you don't carry your clothes out in your arms. It's like he's planning to audition for Mr Incredible in the live-action remake. No man should have a body like that and I don't mean that in a good way. And he's hoiking down the top of his jeans like his pubes got caught in his zip and he's trying to ease them free. I never knew muscle men were Silva's type. I mean, serious, she spent years sighing over Jungkook from BTS. I don't want to dis Jungkook. I mean serious, I don't. His fans would find out where I live and kill me, but three Jungkooks could fit in our man on the bag here with room for half a Jimin.

After all that effort, Azog took a dump on him anyway. Nice work, cat.

I think there's stuff inside the bag but it's gonna be easier to tip it out and throw away the bag, than properly de-poop the chest. Buff-Man won't look so hot with a crap stain across his pecs. I still need to get the worst off, because if I tip it now, Azog's gift's gonna slide down our man's ribs on to the floor. I prepare for battle. Gloves on, kitchen towel ready, breath held. I scoop the poo bomb into a plastic bag. If I release this into a crowd, I'll be sent to prison for years. I tie the bag up and carefully drop it on to the floor.

I pick up Buff-Man, turn him upside down and empty everything out of the wide man's chest. Papers flow on to the carpet. It's not Silva's exam certificates because Justin keeps them all squeaky clean in plastic covers in a folder by the TV. He says he can't wait until mine join them. Hmm. 'See Azog? You've stopped my revision!'

I take a closer look. This is not what I'm expecting. I mean, Silva's old enough to get a tattoo. She can vote. She can buy tequila – if she takes ID. But no, instead she saves grocery delivery receipts in an Abercrombie and Fitch bag under her bed.

I'm looking through them and – I don't get it. There are so many special things you can order to your door, if you want. Jerk pork ribs. A custom Ramona Flowers T-shirt. A biscuit tin that shrieks like a police siren when you lift the lid.

I mean, what the hell, Silva? On the 9th January, between 12.30 p.m. and 1.30 p.m. you got a delivery of a set of mixing bowls, eight bottles of still mineral water – the stuff that gets

25

filtered through a mountain and costs more than the mountain itself – and a pair of jam tongs.

I have to google what a jam tong looks like because a spoon's much easier and way cheaper to get the stuff out the jar. But jam tongs are for making jam. Which I know for sure Silva doesn't do. I check another A4 receipt. On the 13th January, between 12.30 p.m. and 1.30 p.m., Silva received two kilos of Harringtons Complete Cat Salmon and Rice. So that's where that posh stuff came from! I thought it was Mum trying to say sorry to Azog for fixing the tap so she couldn't lick the drips no more. Why did you buy Azog quality food, Silva? You and Azog ain't exactly allies.

And why does she need mixing bowls? I ain't seen no cake coming out of this room, or the kitchen for that matter. Now, I'm starting to think – tongs, mixing bowls, is my sister setting up a drugs cartel? Some of it I get. Yeah, she might use a glue stick, or a stapler or a load of AA batteries, though I don't know what she's planning to do with forty-eight of them. Maybe she's making a life-size Iron Man and if I stay in here too long, he's gonna shoot out from behind the clothes rail and zap me. I sneak a look at the rail. All's quiet.

I check out another receipt. Bubble bath. *She paid how much for it?* I saw that bottle in the bathroom and now I'm never gonna tell her about that the time I used it. It must have cost about £1.20 a splash. And I sure as hell used more than one splash. I would have eaten breakfast, second breakfast and elevenses in that bath if I knew how much those bubbles cost. Four argan oil soap sets. I remember seeing two of them in the wedding hamper we made for Mum and Justin. She's bought tea towels, an oven glove, nail varnish remover and plastic sink covers – they must be the ones that you put over the plughole to stop food lumps jamming up the pipes. Maybe Mum asked her for them after the Saturday she spent unscrewing the S-bend and fighting the monster inside.

Okay, I'm gonna step back and think. Maybe I'm taking all this the wrong way. Silva's been locking herself in here for weeks doing her own thing. Maybe this *is* her thing, buying random stuff online.

That's our family, right? We're messy shaped and we don't always do things the way other people do. There's no piece of paper big enough to draw even the last two generations of our family tree and that don't include the cousins we probably don't know about. If you tried to make a K-drama about us, we'd be a hundred episodes plus a prequel, sequel and an American remake. Man, we *are* complicated.

But even with all that, an eighteen-year-old girl who buys tea towels online is weird. She *could* be buying them for aunties, ready for Christmas. (Though I can't think of no aunties who are gonna smile when they open a package of tea towels.)

And, hey, why would she get them delivered at 2 p.m. on Tuesdays and Fridays? What's special about the time?

Nothing, except . . . that's the time Silva's home from

college. She's only got one lesson in the morning on both those days.

Mum was laughing about it, saying she's gonna make sure I go to a sixth form that locks me in all day. She'd never trust me to motivate myself. Everyone trusts Silva, though. And while they were trusting her, she was getting lunchtime home deliveries of stuff she didn't need. Twice a week.

I turn the last receipt over. It's the one with the earliest date.

Huh?

Five words are written on the back.

I turn the receipt over and check the date on my phone calendar. Man, this was from before Christmas! It wasn't a Tuesday or Friday day time. It was Friday evening – and – God! I was here!

Is this what it's about?

Man. That's just wrong.

4

You are the most beautiful.

Written on the back of the receipt.

The delivery man! Hitting on my sister! Oh. My. Days!

Not unless it was meant for me and she didn't pass it on. Nah. I remember it, I embarrassed the guy about the tampons. Though, that's all I remember so I hope I won't be describing him to the police no time soon. He was white and youngish, and he didn't have a face like Treebeard. Apart from that, Officer . . .

You are the most beautiful.

Yuck! Even if I was into boys, it wouldn't have worked out between us.

I know Silva had a boyfriend when she was sixteen. I'd overheard Justin asking Mum to give Silva the contraception talk. Mum had said no, because she was still traumatised by the condom and banana session from her sex ed lessons when she was fifteen. Mum also said men need to talk about that stuff too. I never knew if Justin did talk to Silva, but none of us met that boyfriend. He didn't last long. Another time, Silva was talking to some guy on a K-pop forum. I only know that because she used something he'd said to win an argument about which members of Exo sing in Mandarin.

Then there was the guy I walked in on in her bedroom. That was just after the wedding. *Was he the delivery man or someone else?* We never ever talked about that. The shock hit me so hard it was like my eyes shut down. I had to style it off with some swears.

I shuffle through the receipts again. I try and add up how much she spent, but when I get to £230, I don't bother no more. Mainly, because I keep wondering how much extra allowance Justin must be giving her. Does Mum know? *No, Becks. That's not the issue here.*

I put the receipts down and crawl back under Silva's bed. There'd been that box under there too. Everyone's got weird crap under their bed. I think my swimsuit's still under mine, drying out after the Year 5 sports gala. Would it make me an even worse person to have a look? We-ell, if Silva had bothered to get in touch with me, I wouldn't have to. I pull the bed out even further. The box is pushed against the wall. If the bed was in the right place, the box would be on the floor beneath Silva's head, like she needed it close to dream about. As I lift it out, I see it's more like a big cardboard drawer with a lid on it. I take a big breath before I lift the lid. Not because I expect something to jump out at me, but because this is so wrong. Going into Silva's bedroom when she's not here is wrong. Searching around under her bed is wrong. Nosing around her private stuff is wrong to infinity and back, but I've got to look.

The first thing I see is a padded, brown envelope.

It's sealed. I put it on the floor. Underneath, there are drain strainers, tea towels, two bars of posh soap and yeah, jam tongs. And so many batteries I'm surprised I wasn't electrocuted when I picked up the box. The stuff's been arranged carefully, but that's Silva, our neat freak. (I think Justin is too, but he's learned to hold back over the years because he loves Mum so much.)

I go back to the envelope. I shake it and squish it. There's something soft inside. I run my finger under the sealed flap. It's not that sticky. It must have been opened before, so it's not like I'm breaking in for the first time. This is Silva's private stuff. I shouldn't but I empty it into my palm. I almost scream and I don't do screaming. My vocal chords can't stretch that far, but this time they try and make an exception. I'm looking at something furry and dead. I chuck it on to the floor.

Then I realise . . . it's a wig. I don't get it. Silva ain't got hair because she don't want hair. She gets it trimmed down every three weeks. A buzzcut suits her because her head is a perfect shape, like every cell was slipped into the right place, one at a time. My head looks like it got dropped and bounced a couple of times.

Then – my heart gives me a sucker punch. *How damn stupid am I?* It must be Silva's mum's wig. Silva first shaved her hair when Marnie started losing hers. Is this Marnie's first wig? Or maybe even her last? Whatever, I've just chucked it on to the floor like it's trash.

31

Becks, you need to stop and think, sometimes.

Becks, you act before your brain's started working.

Becks, just don't!

Sometimes, I need to remember to let my brain click through its notches before I open my mouth or start acting. One thing I do need to do is pick that wig up and put it back with respect. I slide one of the receipts under it because I feel my bare hands are gonna soil it and then I open the envelope and let the wig gently drop back in. It brushes my hand. It's not as soft as I think it's gonna be. Maybe Marnie didn't want to spend too much money on it because she knew she wasn't gonna . . . My heart beats hard thinking about it. I'll just put all this away and make sure Silva never knows I've been in here.

I pick up the bag of poo and Buff-Man, and take them into the kitchen. I drop them both into one of the thick bin bags, knot it tight and leave it by the front door to take to the chute later. Then I have a thought. I go into the sitting room. The wall by the table is edge to edge pictures. It used to be me, me and Mum, and some cousins and aunties. Some of them got shifted to make way for pictures of Justin and Silva, and Silva with her mum. The more recent ones are on the mantelpiece. They're smaller and I think Justin may have used Mum's printer to print them. The one I pick up is the size of those really small school photos that Mum used to send off to the aunties she didn't like.

I think it's taken in the hospice. Silva and her mum are

cuddling each other. I hold the picture closer to my eyes. Silva's hair is shaved. Marnie's is short and brown, mixed with grey. That wig in the envelope seems too long, too dark, too cheap, but I don't know, do I? It's important to Silva and I interfered where I shouldn't have.

I go back into the kitchen and untangle one of the bags-for-life from the bundle in the cupboard under the sink. I take it into Silva's room, flatten out the receipts until they're in a nice, tidy stack and slide them into the bag. I put the lid back on to the box and shove the bed back against the wall. If Silva notices something's wrong, then we'll talk.

5

Becks?

I'm thinking of you. Please believe me.
I can't be with you because something happened.
I don't want you to be alone.
I can't explain. It's too late.
Everything happened so quickly.
Sorry.

6

Silva's been gone for twenty-four hours. Well, more than that, because technically she's missing since she left the airport. She must have got the Piccadilly line and then what? Took the tube to outer space?

Are my messages getting through? I call again. Her phone rings.

BLOODY ANSWER, SILVA! (If you can.)

What if she can't? What if she's in that cellar and . . . No. I'm gonna take what Raych says. Silva's on a big chill out and ignoring us all. She's gonna get over it and come home.

And I'm going to Savannah's tonight. I missed last night's meet-up in central because of Silva. So I'm definitely heading out to this one. It's not just because China's gonna be there. Well, that has *something* to do with it. She was with Poppy for three months, but from what I hear, Poppy's not on the invitation list tonight. I don't know if Savannah planned it that way. I'm kind of hoping so.

Everyone likes China. She's precious. I don't mean delicate. I've seen pure toughness in her eyes, but she's one of those people who's picking through Lauryn Hill lyrics one second, then asking you about your stresses the next. She notices who feels left out of the party and brings them in. And man, she's never, ever gonna look at me. Not in the way I want her to.

I'm still making an effort, though. I've started work already. I've used half a pot of argan gel to smooth down the braid frizz and mould some decent baby hairs. I've cleared out my nose pores, though I'm still not sure the apple vinegar's gonna cancel my spots the same way it sorted Silva's. I hope it don't stop anyone from coming near me. I rub my finger across my cheek then sniff. Nah. I'm not too vinegary. I saw hardcore moisturiser in Silva's room. I'm tempted, but I don't want to risk her walking in when I've got my fingers in her pot.

Though I probably wouldn't mind that now. She'd be mad at me, but at least I could stop stressing.

I can't help thinking of her and that delivery man. I know how it feels when you really like someone and you want them to like you back. The first girl I had that feeling for was Glinda in Year 7. Yep, she was actually named after Miss Green Dude from the musical *Wicked*. Glinda's hair partings were never straight. We had that in common from the start, especially when all the other black girls looked like their mums made them get up three hours before school to perfect their styles. Me and Glinda also had that look, the one where other black people know you're black, but not quite 'proper'. I saw Glinda's dad at parents' evening and realised that her 'not proper' bit was Mauritian.

Glinda knew I liked her. She knew I did more than like her, but it was never gonna be returned. Glinda was as straight as Hawkeye's arrow. No swerving sideways, full on splat-in-the-target straight. Boys were her target and her aim so good that her dad took her out of our school in Year 9 and put her in St Mary's Girls. Glinda wasn't rude to me. She didn't dis me. It wasn't personal. But I still thought my heart would shrink to the size of an apple pip then rot away.

Silva and that delivery man – *You are the most beautiful.* I hope that wasn't just empty lyrics and he liked her as much as she seemed to like him.

I'm still vexed though.

I brush my teeth and I pull on my clean jeans. I really have to pull because they always go down a size when they've been washed. Next on, my Marvel *Black Panther* T-shirt. Justin had them sent from America. Mine's got a full Shuri face on it. Silva's just got the Shuri symbol, because she likes to be subtle.

I tidy everything for when Silva gets back. Not because I'm feeling guilty or nothing. I check that Azog's in, make sure Silva's bedroom is proper shut and leave.

Savannah lives in a house. It used to be her grandparents'. They'd bought it when no one wanted to live in Hackney. Now her street's full of sports cars and windows that don't have curtains, so we can all get a look at cactuses and giant fridges. Some of the places have TVs the size of cinema screens. Yeah, I'm jealous of that, but our flat's too small for one. We'd have to sit on the wall across the road to see the picture.

I'm the second one to arrive. China's here already. I smile at her and she smiles back.

She touches the arm of my T-shirt. 'Cool! Where's it from?'

'Justin got it from America.' *Damn! Maybe I am a bit cool!*

I have to say something else, something good about her. Everything is good, though. She tilts her head and her earrings glitter. They're long, silver Black Panther talons. I reach out and touch one. She holds her head still and suddenly I feel stupid. Who meets up with a girl then starts fiddling with her earrings? I let my hand drop and China raises her eyebrows. She starts to unzip her trackie. Her T-shirt's Janelle Monáe's 'Dirty Computer'. I want to tell her she looks like Janelle, but that's cheese, right?

China touches Janelle, then Shuri. Yeah, for a second, China's finger is pressing just above my belly button. Then she laughs and says:

'Two damn cool sistas!'

I don't know if she means them or us.

Savannah's made spicy chicken stew. She's on this Korean tip at the moment, music, dramas, kimchi, the lot. She's even done up her eyes in blue, black and red make-up, though I don't know if even Savannah would cosplay the Korean flag.

She checks her phone. 'Those two are always late.'

We all look at each other and burst out laughing. Last time Rianna was here, she made the 'black people's time' joke. She thought she was quiet, but Savannah's aunty heard and almost threw her out. Savannah's aunty's got muscles like Hulk and could have done it too.

'What are we gonna do?' I say.

Savannah reaches for her laptop. 'There's only one thing we can do.'

Me and China peer over her shoulder. We both look back at Savannah at the same time.

'You've put in the work, girl,' China says.

Truly, Savannah has. She don't just have a K-pop list. She has a K-pop list for *everything*.

Sexy K-pop boys.

Sexy K-pop girls.

Sexy K-pop boybands.

BTS v Exo.

GIRLS.

Indie boys.

'Indie boys?' China and me are in sync again.

'You want the indie boys?' Savannah looks from me to China.

'Of course not,' China says. 'Let us sort this.'

Savannah smacks a kiss on China's cheek. 'Make it good, honey.'

She goes off to check her food. China clicks on GIRLS.

'What have we got here?' she says. 'EXID, EXID, Blackpink, Twice, IU, EXID, Heize . . .'

'Our girl has a serious vibe for EXID,' I say.

'Yes,' China says. 'So let's go for these honeys.'

Blackpink 'DDU-DU DDU-DU', dance practice. I love this one, but last time my knee clicked hard when I did the bend at the beginning.

I turn up the volume.

'You coming, Savannah?' China calls.

Savannah runs in and takes the place in the middle. Me and China grin round her.

'What?' she says.

China presses play. I bump into Savannah when I move the wrong way, then we do the arm-waving. Those hips? Me, China and Savannah have all got double the hip and twice the butt of those girls, so our shimmies and shakes are mean! I'm good. I know I am. I hike up my T-shirt and tie it into a knot just under my boobs. Sometimes, you gotta give it some belly.

The door knocker goes and Savannah leaves the room to answer it and it's just me and China still dancing, so close our hips bounce off each other. Then she lifts her fingers to her face and elbows me in the head and we're looking at each other and laughing.

Hannah and Rianna have arrived together, still laughing at some joke they must have had on the way over. Rianna changes the music to Burna Boy because her mum complains she ain't Nigerian enough. I ask if 'not Nigerian enough' is her mum saying she knows Rianna's into girls and maybe it was time to tell the truth. Rianna laughs so hard the chilli catches in her throat and she starts coughing.

'You're mad!' she gasps. 'If I give her that news, it's gonna make *Infinity War* look like a dance off. I'm happy to let Mama's brain keep busy just wondering.'

'Your mama keeps it all in her head?' Savannah's eyes go wide and she slaps both her cheeks like that kid from *Home Alone*. 'She doesn't tell you what she thinks? Over and over and again? With some aunties' advice thrown in for extra measure? How does this work, Ri?'

'It works because my mother is clever. She knows I'm not gonna bring no girlfriend home to meet her. Not while I'm at school, anyway.'

'But she'd let you bring home a boy?' Hannah asks.

Rianna screws up her face. 'Good point. But even if when I'm twenty or twenty-one or twenty-five, do you think my mum's gonna throw the door open wide and make tea for my girl? The best thing for me is to go far away. Thirteen top GCSEs, that should do it. Then I blitz the A Levels and head off to Edinburgh University.'

'What course?' China asks.

Rianna winks. 'I'll let Mama choose that.'

Me and China glance at each other. If anything did ever happen between us, I wonder if I could meet her family. Mine have never given me trouble though I still reckon there's a couple of aunties that have been missed off the announcement.

Our glance turns into a longer look.

Savannah whoops. 'What's up with you two?'

Me and China both laugh and carry on eating our stew.

7

It's twenty past midnight. I came back, but Silva didn't. I knew straight away because the door was still double-locked. We can't double lock it from the inside because the key's weird and only works one way. The lights were on in the kitchen and the hallway like I'd left them too.

I tried to call her, but she didn't pick up. I left a message and sent more texts. Nothing. Not even the damn blue ticks to tell me she's seen them.

I've gone back into her room. I'm not gonna disturb her secrets again. I just want to think and my room feels too small. The walls were cramming my thoughts together before they had a chance to open up and help me.

My stomach's hurting. That's not a dis on Savannah's stew. It's like all the feelings I've swallowed are in a bad mix-up. China is everywhere in my head, our hips bumping together and the way we looked at each other. She's into girls, but me? She glows, man. I don't want to dull her shine.

Then there's thoughts about those receipts under Silva's bed, the box that's like a shrine and the envelope with the wig. All that muddles up with Rianna living her secret life and how I'm lucky because I don't have to hide that part of me. Mum always says, I didn't come out to her because I could never be in. But now it seems Silva's been hiding so much of herself from all of us.

I message her again.

Silva, I don't mind if you've got secrets.
Please come home, Silva. Please?

8

Have you ever been afraid, Becks? Have you ever fallen deep into a pocket of darkness and struggled to climb out?

I dipped in and out of that darkness when Mum became ill. After she died, I thought I would tumble down and never come up. I didn't though. There was greyness and heaviness, but as I stumbled over the edge, so many hands reached out to pull me back. I saw those hands. My dad's. Your mum's. Even your little ones. I reached back for them.

But sometimes the darkness rises when you don't expect it. You lock yourself away and wait for it to pass, but you're wrong. It's just waiting.

I made a list of why I should be punished. I wrote it in a notebook on the blank piece of paper in the inside cover. It made it easier to find every time I needed to add to it.

This is how the list started.

He gave up his job for me.
I spoke to his brother without asking him.
I wasn't grateful enough for his gifts.

You never knew about the gifts, Becks. His gifts. The picture and the shoes and the dress and everything else.

Just him, he was a gift. Do you know the first thing he gave me?

His smile.

He looked beyond you and your laugh and your chat and he saw me. I needed to be seen.

9

Azog farts and wakes me up. It's not the volume. Her bottom ain't found the sound function yet. It's the pungency. It smells like she's broken a seal and it's only a small matter of time before the next stage. Then I realise I'm still on Silva's bed. I sit up so quickly my head blips. I blink a couple of times then jump off the bed and run and unlock the front door. It's morning. Azog heads out down the stairs to the first-floor balconies, leaping on to one of the weedy window boxes on the ground floor, and from there, out into open space.

'Don't even think of going to Mr Phan's,' I call after her.

She don't bother to look back. I close the door and stand by it. The fridge is humming again and the tap's still dripping in the bathroom. I can even hear next door's TV through the walls and I've never noticed that before. I need noise. Even if it's *Countryfile* or last night's *Match of the Day*.

I check my phone. Nothing from Silva.

I call her. It goes to answerphone.

What if she's never gonna come back?

Mum's sent me a picture of their apartment. She's surprised how much fits into a tiny space. She jokes about coming home and moving us into somewhere smaller. Yeah, at this rate, we're not gonna need three bedrooms. I spot a big bottle of Asahi beer on the table and two glasses. This ain't just their honeymoon, it's their first proper holiday by themselves. It took them more than a year to save up money for it.

I want to message Mum about Silva. I *will* message her. I'm gonna cover all bases first, though. If her and Justin think there's a problem, they'll fly right back. I reckon Silva must have been messaging Justin, otherwise Mum would have been on to me about it straight away.

Silva's an adult, so she can do what she wants. Still, I look online and google 'what to do if you think someone might be missing?'. One website lists things to think about before calling to report a disappearance. Is it out of character? Yes, but she does spend loads of time by herself. Is she in danger? I don't know. Does she need medication? Not that I know of. Is she vulnerable?

I DON'T KNOW!

I don't know nothing about my sister. Why am I still calling her my sister, when she's like a stranger?

She's the stranger who took my room and my mum and—

This is why China doesn't want me. She must know the person I really am, mad at a girl who's still sad because her mum died.

The girl who takes all the attention.

Silva knows I'm gonna be worried. She knows Mum and Justin would come straight home if they knew anything

48

was wrong. But, still she won't get in touch. (*If she can get in touch, Becks.*)

I should just call the police, straight off, but once I've said my bit, what are they gonna ask me? How old are you? Are you by yourself? Where's your family? What if they send round social services? Mum and Justin will get in trouble for leaving me and their honeymoon will end up one of those news stories about bad parents that abandon their kids.

So what *am* I gonna to do?

Find her. That's what. Or know I've tried everything I can before I call them.

I rub my hands together like I'm warming up my luck. First thing I need to know – is she with anyone? If she is, and they're not a psycho serial killer, then I can calm down a bit.

I go back into Silva's room, heave the bed away from the wall and pull out the bag of receipts. I don't know if this has got anything to do with her disappearing off, but what else have I got to go on?

I empty the receipts again. They might have the name of the driver on them, like when they text you to say your delivery's coming. No. No name. I hold up the You are the most beautiful one to the light. I don't know what I expect to see. His name written in invisible ink would be good. Or in pencil that's been rubbed off, but with still enough on there for me to work it out. Nope. Nothing.

Did he leave off his name on purpose? So no one can trace him? The sick feeling is coming back.

49

I message Silva.

I call her.

Jesus, Silva! Answer me! I will try and be a better sister, I promise.

There's nothing here to help me. I don't know where she is or if she's okay. She is a missing person.

I call the police. Not 999 emergency, but the 101 number. I say that I think my sister's gone missing. The woman on the other end of the line sounds sorry for me and doesn't tell me to go away. She asks me lots of questions about Silva. *Is she vulnerable?* I don't tell her that Silva stays in her room all the time and only comes out at meal times. I used to do that too. I don't mention the delivery man, neither, because I still don't know for sure. In the end, none of my answers make it sound like Silva needs help. The woman's still patient though and takes the details and gives me a reference number. She says that I should call back if I don't hear from Silva by tomorrow or the emergency line if I think Silva's in danger.

I feel a bit better for making the call, like I've cleared enough out of my head to have room to think. The delivery man crams himself into that free brain space. I have to find him.

I actually give myself a comedy slap on the forehead. What did Silva do when she was looking for him? The obvious thing! I'll order some shopping. The chances of him actually delivering it are probably thousands to one, but weird things happen. Mum was once seriously freaked when she found out she was sharing a taxi pool with a man who went to the same primary school as her, in a village, in Sussex.

I go into the kitchen. Mum left the website password on a scrap of paper on the fridge, just in case . . . I'd wanted to ask her, 'Just in case of what, Mum? In case there really is an apocalypse and we need more chickpeas?' I suppose we could use the tins as weaponry. I look around. What else can I buy? Mum bought half the shop before she went away and got it delivered yesterday. Washing-up liquid, washing powder, toilet roll, they're always needed. More cat food? Always. But Mum's gonna be really suspicious if she gets a notification for another shopping delivery on her phone. I wish I had my own card like Silva, then I wouldn't have to use Mu— But I don't have to use Mum's! I know Silva's password. She gave it to me so I could order the Bobblehead Okoye, the one where she's about to kick ass in the Busan casino. I just got to hope she uses the same password for all her accounts. I bring my laptop into the kitchen and go on to the grocery site. I enter Silva's email address and the (maybe) password. Fak3Lov3. 'Fake Love'. BTS broke some good moves to that tune.

The screen blinks and I'm in! They can deliver tomorrow, first thing. Maybe I should have gone for a Tuesday or Friday, like Silva, but I ain't got time. So what's it gonna be? Nutella, the biggest jar they got. Crisps multi-packs. Yoghurt. The type from soya beans, for Silva. Oh and there's a deal on Palmer's cocoa butter. Tub, body oil, foot lotion and some sheen stuff for the hair. Yeah, that's added up enough for delivery. I just hope Silva's got money in her account. I go to checkout and confirm. Then – yeah! Done! Maybe Silva will be home by then. She can put the damn stuff away.

She'll get an email telling her she's made an order. That should make her phone me.

I want to call up China. I just want to hear her voice, but last night she told me she's going down Coulsdon to see her new baby cousin today.

I *could* head back round to Savannah's. I could tell her about Silva because we all made a pact to help each other when we're stressed. *My sister's obsessed with a delivery driver and she's disappeared.* It sounds like one of them captions on daytime TV. Even I would laugh aloud at that one. I don't want Savannah to laugh at my sister.

I phone Raych. It's automatic. I almost don't realise I've done it until she answers. She picks up straight away.

She says, 'I was just thinking about you. How's things?'

'I don't know.'

'What's wrong? Is it last night?'

'Last night?'

'With China, Becks!'

'Oh. No. That's good. China's good. Really good and—' I clamp my lips together to stop my mouth running off. 'It's not China, Raych. It's Silva. I think she's gone missing.'

'Missing?'

'Yeah. I've messaged her and phoned her and I still ain't heard nothing. I've even reported her missing to the police now.'

'Wow! That's hardcore!'

'Not the emergency police. The other one. But it's Silva's fault if they have a go at her. She broke her promise to our parents. She was supposed to be here, with me, but all she's doing is stressing me out.'

Raych sighs. 'You're mad at her, right?'

'Yeah! And she deserves it!'

'I understand,' Raych says, 'but what if Silva can't deal with that right now?'

'What do you mean?'

'You're one of my best friends and everything, but sometimes you get a bit intense.' *Intense?*

'It's like you have to tell everybody everything even if they don't want to hear it. Maybe Silva isn't ready to hear your opinions.'

My opinions? The only opinion I've got is that Silva should call me back and tell me where she is.

It was one of them moments. Me and Raych have years of 'good mates' stuff stored up. When I was eleven, her parents took me on holiday with them. The hotel had one of those bars where you didn't need money. You just showed your wristband and they served you as much mocktail and ice cream soda you could drink. Raych taught me backstroke in the hotel pool, holding me up until I stopped whipping water and relaxed enough to float. I could never have done that without her.

And there's the time when we were twelve, and me and Mum went to see her play in the orchestra at the Round Chapel? She'd been so happy to see us all sitting in the front row. Or the time I'd lied my guilty ass off to her mum, saying she was here when she'd gone cinema with Scott from St Chad's Boys?

Loads of good mates stuff. I have to try and remember it when our friendship feels like one of them glaciers on the nature programmes, all cracking and falling apart. I want David Attenborough to turn up and make everything right again.

She says, 'Are you mad with me now?'

Sort of.

'I just thought maybe I was helping, Becks.'

'Yeah,' I say. 'Thanks.'

'Becks?'

I ring off.

I'm intense? I'm the one stopping Silva from coming home? I throw my phone across the bed. Why does everybody always think things are easy for me? I didn't ask for none of this, but I've tried so hard. It seems like that's not enough.

I like Justin. I do. He's so into Mum. I can tell just by the way he looks at her. He wants all of us to be happy and he's trying so hard to be happy himself. I still reckon he's not over

Silva's mum dying even though he split up with her before she knew she was ill. Mum says you don't get over things like that. You just learn to live with them.

Justin used to bring Silva to see us when her mum got ill. The first time, she looked round our sitting room then burst into tears. Mum joked that maybe she got an instant migraine from our decoration. But it wasn't that. Silva didn't want to be here. She must have sensed that her mum wouldn't get better. If that was me, I know I wouldn't want to be dragged round to strangers. I'd want to spend every second with my mother.

Mum made me show Silva my room. I remember her looking back at Justin and him giving a little nod. I probably gave Mum the same look. *What was I supposed to show her?* Silva must have seen a wardrobe and a bed before, and mine weren't particularly special, apart from the chunk missing from the corner of the drawer where Mum's drill had slipped as she was putting it together. Silva stood in my doorway, her eyes open so wide I thought she'd have to go to A&E to get them closed again. Her mouth moved.

'SHINee?'

SHINee is for the originals. All of them BTS K-pop newcomers have to look SHINee in the face and apologise. These boys were there first. They've even had to overcome their own tragedies when Jonghyun died.

I didn't exactly have a poster of them. I'd found a picture online and made Mum use up all her colour cartridge printing it out for me. I'd stuck it on the wall above my bed, with Loctite, because I was never, ever gonna take it down. I'd nodded, slowly, because this was a serious moment between the two of us. I borrowed Mum's laptop and set up my K-pop video playlist. We didn't talk much. We definitely didn't dance, not that time. Maybe not the next time, neither. But some time we did.

It's always me. I'm always trying to make things good. *Who's trying to make things good for me?*

10

I'll try and explain, Becks. I owe you that.

I was coming home to you. My head was full of saying goodbye, the hustle and kisses and hugs of the airport. I'd taken a bus to give myself time to slowly build my defences. Dad and Win were finally away on their honeymoon. I should be happy. Our parents deserve this.

I would come home to you and be the sister I'd promised.

That's when it happened.

I saw him.

I closed my eyes, tried to stop it. My heartbeat filled up my whole body. Perhaps one day you will understand. Love can grow and grow and then suddenly, love stops. But, when you think it's dead, it explodes again.

I breathed in, out, in again slowly. I could smell cologne on skin, as deep as bronze. Strong beer that stuck in my throat and coated my tongue. The old woman's shopping trolley filled with oranges. There was a boy sitting next to me. I could smell his jacket sleeve speckled with chip grease. I heard the creak as a window slid apart and the cool air broke up the fug.

I made myself open my eyes. I looked at the woman who had opened the window. Her hair was twisted into solid curls and the breeze blew the slick scent of her hairspray to me.

My body was just heartbeat.

The bus stopped. Temporary traffic lights jammed on red. The man in the seat in front of me was sipping from a can wrapped in a paper bag. His suit was grey and a little shiny, the jacket collar twisted up as if it had hung crooked in his wardrobe, squashed against his other clothes, never loved. He drained the last dregs of beer and let the can fall to the floor. It rolled beneath his seat to my feet, leaving a damp trail. It was the smell of fights.

I took out my earbuds, hoping my heart would quieten down. Other sounds leaked through – the hum of the bus engine, the crackling voice in the driver's cab describing a diversion – but they were still faint beneath my heart.

This was not the time to see him, not when I was still soaked in goodbyes. I wasn't ready. Now I know I never will be.

I had only seen him for a second, but I had known. He is still part of me. Didn't he understand that?

He was alone. I could just go up the stairs, sit next to him, explain again why we should be together. I wouldn't go upstairs. I would not look at him. There was too much to lose.

I had to get off the bus. It hurt too much. There was so little space between us, but he didn't know I was there. I pushed the bell and stood up. My heartbeat was louder.

I was all noise. I looked at my feet, the aisle, the stairs, my hand on the rail, everything except the screen in case it blinked back to the upper deck.

A young woman had nudged her way in front of me, waiting for the door to open. I caught a whisper of her deodorant and for a moment my own beat changed. It was dancing with you to BTS and early SHINee. It was Right Guard Women Xtreme sprayed across our socks and T-shirt armpits.

My mind jumped back from you to him, Becks.

The smells that remind me of him, they should be warm, like a bakery when they unlock the door in the morning. But that's not it. He is burnt cheese from the pizza you forgot in the oven and the lemon bubbles from the tray left soaking in the sink. Do you remember? His smell is sharp and heavy and catches in my throat.

The bus stopped.

A boy pushed past me out of the door, trailing a stink of strong weed. He looked so like him. I glanced up at the CCTV screen. The images blinked from camera to camera, but they didn't land on him again.

I stumbled out and the door closed. I had done it. I had escaped him. The bus indicators flashed as it started to pull away. And then I looked up.

He must have changed sides of the bus. He was staring down at me through the window. Our eyes met. I can read him, Becks. I knew what he was feeling. Perhaps he had tried as hard as me to pretend our love had ended. But he knew that was wrong.

I stood watching the bus until it was gone. The smell of weed stayed at the bus stop like it was waiting for the boy to return. People say that a person you want to get rid of hangs around like a bad smell. Someone who's good for you is a breath of fresh air.

We need air to breathe.

Starve us of it and we die.

I felt myself coming alive again.

I knew I had to find him, Becks. We had to be together.

This was my chance for life.

11

Am I intense? I check Google for opinions. Some dude's got more than three thousand thumbs up on his blog telling people like me about ourselves. Intense folk *care*. We're honest. We don't try and hide nothing. You don't even have to be real life for us to care about you. One time, I cried so hard at the end of a K-drama that Savannah's mum rushed into her room to find out what was wrong with me. So I take my intense self back into Silva's bedroom and that box.

When I was about nine, I was at my friend Kieron's Halloween party. We played this game where they turned the lights down low and his mum told a ghost story. While she was talking, we all passed round a bag, like one of those little kids' PE bags with a drawstring. Whenever she stopped, the person who had the bag had to stick their hand in and draw something out. I got a couple of peeled lychees that were meant to be like eyeballs.

Silva's box is the opposite. It's got an envelope with a wig in it. That's all. I can see that, but . . . Oh. Lord. One of the aunties once told Mum that when God was giving out brains, I was last in line. Mum hasn't spoken to her since. But maybe Aunty Iz had the sight and it's true. All I'd seen was a shallow tray with an envelope in it. The box is way deeper than that.

I lift out the box again. It's got that drawer underneath. For a second, I imagine that my sister's got Mad-Eye Moody's magical trunk beneath her bed. If I open the drawer, there's twenty more drawers inside and the smallest one's got the delivery man tied up inside.

I say a prayer. I'm not sure who to. Whoever it is has to be cool with forgiving me for rummaging through my sister's secrets.

I ease open the drawer and lay it on the bed.

What the hell *is* all this? The drawer's lined with red material, like some sort of weird shrine, but the stuff in it is just random. I take out the first thing and hold it up to my eyes. It's a green plastic counter, like the ones you use for board games, but bigger. It reminds me of plastic coins Mum used to get after she'd finish shopping at the supermarket. I was allowed to choose a charity and drop the coins down a chute. There's no shop brand on it, though. I place it down on the duvet like it's a diamond.

Next, I take out a medal hanging on stripy red, white and blue ribbon that looks like it's got a rub of neck grease along it. The medal's bronze-coloured, so whoever wore it came third, though I don't know what in. The metal's so thin that if I drop it in a puddle it's gonna float. The word 'Inspired' is engraved in the middle. I wonder what you're supposed to be if you're silver or gold. I lay it down next to the counter.

I pick up a roll of white tape, stretch some out and stick

it to the back of my hand. It's proper sticky. When I pull it away, I think my hand-skin's gonna be swinging from it. You could tape a polar bear to the wall with that stuff. Is my sister Spiderman? She could be guarding the Multiverse right now.

Be serious, Becks. Be intense.

I take out a sheet of printed paper inside a plastic sleeve that's been folded around it and held tight with three tiny bulldog clips. I look up at Silva's desk. There's a whole jar of those clips on there.

Underneath that, there's a brown paper bag with something square and solid inside. I unwrap it. It's a picture in a clip-frame. I see straight away who it is and drop it on the floor. Lucky, it don't have far to fall. I wipe my fingers on the rug like they're dirty. I mean, Silva! I just don't get it! Why d'you have this?

I turn the picture face down and go back to the paper in the plastic folder. I take it out. It's been printed just as the ink ran out. It's about a football game. The picture's taken mid-action. One player's high in the air with his leg out ready to shoot. The goalie is diving towards him. I squint hard at the caption underneath. **Action from Finsbury FC v Stamford Lions**. There's more writing beneath that but the ink didn't stretch that far. Is this about the delivery driver? Is one of them dudes him? Though that picture don't help. The only way I'd recognise either of these boys in real life was if they poured ink on their face and scraped half of it off.

I look for a date or a place. Nothing. But I've got Stamford Lions and Finsbury FC. Somewhere to start.

I look them both up online. Stamford Lions ain't got no website. I see them mentioned a few times in match reports but I've got a feeling they're not properly formal. Finsbury FC have got a website, mostly full of Insta and Twitter pictures. There's dudes of all different colours either kicking a ball or holding up a trophy. I click on every caption looking for clues. I see a picture of their youth team, all of them grinning apart from one little black kid next to the ref who's staring at the sky. I see you, mate. That would have been me. In February, a girl called Shanika's shaking hands with the Mayor because her team's just won a tournament. I find a snap of the under-25 team, though it's from last year. I hold my sister's printout next to my screen to see if I can match either of the dudes to the team shot. I make the screen picture as big as I can. It just goes blurry. I stare at them some more. There's only three white dudes in there. None of them remind me of the boy who dropped off our bags that day. Though, maybe I just remember girls better.

I place the picture next to the medal and go back to the Finsbury FC homepage. It says that they practise on Hackney Marshes on Sunday afternoons. If I want to find them, it has to be now. I can't wait another week.

I let Azog back in. She's been doing vertical trampoline off the front door for the last ten minutes. Then I write a note for Silva just in case she gets back.

Gone out. Please call me.

I fold up the article and slip it into the plastic folder, then put it back in the drawer with the counter and medal. I tidy it under the bed. Then I pick up my phone, my keys and a notebook, and drop all of it into my bag.

I've only been on Hackney Marshes one time before. They had a free concert there when the Olympics came to London. Mum took me and we saw Labyrinth and Dizzie Rascal, but she brought me home before Rhianna came on because she said her songs are too rude.

I can tell you one more thing about the Marshes now. It's where cold winds go to try out their superpowers. I dodge mad cyclists on the canal path and a cloud of blood-sucking bugs partying beneath the trees. When I step out on to the grass, I get slapped round the face by the wind. When I manage to open my eyes again, I see that nearly all of the pitches are occupied. I'm gonna have to go round every single one. I try and count, but there must be more than forty. Some have proper games with people gathered round them cheering. Other ones are covered in cones and spare balls and piles of sweatshirts and bags.

I check my phone. In a film, this is where I'd get a call from Silva telling me she's safe at home. *Where are you, Becks? I've been waiting ages for you.* This ain't no film, though. There ain't no message, nor missed calls. I'm gonna have to put in the leg work.

The first two pitches are boys' teams, but they look like Year 11s and 12s, too young. The next pitch, they're all older, mainly Somali, I think. I move on. Women, mostly about Silva's age though a few look a bit older. Their coach smiles at me and I smile back. I think about asking her if she knows where Finsbury FC practise but she blows a whistle and the team gather around her. I carry on walking, trying to sneak a look at bags and bibs, just in case Finsbury have cash for branded merch. Then I see them. Finsbury FC, doing their drills, shuttle runs from the goal to the midway line and back again. I know it's them because someone's planted a little flag with Finsbury FC printed on it at the corner of the pitch.

As the boys finish running, they collapse on to the grass. A couple of them look like they're trying to style off their pain, but I can see their chests going up and down like they're being stamped on. I take a deep breath and go over to one of the boys sitting by himself. As I get closer, I smell him. It's like all his bacteria have opened their mouths and coughed at the same time. This must be what it's like to be Silva. She always smells stuff bigger and sooner than anyone else. It's the superpower that no one would ever want, unless you end up saving a baby from a burning house because your nose caught a sniff of the villain striking the match.

'Hi,' I say and crouch next to him. 'Can you help me? I'm looking for my sister.' He scowls at me when he sees the others looking over.

He points back to where I came from. 'Girls' team is over there.'

'She's not on a team. I think she's one of your players' girl. I came to see if he's here.'

The coach comes over. I stand up slowly, trying to find a better way to explain myself. I can't.

I say, 'I'm looking for my sister. She's sort of gone missing.'

He could have made another joke about looking in the wrong team, but he frowns.

'Gone missing? Sorry to hear that. What can I do?'

It's stupid. I feel like crying. Nothing bad has even happened, just this man being kind to me. It's like none of it has been true until I say the words to someone I've never met before and they feel sorry for me.

I say, 'I don't know for sure, but I think she had a boyfriend who played on your team.'

He raises his eyebrows. 'We've had a whole load of players over the years. Not everyone's got the commitment.' He sweeps a hand towards the boy lying in the grass. 'Or the fitness.' The boy ignores him.

'I think he was playing at the beginning of this year.'

'Do you have a name?'

'No, sorry.'

'Any idea what he looks like?'

'I think he's white.'

'We have a few white boys. Anything else?'

'Maybe he works as a delivery man.'

67

'A delivery man?' The coach steps back. 'You mean Logan?'
Logan? Like Wolverine?

'I just need to know more about him because my sister . . .'

'Your sister?'

'My sister, yes.'

He stares at me. I wait for it. *'You two don't look alike . . .'*

Instead, he says, 'Is your sister the girl who was following him round all the time? The one who wouldn't leave him alone?' He's shaking his head the way teachers do when they think they've caught you lying. 'And now she's sent you?' He blows out his breath.

'No one sent me!'

I get a long look back from him. I want to look away, but I need him to see I'm not lying. I also want to check his expression too.

I say, 'You're talking about someone else. My sister ain't no stalker.'

I take my phone out my pocket and find a picture of me and Silva at the wedding.

'This is her,' I say. 'My sister.'

'Yes,' he says. 'That's her.'

He doesn't drop his eyes or even looked shamed. 'I don't know what you know and what you don't know, but Logan doesn't play here no more. He was one of our best players. He strained a tendon in February and never came back. At least that's what he told us. Truth be told, I think he was scared that girl, your sister, would come and find him.'

The coach turns his back on me and walks away. I run after him.

'My sister ain't "*that* girl". Ain't no stalker neither. She's gone missing and . . .'

He stops. 'No stalker? Logan's told me about all the tricks she used to get him back. She was here, every single practice, long after Logan told her nothing was doing. It was like she'd got an obsession and nothing was going to change her mind. I even asked him if he wanted me to talk to her, but he said he could handle it. We'd see her coming along the path from the canal and she'd sit over there.' He points to some random grass slope.

'I'm sorry. I can't give out my players' details anyway, it's against policy. I hope you find your sister.' He walks away. I watch him sweep up an armful of bibs from the sideline and carry on. 'Ritchie and Stirling, you're captains. Pick your teams quick and let's get going.'

He doesn't give me another look. My eyes sting.

Silva, a stalker? Nah! The man's confusing her for someone else. She spends all her time in her room, except when she's – when she's what? I don't even know no more. Maybe she wasn't in her room. Maybe she waited until we were all asleep then crept out again. Or when I came home from school and thought she was in there, she really wasn't. One thing I do know is that she was spending more than two hundred quid getting stuff delivered that no one knew about.

My sister's definitely got secrets. Maybe some of them are ones I don't want to know.

My chest hurts. I feel like it's me who's been running up and down the pitch until I want to throw up. I walk away across the marshes until I'm on the main road. I don't look back neither. I see a bus stop and get on the first bus that comes. I try and call Silva again but it's still straight to messages. A few stops on, a crowd of girls my age get on, snatched belly tops, hair and eyelashes, lots of noise and jokes. They go upstairs but I can still hear them from below. I watch them on the CCTV screen. I want to be with them. I want to be them. I also want to put on my headphones and turn up Odunsi so loud my head hurts, but I just listen to their fun and look out the window.

They get off long before me, not even glancing my way. I stay on until we reach St Paul's. I cross the road and head towards the river. I go over the Millennium Bridge feeling the clonk of my feet on the metal. We used to come down here on Saturday afternoons with Mum. Silva would make us stop in the middle. Mum and me thought it was because she was enjoying the view, but later she told us she liked the way the river smells. I think the river smells like Mum's trainers, but Silva said that if she closed her eyes and took a deep breath, she smelled ghost ships. I thought that was a bit mad. Mum thought Silva was wonderful.

The tide's out. As I cross the river, I see the mud and sand stretching from the water to the river wall. I reach the south bank and go down on to the shore.

This was another one of Mum's trips, but mainly when it was just me and her and we had no money at all. Mum said we were searching for treasure. The river washes up secret stuff then takes it away again. I'd wear wellies and she'd make me put on plastic gloves in case I got infected by rats' pee. The gloves almost always ripped and I'd carry on without them. We'd pick up old bits of crockery and fossilised wood and clay pipe stems. All of them must have been shifting across the riverbed for hundreds of years. Thinking about it, Silva was right about the ghosts after all.

I'm standing as close to the water as I can without getting my Vans too mucked up. The sun's shining down hard now, but it don't make the water shine. I look around for flat stones, not too big, not too tiddly. One of the police boats shoots by and then a tourist boat. The guide's saying something about Shakespeare. When the water's settled again, I skim my stones. The first one sinks. The second one manages two jumps before plopping into the water. The third one seems to catch the tide and skips three, four, five times before it gets tired. It's my best yet, but it's not the same when there's no one else to see it.

12

I've lied to you, Becks. I've broken my promises. Now I've left you alone. I want to tell you not to worry about me. I'm the oldest sister. I'm the adult. You shouldn't be responsible for me.

I can't sleep. The sounds here are different, they have to drift higher to reach me. I've scrolled through the memories and, Becks, I wish I'd told you. I think I was frightened you wouldn't believe me. In real life, love shouldn't strike hard like this, should it?

I'll try and explain. I'll start slowly, following the path of our story. Ours. Me and him. I want you to understand.

I created an album on my phone. If you were here, Becks, I could show you. The cafe and the restaurant, the clothes shop and the football pitches. I've captured pictures of them all. The pub on the canal bridge. The club. All of these places were ours. Mine and his. They will be again. We just need to be together.

But I'll take you right back to the beginning to the place I still can't quite call home.

The night I met him, I was taken by surprise. After Mum died, part of me closed down. Even when Dad and Win and you reached out to help me, shadows still tried to pull me down. They wouldn't give up. I'd see splashes of light but so much was in darkness.

The evening we met, my bedroom door was open. That was fate. I usually keep it closed. The flat is noise and colour and sometimes it's so hard to fight through it all. You're used to it, Becks. For me, it's harder. But that was the destiny. An open door. I was meant to meet him.

But you should remember. Dad and Win were out on wedding business. You were there. We're so different, little sister. I hide everything away. You cannot be embarrassed. You can't hold anything inside you. Do you remember when you were twelve? You told me about that girl in your textiles class. *Ached*. That was the word you used. You told me your heart was being pulled out. I didn't know what to say to you. Sorry. But when I saw him that evening, I finally understood what you meant.

You opened the front door, Becks. I was sitting on the floor by my bed trying to read a book on Greek architecture. Every time I turned a page, my eyes slid to the bottom without catching any of the words. I heard you laugh out loud and I eased myself closer to the door. A split plastic bag was dangling from his fingers and he was surrounded by packets of sanitary pads and tampons. He picked up some Always. He glanced down at the rest of it, back to the bag, and then at you. You had your hands on your hips. I couldn't see your face, but I know you, Becks. You had your eyebrows raised, didn't you? They must have lifted even higher when he spoke.

'I didn't think no one uses these things now.'

'Some people do,' you said. 'But some girls prefer tampons . . . or mooncups.'

I could almost feel his blush from my bedroom. I was blushing with him. I wanted to race out and help him but I couldn't move.

'I don't really know about them things.' As he said it, he twisted his finger up like he was . . . putting in a . . . You were there, Becks. You saw. And you laughed so loud your whole body shook.

You gave me courage to come out of my room.

He and I looked at each other. It's a cliché, but love at first sight is real, Becks. Scientists are trying to prove it.

I wonder what he saw in me. I was wearing old jeans, the hoodie with the bleach mark, no make-up. My hair – he saw that too. He didn't turn away.

And him? You would never have suspected, Becks. He's skinny and white, isn't he, not like the usual boys who try and talk to me. He was wearing hi-vis over a dark T-shirt, dark trousers, nothing that made him stand out.

You raced off to rescue the food. Burnt cheese from the pizza you forgot in the oven filled the hallway. He took a pen from his pocket, scribbled on the back of the receipt and dropped it into the last bag. He handed it to me, smiled and left. I took that bag into the kitchen, and emptied it while you were trying to scrape the pizza off the baking tray. You didn't see me take the receipt out and back into my bedroom. My heart was beating so hard.

There were five words written on the back of it, Becks. This wasn't just chat. I knew it.

He'd looked at me and loved me. I knew I loved him too.

But then . . . It hurts so much to remember.

I promise, though. I promise to take you down the path with me.

13

When I get home from the river, Azog's waiting for me. It's not her usual type of waiting. Furry side eye and a meow that says 'Open that damn pouch!' She rubs herself against my legs, gives out a few purrs and strokes her cheek against mine when I pick her up. It's like she knows she started this by taking a dump under Silva's bed and she wants me to know she's sorry.

Yeah, I'm sorry too. Thanks to that dump I've been sucked into Silva's secrets and can't go back. *That girl*. That's what the coach had called her. He really did think my sister's a stalker. Maybe – and this hurts – he's speaking the truth.

I let Azog go, crouching down so she don't drop like a rock. She steps out of my arms then looks back at me. Her face says, 'You sure you're all right, Becks?'

Nope, Azog. I'm not.

So how am I gonna find Logan? Of course, I try the obvious and do a search of 'Logan' and 'delivery man' online. Well, I can tell you something. There's a bad Chris Pratt film called *Delivery Man* where an actor called Logan played a reporter. And something else I don't need to know? Paul Logan from Consett got killed while delivering food from the Golden Flower Chinese restaurant. It looks like no one ever

76

found his murderer. And a dog called Logan stopped a delivery man walking into a house without knocking. I'm gonna tell that to Azog. She needs to earn her keep.

The Logan I don't see is the one who delivered chickpeas to us before Christmas.

It's still not easy to go into Silva's room, but I do it anyway. Looking through the stuff in the box felt bad, but it took me to the football pitch and gave me his name. He's Logan. A skinny, un-hairy, un-Wolveriney Logan.

Now I need to do a proper snoop. I don't even know what I'm looking for. I suppose it's something that will turn Silva from my sister into 'that girl'. I'm looking for something that I don't want to find.

When I gave Silva my room, I took out most of the things I cared about. All my old picture books, the knitted Handa from *Handa's Surprise* with her bowl of bobbly fruit on her head (Grandma really put time into making that), the ticket from *Matilda* that I'd stuck bang in the middle of the door. Mum and Justin got us both new beds, though when mine was fixed up in the small room, there was hardly any space for me. Lucky, there was already a built-in cupboard for my clothes. Silva took down the old curtains in my – her – room and Mum put up a wooden blind. I wish Mum had let me keep the curtains, but she took them off to the charity shop. I hope whichever kid got them enjoys them.

I pull the cord until the blind lifts as high as it can go. The room faces west so sunlight pours in. I check the walls just in case secret writing magically appears. Then I smile. When Mum and I first moved into this flat, she painted giant bubbles on the bedroom wall. She said they would help my bad dreams float away. It must have worked, because when I did remember my dreams, they were always happy. As the sun hits the wall, I can just see the bubbles shining beneath the light grey paint. It makes me feel better.

I have a quick look through Silva's clothes. They're just there on a rail – she got rid of my crooked old wardrobe – so it don't feel like the worst snooping, though dipping my hands in and out the pockets of her jackets and trousers don't make me feel good about myself. I don't find nothing. Not even a wrinkled receipt. Silva's always dragging me for destroying anything paper that goes in my bag or pockets. She says when I get it, it looks like it just slid out the printer, but once it's spent two minutes in my bag, you think it's been pulled out from beneath the bin. Suddenly, I feel guilty. Those delivery receipts don't look as flat and bright-white as they did before I took them out Buff-Man's tote.

I give her trainers a shake and turn her boots upside down. More nothing. I don't touch her shelves. It's like she used a tape measure to make sure everything's in the right place and I don't dare move a thing. I don't notice nothing new, nothing that shouldn't be there. There's stuff she brought over from her old house, like the glowing globe that shines stars across the ceiling. I've always been jealous of that because I spent ages scraping my old fluorescent stars off the ceiling before she moved in. There's a white mug with a black 'S' on it holding three silver pencils. They look as sharp as spears. There's some little bottles of oil for her diffuser. Sometimes I walk past her room and wonder why I can smell mangoes. Here's why. Mango oil, and orange blossom and rosemary. I sniff the orange blossom and think of her in here curled up on the bed, by herself. My stomach does a little twist.

Of course there's some photos too. This is the first time I've had a good look at them. That's Silva when she was a baby with her parents. It's weird seeing Justin with hair. It's weird seeing *Silva* with hair. I mean, for a baby, she really had a lot of hair. In another picture, her fringe has been pulled into a band to stop it flopping in her eyes. It sticks out of her forehead like a unicorn horn. She's being cuddled by her mum so I think Justin must have taken the photo. It's in a white frame with a tiny little pink footprint on it. I move over to her books. She's still got the Korean and English dictionary that we picked up in a secondhand shop. We reckoned that if we worked hard enough we could understand every BTS song in eighteen months. Of course, we didn't get past two weeks.

Then something in my brain clicks and I go back to the picture of Silva as a baby. It's not Silva I'm looking at, it's her mum. She's got brown hair. It's long enough for the wind to blow it and make it stick to her face. I pick it up and stare at it. Then I turn the picture over. It's automatic. I've got a picture of me and Mum that Grandma took. I was tiny, not even a month old. Grandma put the picture in a photo frame and last year, Mum unclipped the back to show me that she'd saved a lock of my real baby hair. It was so soft, a little curl from the back of my neck.

I unclip the back of Silva's baby picture carefully. The last thing I need is for the glass to fall out and smash. I lift the back away. It's empty. I clip it closed again. I go into the sitting room and get the picture of Silva and her mum off the mantelpiece. Silva's mum's hair is a little darker and shorter in this picture. I know that it was already starting to fall out. Maybe – I turn the picture over and unclip the back and pull it away.

There is something underneath. It's a tiny pouch. I pluck it out and loosen the drawstring. I tip the bag on to my hand and a lock of hair falls out. It's tied up with a pink ribbon. Then I see that it's two locks, one darker and one lighter. I can feel rubber bands beneath the ribbon, holding the hair tight. There's still something else inside the pouch. I give it a little shake and a slip of paper falls out, like the ones they print jokes on in Christmas crackers. I read it. It doesn't make me laugh.

It's written in ink pen.

You and me, my darling, Silva. Always together.

I go and sit on Silva's bed. Baby Silva and her mum stare up at me from the picture. The thing that's bothering me again is that wig. The hair's too – I don't know. It felt like

80

it was made from cut-up drinking straws. It's the wrong colour for Marnie. If Silva shaved off all her hair to keep her mum company, why would her mum wear a really cheap wig? Why would Silva keep it when she's already got this picture?

I don't want to cry, but my body won't listen. I lie on Silva's bed. I don't care that all my tears must be making her duvet dank. I don't hear Azog pad in, but I feel her curl up next to my stomach. I scratch her head and she purrs. That makes me cry some more.

I feel my phone buzz in my pocket. I wipe my eyes on my sleeve, take my phone out and have a look.

14

I waited, Becks. I waited for him. I knew we would be together. I wanted it to happen soon. I looked through his company's website searching for pictures of him, just in case his smile started to fade in my head. He wasn't there.

I was frightened. The shadows were swirling around me. But how could I tell you all when you were so excited about the wedding?

I opened my own shopping account. I started off ordering things I could sneak into the kitchen – cat food, cling film, chickpeas. You know how small our kitchen is, Becks, it soon fills up. So I ordered things I'd hope I'd use. Glue sticks, staplers, sticky tape, even a mug stand. I took that to college and left it in the common room. Each time the text came through about the deliveries, I hoped it would be him.

I would open the door and it wasn't. I even started to ask other delivery drivers after him, but no one could help.

Just when I was about to give up, he sent me a letter, a real letter. I have it with me now.

I know that you've received letters, Becks. Dad told me. He said your mum was furious, but he made her tell you. I knew too. I hoped you'd tell me yourself. We haven't been very good at trusting each other, have we?

But do you remember how you felt when you opened the envelope for the first time? Did your heart beat harder?

I don't like letters. Dad says they bring only bad news or bills. Grandma wrote to me after Mum died, but the ink was smeared. I knew she'd been crying. Mum wrote a letter for me too, when she knew things were getting worse. I read it the week after she died, but I don't think I'll ever read it again.

But this letter, Becks, this letter was different. These were words I could read again and keep. He said there was a warmth and sadness in me. He'd seen it straight away and wanted to talk to me there and then. Life was complicated for him. Drivers were forbidden from dating customers, but the way he felt about me was too strong. I could ignore his letter. I could throw it away, if I wanted. But, could I give him a chance?

Chance? It was fate.

I held the letter so long I could see the shape of my fingerprints on the paper. I thought of all the stories Mum and Dad read to me when I was little, the stories where you close the book feeling happy. That's how I felt when I held his letter. My stomach hurt when I tapped the number he gave me into my phone.

We spoke every day. Sometimes for minutes when he was between deliveries. Sometimes, when I was sitting in the park near college watching the Year 12s flicking zoot ash across their Vans. Sometimes, we'd talk late at night, when I crawled to the bottom of the bed with the duvet covering my voice. Did you ever hear me, Becks?

I don't think so. You never knew. Nobody did.

Then, at last, I met him.

15

It was a message from China. She's invited me round to her place tonight to watch *Black Panther*. Just me and her, alone. Alone! My head needs to sort itself. China. Me. Alone. I said yes. Don't judge me. It don't mean that I don't care about Silva, it's just . . . I don't want to be at home holding it all down while everyone else goes off and has fun. I want something for myself too. Even if it's just a few hours.

I know I should be looking for Silva. But I've been doing that all day. I've even found out the boy's name. If I don't hear nothing soon, I can tell the police to go and interview that coach. He had enough to say for himself.

So what do I wear?

Going over to Savannah's was different. I'd looked good, but that was an accident. I can't wear the same clothes. I don't want China to think I ain't got nothing else. And my hair! Man, it's starting to look really mashed. I might have to use some of Mum's metal chopsticks to push all the frizzy bits back into the braids. If I keep this style in much longer, I'm gonna have to wear a head wrap. Mum's got a collection in a drawer somewhere from when she was discovering her African side.

I *could* go all Ghana for China. Man, this April's been so

hot, it could be Ghana. At Savannah's, China showed us pictures of her dad. He was full dashiki. China's more 80s b-girl, vintage tracksuit and baseball cap. So does that mean I can't wear my tracksuit in case she thinks I'm copying her? I can't even raid Silva's clothes because she's two sizes skinnier than me and got a different style. Funny, if we stood side by side and you had to pick the lesbian, most straight folks would say it was her. Maybe even some lesbians.

I put the locks of hair back in the pouch. Tied together in that ribbon, they look like they're cuddling each other. I clip them back inside the frame, then make sure the picture is in exactly the same place it was before on the mantelpiece. Right there, next to a photo from Mum and Justin's wedding. I love this photo. Mum looks amazing. She's wearing a tight, sunshine-yellow dress and carrying a bunch of bright blue flowers. I'd twisted some of the same flowers into my hair and Silva had pinned some to her bodycon. Justin's suit sort of matches the flowers and his tie matches Mum's dress. The sun's shining even though it rained for the whole week before and Mum made me get some quotes for fifty umbrellas for the walk from the registry office to the restaurant. It was a good job I didn't buy them.

I'm standing behind Mum and Silva's behind Justin. We're both slightly in a shadow. It was the parents' time to shine. Though when I look at it closely, I see that I'm smiling, Silva's not. She doesn't look cross or sad, or nothing.

It just looks like it's only her body that's there. Her mind is somewhere else.

You are the most beautiful. Was that what she was thinking about?

How am I supposed to know if she didn't tell no one?

China. That's what I'm gonna think now. China. Not Silva.

I go into my room and look through the pile of clean clothes Mum left for me to put away. All I've got is jeans. Not the black ones, though, because Azog slept on them and left her shape in fur across the legs. It's the washed out high-waist ones. They hold my shape well and I've got that polo neck that stops just where the jeans start. It's not a belly top but a little skin gets shown sometimes. My eyebrows have got a good shape but my nose pores look like they could suck in a spaceship.

It don't matter. We're just watching a film. Me and China are friends. That's all. No one cares if your friend's got nose pores like sinkholes.

My stomach's hurting again. I don't know if it's China or Silva making that happen. I run myself a deep bath and use some of Silva's bubbles, at least a fiver's worth. I think of Silva's shopping coming twice a week, when all of us were out. Did she dash open the door every time, hoping it was Logan? How did she feel when it wasn't?

Azog sits on the edge of the bath sweeping the bubbles out with her paw. (That's £1.60's worth, orc-cat.) I think about the wig and the locks of hair and wonder what the hell my sister's up to.

I flick bubbles on to Azog's nose.

'Pray to the cat-gods, Defiler, that Silva's gonna be here when I get back.'

16

China lives south, on one of those streets where all the buses stop too far away from the station to make it worth taking one. Then you start walking and wish you took the bus after all.

It's still light, so I'm not stressed and I don't get lost. I pick up some doughnuts and a big bottle of ginger beer to bring with me. I have to stop and take a breath before I knock on China's door. It's the same bright blue as ours and that makes me relax.

China opens straight away and grins at me. 'You found me okay?'

Yeah! I grin back.

China's not wearing a tracksuit. She's in a skirt. The first time ever I've seen that. It's kind of denim, button up the front and comes down to her knees. She's got an old Run-DMC tee tucked in the front. Both sides of her nose are pierced. She did it because her mum wouldn't let her get her septum done. Tonight she's got different coloured studs on each side. Her eyeliner's got perfect flicks and that looks like the only make-up she's wearing. I'm glad I went light on that too.

She shuts the door behind me. I smell cooking smells.

I realise that I've barely eaten all day.

'Doughnuts,' she says, holding her hands out. 'We can have them for pudding.'

My nose twitches. Man, I'm turning into my cat. 'Something smells really good.'

'Barbecue ribs. Just the ones you buy and stick straight in the oven but it was cheaper than getting takeaway.'

I nod.

'What do you think?' She holds her nails up for me to see. Red, black and gold – *Black Panther* colours.

I want to kiss her there and then, but – we're just friends. This is not a date.

'I better check the rice,' she says. 'If there's no rice, you can't call it a meal.'

'In my family too.'

'Even when you've got roast potatoes?'

'Yeah!'

We smile at each other again.

'Can you cut the cucumber for me?' she asks.

'D'you want it sliced or diced?'

She raises her eyebrows. It must have sounded like I was showing off. She don't know that I've been helping Mum out with meal prep since I was seven. There ain't no type of chopping that I don't do quicker and better than Jamie Oliver.

'Diced if you want a proper pretty salad,' she says. 'I've got tomato, avocado and baby spinach. There's sweetcorn too, if you think sweetcorn has a place in a salad.'

'I don't.'

She squeezes my shoulder. 'My girl!'

My heart almost stops, but she moves away and lifts the saucepan lid and checks the rice like those last words were just an accident. The heat makes her face damp.

I say, 'Dicing can make them too watery. If I cut the cucumber into sticks, we can just pick them up and dip them in the barbecue sauce.'

Because the shape of cucumber is the most important thing right now, huh?

China dabs her face with some kitchen towel. I see little spots of foundation on the paper. So she's got on more than just eye flicks. Did she try and make her skin look top just for me? She's invited me here alone. She wants her face to look good. So that must mean –

I DON'T KNOW WHAT IT MEANS!

I finish with the cucumber and China takes the ribs out and empties the rice into a bowl. She tells me where to find plates and trays. She puts the ginger beer in the fridge to cool. Meanwhile we've got sorrel to drink. China's mum's made it with lots of spices and sugar, just how my grandma makes it and my mum wants to learn to make it. Me, I just buy a bottle of Tropical Rhythms Sorrel and Ginger and twist the lid. This reminds me that homemade sorrel is so much better.

Finally, we're all assembled and ready. We load everything

on to our trays and take it into the sitting room. China's got one of them TVs that take up a whole wall but her sofa's just the right distance away for maximum enjoyment. We're gonna be sitting on there together. The film's set up and waiting for us.

How the hell do I eat ribs without spraying me and her with barbecue sauce?

I hear a swear word and see that China's dropped her rib in a splatter of sauce. There's a little trickle across the front of her T-shirt.

'I borrowed this from my brother.' She rubs at it with the kitchen towel. I wonder if I should offer to help when she just shakes her head and laughs. 'It doesn't matter. It's his punishment for being such a dick to me when we were little.' She picks up the remote control. 'Ready for Wakanda?'

I cross my wrists over my chest, pleased I remember to put my ribs down first.

We eat our food. We watch the film. We open our sachets of wet wipe things that must have been left over from a takeaway some time back and clean our hands. We put our trays down on the table in front. Martin Freeman appears and we both giggle, because even though we both expect him now, we're still laughing at our surprise when it happened the first time we saw the film. And somehow we've moved closer on the sofa.

It's just the way sisters sit. And friends. Good friends.

Shoulder to shoulder, my arm touching China's. Every

time I breathe out, it feels like we're even closer. Then her head is on my shoulder and I don't think I can breathe at all. T'Challa and Nakia and Okoye are in the underground casino in Busan. I got one eye on the Wakanda sistren strutting beside Panther there and another on my right hand trying to tell it that if China don't want me to put my arm round her, her head would still be upright. My hand ain't buying it.

Then suddenly I see something. I sit forward so quickly I'm sure I hear China's neck go crick. I want to say sorry, but I can't stop watching the film. It's *that* bit, the bit where the natural hair girls in the cinema cheer and the girls with weave suck their teeth. Yes! That bit! When Okoye dashes off her wig and throws it at the hoodlum.

'The hair,' I say.

'You knew the sista's bald,' China says. 'Or did you think she grew a full bob between Wakanda and Busan?'

'I mean the wig.'

'Yeah, Becks.' China makes those two words sound proper vexed. 'You have seen that bit before, right?'

I look at China. I see a whole faceful of disappointment looking back at me. She presses the remote and Okoye is frozen on the screen.

I say, 'I got to go.'

'You got to go?'

I nod.

'There's more food and the doughnuts and—'

'I'm sorry.' I fight against myself to tell her why, but even when I tell the story to myself, Silva comes out the worst. I don't want to do that to my sister. 'It's a weird family thing.'

China picks up her tray and stands up. I pick up mine. I follow her into the kitchen and wait while she scrapes her rib bones into the food caddy. Then I take my turn. I feel China watching me while I do it.

Her voice is quiet. 'Is it something I've done?'

I want to run up to her, put my arms round her and kiss her. I just shake my head.

'It's something at home. It's . . . it's a bit weird and I don't want to make someone look bad if I'm wrong.'

'And you really can't tell me? I'm not going to judge you, Becks.'

'Not yet. I'm sorry.'

'Right.' But she looks more sad than cross now. 'Do you need help with anything?'

'I don't know yet. Sorry. I'll . . .'

'Okay.' She takes out her phone. 'I'll get you a cab.'

I shake my head so hard I'm surprised all my braids don't shoot free in one go. 'It's all right! Mum only left enough money for . . .'

'Me and my brother have got a joint account. I think it's so Dad can keep track on us.' She gives me a little smile. 'This journey's going to confuse the hell out of them. Post code?'

I tell her. She nods and waits. 'It'll be here in three minutes.'

She comes with me to the hallway and opens the front door. 'Do you want to take your ginger beer?'

'No,' I say. 'Maybe we can save it and finish watching the film.'

She smiles. 'Good idea.' She goes back into the kitchen and comes back with the bag of doughnuts.

'Two for you and two for me?' she says.

We look at each other and for a moment I wonder if we should be kissing goodbye. She glances at her phone.

'Your cab's here,' she says.

I put my key in the front door. The double lock's still on. Nobody's in. I nearly turn round and go right back to China's. I don't want to be here alone. I want to walk into the kitchen and see Silva blitzing up one of her strange smoothies with Mum. I'd even offer to drink some of that bright green gunky one with cabbage and seeds and stuff right now. Another time, she used beetroot and it turned out the same purple as the potion they give Wakanda kings to make them into Panther. I got ready to bury her in sand while she had a vision.

But she's not here. It's just me and Azog again.

I need Mum. I need her right here and right now. I start up a message.

Sorry, Mum. I don't mean to stress you, but Silva's . . .

Delete. Try again.

**Sorry, Mum. Do you know if Justin's heard from Silva,
because she's . . .**

I stare at the phone until the screen goes blank.

Because she's disappeared. But no one just disappears,
not in real life. You leave pieces of yourself where you don't
mean to and end up getting found. Just like my wasteman
father.

Me and orc-cat go into Silva's room. Azog styles it so she's
heading that way and I'm just following her. I pull back the
bed and lift up the box of clues. I pull out the envelope and
empty the wig on to the bed. Then I get up a still on my
phone of wigged-up Okoye in the casino and lay it next to
Silva's wig. It's the same style. Definitely.

When people get crapped on by a friend or a girlfriend,
you can be sure that some folk always comes up with the
'you never really know someone' line. It's not that deep.
Course, you damn well don't really know someone. We all
keep a bit of ourselves locked away. But cosplay? Is that
the bit Silva's holding back? Serious? She's a secret *Black
Panther* cosplayer? *And she didn't even tell me?* Where's she
hidden the red dress and gold shoes? I've looked through her
stuff and didn't see nothing. We don't have floorboards to
hide them under.

Whatever Silva was doing with that wig, it must have

been important enough for her to keep it in the envelope in the box. A scary thought: what if it wasn't Silva wearing it? What if it was Logan? I flip the wig over and hold it close to see if there are other hairs in there. Nothing. I sigh and let the wig drop on to the envelope. I mean, this whole thing is mucked up, but not as mucked up as the thought of Silva dating a white dude playing a bald warrior sista from Wakanda – in a wig.

I feel like all my air has been let out. This is what I rushed away from China for. I send her a text. I tell her there's something happening with my sister and it's easier to explain when we meet up again. She sends me three hearts. I send back four. Then I lie down on Silva's bed next to the envelope. I plug in my headphones and scroll through my tunes. I end up with a mix of K-drama ballads with all them pretty straight couples staring at each other in slow motion. The music's cheesy, and imagining me and China staring at each other is even cheesier. But I don't care. Azog curls up by my stomach and I try to fall asleep.

17

Bang!

What the hell, man?

Bang! Bang!

Who's hitting my door like they're coming to take me away? I blink because my head's all fuzzed up. My eyeliner's splodged all over Silva's pillow.

The door bangs again. I push myself out of bed and try and pull on my jeans, and – how the hell did my own duvet get on top of me? Do my bedclothes come alive like *Toy Story* when no one's looking, or have I been sleepwalking? Heck! My head goes fuzzy again.

Bang! Bang! Bang! Bang!

'Hang on!'

I stagger over to the door with one leg in and one out of my trousers. I manage to sort it out and zip up. I lunge at the door and open it. A grocery delivery woman stands there scowling at me, the same one that came a couple of days ago.

'Hi,' I say. 'I'm really sorry. I was asleep.'

'Where do you want your bags? Kitchen or doorstep?'

'Hallway, please.'

She hauls the bags off the plastic crates and dumps them half a centimetre past the door frame. She swings back from the stack of crates to get more. One lands on my toe. Lucky, it's got light stuff in it.

She don't look like she's gonna welcome my conversation, but I have to try. I smile and say, 'Do you know any of the other drivers?'

A bag lands on my other foot. This one's heavier. I lift it off and try and keep my voice sweet, because her face is still fixed on full-vexed.

'I'm looking for this driver,' I say. 'He used to date my sister and—'

'Drivers are not allowed to date customers.'

I carry on. 'They met when he delivered some shopping last December.'

The last bag comes out the crate. I'm surprised there's so many. There must be one thing in each bag. She dumps it down and turns away.

'His name's Logan,' I say. 'Do you know him?'

'Logan?'

Her face is still and I wonder if some of her thoughts are Logan-shaped.

'I don't know anyone.' She shakes her head. 'I just do my job.'

'Please,' I say. 'I think my sister's in trouble.'

She frowns. 'Your sister, is she pregnant?'

Shit! That hadn't even been a thought, but now it's burning through my head. She sees my face and something in her softens.

99

'She's missing,' I say. 'And I think she might be with him.'

'Missing?'

I nod.

'You called the police?'

I nod again.

'I don't tell bad stories about people.' She leans towards me. 'Especially if I don't know if they're true. But there was a boy who hurt his ankle, not too bad, and he was supposed to come back to work. Then suddenly the managers are looking for drivers to cover his shifts. I heard he left because of a girl. Some of the drivers said she wouldn't leave him alone, and it wasn't fair that he was the one who had to go.'

'He left his job because of a girl?'

'From what I heard, it was a big problem for him, this girl. Not just this girl, lots of girls.'

Lots of girls?

She sighs. 'You hear some of the ways the drivers talk, it's like they're fighting off beautiful women every time they knock on the door. Especially the ugly drivers, they got more beautiful women than anyone. You know what I mean?'

Yeah, I know how boys like to big themselves up. Especially the ones that think they're owed. There was this boy in my class with a squashed face who was always yelling stuff at me on the bus after school. It's like he was trying to dig beneath me to find out my secrets. Lucky, I've got good friends who could tell him about himself in words he understood. Who did Silva trust?

The driver says, 'Any bags to take away?'

I shake my head and watch her stack the crates on the trolley.

'Logan the Legend,' she says. 'That's what some of the other drivers called him. I hope your sister comes home.'

'Thank you. So do I.'

She wheels the trolley towards the lift.

I lean over the shopping and close the door. I take two bags into the kitchen and dump them on the table. I open the fridge. There's a piece of paper wrapped round the smoothie bottle and it's got my name on it.

Of course, I recognise the writing. Mum wanted me and Silva to write all their wedding invitations by hand. She even bought gold and silver pens for the purpose. I spent ages practising because it seemed wrong to use my school writing, but when I tried to do fancy letters with flicks and joins, no one could read it. So in the end I let Silva write them all and I stuck them in the envelopes then chugged off to the post box.

I unwind the paper and spread it out across the shopping.

여동생

I came home to check on you! I didn't want to wake you up. Don't worry. I'm okay.

Speak soon.

잘 가

Silva xxxx

여동생. *Yeodongsaeng.* 'Little sister' in Korean.
잘 가. *Jal ga.* Go well.

Well, that's definitely Silva. And I damn well hope she *is* well, but still. Girl's taking the piss, no matter how many kisses she adds afterwards! How the hell am *I* supposed to *go well* if she creeps in like Ant-Man and disappears again? Doesn't wake me up. Don't ask how I am. Don't stay.

I find my phone and delete the draft message to Mum.

All of them are taking the piss, not just Silva. So what if Mum and Justin deserve a break? They've gone off and left me with a sister who don't want to be with me. Did they ask me if I minded? Well, yeah, okay, they did.

But was I ever gonna say, 'Mum, you've saved your money but you can't live your dream'? Mum's wanted to go to Japan since we saw *Spirited Away* together when I was six. She knew I'd never say no. She shouldn't have even asked.

And Justin, mate! You know your daughter. Remember how you told me what to do when she goes into herself? Leave her alone. That's all right when you're around, but not when you're not here. The only person I should be taking care of is Azog and mostly, she just cares for herself.

Mum and Justin, you should have been here dealing with this. Not me.

I go into my room. If I'd come in here first, I would have definitely known Silva visited. I'd thrown clothes on the bed from when I was deciding what to wear last night. Now they're sprawled on my sheet, but more neatly sprawled. Of course, my duvet's gone because she took it off my bed to cover me. My crossness is really stabbing at me now. I could have stayed with China longer! Instead I ran home to find a damn wig. Meanwhile, the wig owner left me a note wrapped round some damn smoothie!

It's like I don't matter to no one.

I pick up my pillow and throw it. My room's so small, it hits a wall half a second later and flops to the floor.

I take a breath. Then another one. I lift up my mattress and slip my hand underneath. I know I'm not winning no prizes for originality, but there ain't no place to hide nothing in here. My fingertips touch paper, then I hook in my nails and ease out my own big envelope.

DNA-Dad started writing me letters about a year ago. I came home from school and Mum handed me his first one. Her face made me feel wrong for taking it from her. I'd looked at it and wondered who the hell was gonna write to me. My grandmas send me cards now and again, sometimes with a cheque in them and Mum groans because they're always in her name and she has to spend ages queuing at the bank to pay them in. This envelope was small and straining, like there was a big letter folded up inside. The writing wasn't all that. They'd used my full name too. Rudbeckia Alicia.

Mum had said, 'Justin thought you should have it. It's from your father.'

I told her I wouldn't open it if she didn't want me to and

tried to give it back to her. She'd shaken her head and told me it wasn't *my* fault he was my father.

'I really don't know what he wants,' she'd said. 'But if he's giving you stress, give the thing back to me and I'll sort it out.'

She'd walked the two steps out of the kitchen into the sitting room. I'd watched her rearranging some placemats on the table then took the envelope into my bedroom and closed the door. I put on some music, the *Hamilton* soundtrack, because it makes me feel like I should be banging a drum and marching and I wanted loud beats. I don't know why, but I didn't want Mum to hear me opening the envelope. I slid my thumbnail under the flap then changed my mind and tore off the whole top edge like it was a pouch of Azog's cat food.

It was just one sheet of thin paper, the sort with blue lines on it so you can write straight. It had been folded over a few times, like a treasure map. I had to keep flattening it out before I could read it.

Yeah. DNA-Dad. He was still in prison. I knew that straight away because his name and prison number was written at the top. He wanted me to know that he was sorry. The first time I'd read it, I had to stop there and turn the letter face down on my bed. I didn't want to deal with it, the same way I don't want to deal with what's going on now.

I empty out the letters and pick out that first one. That time I'd stared at his writing, all I could think was I have no idea what you look like now. (Mum had given me a picture of him holding me when I was a baby. It was one of his quiet moments between doing criminal stuff and making other women pregnant.) I'd wanted to know what made him decide to write to me now. I'd wanted him to be sitting at a tiny desk in his cruddy cell with tears pouring down his cheek as he realised how wrong he'd been to desert me. I couldn't picture it though. I still didn't know his face.

I'd made myself read the whole letter later. If I was reading it, he'd said, Mum had managed to stop herself setting fire to it. For some reason, that had made me laugh. We've got so many smoke alarms, they go off even when the toaster's set to light brown. He was writing because he was out on licence soon. He'd already done ROTL. I had to look that up. Release On Temporary Licence, so he could go and work and see family. Well, he sure as hell hadn't seen me. I'd googled the prison address. It was about a hundred miles away. I supposed that's why he couldn't pop around.

He told me he'd had enough of prison and wanted to turn his life around and connect with all his children. *ALL*? Damn! How many of us were there? I was his first and the most special, though. Ah ha? Really?

I'd left it on my bed. I'd wanted Mum to ask me about it, but she just slammed things around for the rest of the day, especially when Justin was in the same room. Then I'd taken it into the kitchen and put it in the recycling, right on top so Mum could see it. It was still on top the next day, even though more recycling had been put in. I'd taken it out and squashed it into my jeans pocket, keeping it close in case Mum asked about it.

Another letter came two weeks later. It was left on the kitchen table under the pepper grinder. DNA-Dad had hoped I didn't mind him writing to me. If I did, I should let Mum know and he would stop. I didn't let Mum know and he carried on writing.

At last, Mum did ask me about the letters. I think she had to, or she would have burst. I'd come home from school and the new letter was stuck on the fridge with a giant ice cream magnet next to the Golden Stool takeaway menu.

I'd unstuck the magnet. The menu and three Boots vouchers fell off too. I'd swept the lot off the floor and managed to get them back on to the fridge. I'd stuck the letter in my blazer pocket.

Mum watched me. 'How's it going with your father?'

I'd tried to read her face but she wasn't giving nothing away.

'He seems to like writing you letters,' she said.

'Yeah, he's planning a break-out and wants me to mastermind it.'

'That's not funny, Becks. He can be quite . . . charming. But it's all surface. And he's not very good at keeping promises.'

'Promises? Like what?'

'Like staying out of prison.'

Mum's face had wrinkled up like her words tasted nasty.

Promises? Yeah, he'd promised he'd be the father he should be. He'd even been on special courses in prison about learning to be a better dad. He'd promised to stop making excuses because he hadn't had role models. Now *he* had to be the role model himself. He was my dad and wanted me to fly high, but if I found myself falling, he promised to be my safety net. All I had to do was ask.

I haven't. I've never replied at all. But he's still carried on writing to me. I'd felt I was doing something bad to Mum just by reading his letters. How would I feel if I actually wrote back?

A new letter came last week. DNA-Dad is out of prison and staying down in south London. He'd given me his phone number.

My safety net when there's no one else to hold me up?

18

London's awake now. I can feel it rumbling below me.

Are *you* awake yet, Becks?

I want you to know what happened next, after I left the bus. I couldn't come home, not when I knew for sure me and him should never have been apart. I had to find him or make it easier for him to find me. I'd cleaned everything to do with him out of my phone. It was a stupid thing to do, but I'd let myself be convinced it was best.

After I left the bus, I went to the Muster Cafe near Brick Lane. I stood outside looking through the window. Single people on separate tables were tapping at their laptops. Two women near the window were sharing chocolate cake. The older one dropped her fork on to the plate and laughed. For a second I could see two more blurry reflections in the glass.

Him and me.

It was our first real date. He'd been working extra shifts so it was hard for us to meet. Finally, we did. A Tuesday afternoon at the end of January.

The night before, I'd been out on a wedding food trial. Dad and your mum knew what they wanted for their wedding, didn't they? Nothing expensive, or over the top.

They were saving their money for this trip to Japan. But they did want a good meal for everyone afterwards. How many restaurants did we have to try out, Becks? I know you kept count.

Do you remember that time you couldn't come because you were late with your English essay? Your head of progress had phoned your mum. I heard her swearing about it afterwards.

I'd just wanted to stay in and plan what I should wear to meet him. I was so desperate for a friend to give me advice. A skirt or jeans, trainers or brogues? When my life swept uphill, all my friends flowed back down again.

Could I have asked you, Becks? Perhaps. Shall I be honest? I wanted to keep him my secret. He was something that was just mine. You wouldn't understand.

I worried that I would arrive at the cafe early and be sitting there alone. He messaged me when I was close to say he was already inside, towards the back. I opened the door and took a deep breath – warm pasta and cinnamon. A kind smell.

I hated weaving past the buggies and the pushed-out chairs to find him. I hated how my legs wanted to stop working and how I could feel every word in my head sparking out with each step I took. Have you ever felt that, Becks? How hard it is to get closer to the thing you want?

I worried that I wanted the thought of him, rather than the whole of him. That perhaps, I just wanted his smile.

He stood up. I saw him properly. I saw how his hair flicked up at the front and a hole in his left ear where an earring should be and how his lips reminded me of Jin from BTS. I imagine you grinning at that, Becks, but you know what I mean.

He smiled again and it felt right.

19

I've added DNA-Dad's number to my contacts. And what? It don't mean I'm gonna call him. To push that 'call' button, to hear his voice, to answer back – that's something I could never hide from Mum. Everything about the way me and Mum are together would change. I don't think I'm ready for that.

I go back to the box of clues. I pull it out from under the bed and take it into my room. Funny how I don't feel so stressed out coming into Silva's room this time. Man, I wonder what she was feeling when she saw me sprawled across her bed. Maybe her head was so full up with her own business, she didn't care. I line the stuff from the box up on the carpet. It takes up so much space I have to lie on my bed and look down at it. So what've I got an idea about?

All the tea towels and batteries and stuff, that was Silva's delivery calls, my sister burning through her allowance, hoping the same guy would turn up to tell her she's the most beautiful again. Then I suppose, he did come again and they got together. So I've got the receipts, especially that first one.

The Finsbury FC football article. Got that sorted.

The medal. No idea.

A roll of tape. Hardcore stick. Maybe that just came with all the other delivery stuff and ended up in the wrong place.

A counter. Or cloakroom token, or something.

An Okoye cosplay wig.

That clip-frame picture.

That stupid, stupid picture. Like there's nothing about this whole situation that don't vex me, but that this vexes me the most, even more than the cosplay. I think it's because K-pop brought me and Silva closer. We knew what we liked. Not always the same, but mostly. But some things we knew we definitely didn't like and Rain, man, we didn't like him. The first time we looked at *that* video, Silva swore out loud. (And Silva never swears.) But here he is, smirking out from under the glass, with his autograph underneath.

Was everything Silva did a lie? Pretending to like things. Pretending not to like things. Did she just pretend to like me?

I don't know now. I've got to find her to find out though.

I pick up the bobble-head Okoye from my bedside table. 'You got any bright ideas?'

I flick off her plastic wig and hold her far away from my eyes like I'm really waiting for her to answer. Even if she did, that would still be more normal than Silva having a signed Rain picture under her bed.

'If Silva did cosplay you, she'd need a dress, right?'

112

I prop Okoye up against my pillow, pick up the wig and place it in the box. It spreads across the red shrine material that's lining the inside. I look from Okoye to the material. It's the right colour, but there's not enough for a dress. It looks like leftovers. Did Silva make her own dress? Nah, if there was a sewing machine going in here, we sure as hell would have heard it.

It don't matter. I'm still nowhere near knowing where Silva is or what she's doing. I kiss bobble-head Okoye on her bald head and carefully balance her against the light on my table.

'Thanks, Warrior.'

The counter catches my eye. It all looks random, but nothing is. I learnt that from *Signal*. No one tell me that Korean dramas don't teach you nothing. No clue is too small. Silva saved this stuff for a special reason. I hold the counter between my finger and thumb and close my eyes. I'm not expecting magic or nothing stupid like that. Maybe, if I'm not looking at it, I might have different thoughts. None are coming. I drop it into the palm of my other hand and then close it inside a fist.

First, I think of playing Connect Four when it was just me and Mum. Those counters were bigger, though, with marks on them. And they were red and yellow, not green. Next, I think of the counters the cashier gave us in the supermarket.

Then, I get Silva superpowers and I can smell it in my

113

head, tramped-down grass and candy floss. When Silva's at a fair, she can probably smell the difference between all the rides and tell you what kind of toothpaste the woman behind the shooting range uses. I can't do that. But I can smell food, fried onions and burgers and caramelised peanuts, all of it wafting behind my nose.

This is a counter from a fair. The ones you've got to buy from a booth because they don't want the people operating the rides to stress out taking money.

I open my eyes. I should have got this straight away. I've got a counter exactly the same from the time I *didn't* go to the fair. I think I was so vexed my brain's blanked it out, even though it was only last month.

Me and Raych were supposed to go together, but I got a sore throat and a temperature. It hurt just to lift my head off the pillow and groan 'hello'. Raych came round to see me and somehow ended up going with Silva. They came home when it started to rain. They had a couple of leftover counters. Raych gave me hers in case I got to go later that week. Silva must have dropped hers in her Logan shrine.

Why though? Silva wasn't even supposed to go to the fair.

I go back into the kitchen and make myself put away the shopping, though there's barely room. I might have to stack spare stuff under my bed, like Silva. Except I've got drawers where she's got space. I hold up the jar of Nutella. It's so heavy I nearly need two hands. It still won't last long, though. I unscrew the lid and dip my finger right in to the bottom. I

114

scoop out a load straight on to my tongue. The sugar whack's so hard my eyes almost pop out.

A thought pops out too. *Who's gonna know what happened at the fair?* Raych, of course.

20

His smile was right, Becks.

Do you know what else was right? He listened.

He wouldn't talk about himself. He listened while I emptied out my life. Not in the way counsellors do because he wasn't trying to fix me.

Whenever my grandmother writes to me, she's always reminding me about the stages of grief – denial, anger, bargaining, depression and acceptance. I know them by heart now. Granny will always tell me which stage she's reached, bouncing between one and two. Mostly, though she's still angry. I think Dad's at stage five. He must be, to get married.

Me? I don't know, but wherever I go, people know about Mum. Teachers, counsellors, you and Win. It's like everyone else is trying to work out how I feel when I don't know myself.

He didn't do that, Becks. He smiled and asked me more about my dreams and ambitions and the things that mean the most to me. I even told him about you and me and K-pop. He didn't make a face or laugh. Afterwards, he told me about his life – that he lives with his sister and helps her look after her baby. His dad died last year and his mother moved back to Durham, leaving the flat to him and his sister. His older brother runs a boxing club.

We sat in the cafe for hours, even though I had my essay to finish and he was supposed to go to football practice. Instead we bought cake to share and leaned closer and closer to talk until we were tidied out the door.

We talked every day. It was like I had found all the words I'd lost.

I stood outside that cafe last Friday, feeling that warmth fill me again. Then I walked around the corner to the restaurant.

It had closed down. It was surrounded by a hoarding. An artist had painted it with army tanks and palm trees, a child peering out from behind a tree trunk, watching the soldiers advance. I closed my eyes and pressed my forehead against the wood. *Were we some of the last people to eat here?* I hope all our good memories are still held inside.

I don't like saying goodbye, Becks. It was hard for me not to cry at the airport. I knew Dad was watching me, like he was caught between me and Win. He sent me a message from the departure lounge. I think I convinced him I was fine. I convinced everyone, didn't I?

That first Tuesday, I didn't want to leave Logan. He didn't want to leave me. We'd stood outside the cafe as the owner pulled down the shutter, trying to hold that moment before we went our different ways.

We had walked part of the way together. The restaurant was on the corner. We agreed that we would meet there next time and for that night we would pretend to be different. He would be a vegan and I would be . . . I would be the girl I never am. No hoody. No T-shirt. No long skirt or jeans. I'd crept out in that second dress I bought with the wedding money, covered by a long coat. I'd found shoes in a charity shop, gold stack heels, high, tapering down at the toe. I even walked like someone else too.

He booked a table near the window, so we could watch the people passing by and invent lives for them. The man in the camouflage boiler suit was really a banker who changed out of his work clothes in Liverpool Street station and wanted everyone to think he was a badass vigilante. The woman in the lacy jumper and red lipstick did ballet in the park at lunchtime still wearing her high heels.

Afterwards, we went on to a basement club in Kings Cross and danced. When my feet hurt, he called me a taxi and came in it to drop me home. I was caught in the mist of his aftershave and car freshener and the heater made my stomach turn. I opened the door quickly like I wanted to escape, even though he offered to walk me to the door of our block. I wanted to wave from the sitting room window, but Dad was up and waiting. He'd just wanted to know I was safe.

We messaged. We talked. I know how these things work, Becks. I know how girls like me can be played, how our hearts can be prised open. Guys say the right words. Guys make us feel good. When we adore them, they abandon us.

I had my guard up. Believe me, I did.

21

Raych, I'm coming for you. You've got questions to answer. I'm not gonna let you wriggle out of this. I'm coming straight to your doorstep.

I have a quick shower, pull on some trackies and push the counter deep into a pocket. My head's hurting. I know it's not just the sugar. It's my brain trying to push through all the recent stuff and put it in good, proper order.

Good and proper ain't coming. Everything's wiggling round as I leave the flat. Still wiggling round as I sit in the bus. Nothing's close to making sense as I get off near Raych's street. And man, it's hot. Soon Accra's gonna be phoning London asking for its sun back. My trackie's gonna be dripping sweat on Raych's wooden floors.

Raych's house, man. Savannah, she lives in a house too. Raych, though. If you could roll my flat into a ball, it would fit in Raych's bedroom. She lives off one of those squares with railings round them and a locked gate so people like me can't walk in and enjoy the grass. I sometimes forget that our homes are so opposite. It's not just that I live in a flat. Rich people buy flats in Hackney now. We're in the not-rich flats, the ones with a Costcutters and a dry cleaner and a Chinese takeaway underneath. There's a community hall above the shops opposite. Every Sunday, it gets taken over by an African evangelical church. The preacher's got a microphone and he's so loud and goes on so long, I'm surprised no one in my house ain't converted yet. Whoever's on guitar ain't bad though and some of them sistas know how to praise God in harmony.

I don't think Raych's family can hear each other when they're in different rooms. No pastor's bawling through their windows trying to convert them. If he tried, he wouldn't last long. Raych's parents are lawyers. Though her dad works with poor families and refugees. It's her mum who helps big businesses, though Raych has never told me what help that is.

Raych's mum opens the front door. She's wearing tight trackies – definitely not Primark ones, like mine – and her hair's tied up in a ponytail.

She smiles at me. 'Nice to see you, Beckie.'

I've never had the heart to tell her I changed it to Becks in Year 7.

I say, 'Is it okay to see Ray – Rafaella?'

Her mum looks surprised. 'I'm afraid she's not here. Didn't she tell you?'

I run through what I remember of her schedule. 'Is she swimming?'

Raych's mum cuts her smile. 'That's slipped, of late. Maybe you can have a word with her.'

'Sure.' I keep my face straight and cross my fingers behind

my back. 'Do you know where she is?'

'She's on her way back from Melissa's.'

'In Leeds?' Raych hadn't said nothing about going to see her sister at uni.

'No, she's over at the flat. We want to rent it out again but the last tenants left it in such a state. We will never *ever* rent to students again.' She laughs. 'We wanted professional people, but who wants to live in Tottenham?'

Maybe people who already live in Tottenham? My polite face is so tight it feels like it's gonna tear.

Melissa definitely didn't want to live in Tottenham. Before heading up north, she was gonna go uni in London so her parents had bought her a flat. A real life one. Not even *Sims*. When Raych first told me that, there'd been a small pause. What could I say? We rent our flat from the council. Mum and I can't even afford to buy a bus stop in London.

My polite face stretches so hard it snaps and gives my mouth room to open.

'My grandma lives in Tottenham,' I say.

Raych's mum smiles at me again. 'I know. And I realise how bad that sounded. Tottenham has this – history that people outside of London don't really understand. Would you like to come in and wait?'

I can hear a hoover in the background. I can bet my last Wakandan dollar that it's not Raych's dad digging for dirt in the corners.

122

'It's okay,' I say. 'Thank you. I'll try and catch up with her later.'

I decide to walk part of the way home and end up on Fonthill Road. Man, this place makes me smile again. It's the bodycon, super-stretchy capital of London. It's where sequins land when they've run away from home. I wish I went to places where I could wear them types of dresses. Though I suppose when I had the chance to at the wedding, I wore a tux.

Folks are buzzing in and out of the shops. I see every kind of belly top and cut-off jeans enjoying the sunshine. Best Finish on the corner still has the same display, mad-coloured leggings squeezed over cut-off mannequin legs. Once, I filmed Savannah tick-tocking in front of them. The shop owner saw us and shooed us away. His loss. He could have used it for advertising.

I turn into the tunnel by the station. Heck, there's always been homeless folk and street drinkers in Finsbury, but it's like it's reached a new dimension. I'm walking past a whole town.

Is this my London? It's like I've been seeing the whole city wrong. I've been seeing everything wrong.

My phone goes. It's Raych. I stare at her name then answer.

'Hi Becks,' she says. 'How are you?'

'Did your mum tell you I've just been round?'

'Yeah. Has something happened? Are you okay?'

'Sort of. I need to ask you something.'

'You could have called.'

'I need to see you face to face.'

'Serious? Now you're making me really worried.'

'There's something I need to show you. It's about Silva.'

'Can't you just snap it?'

Yeah. I could. Just take the token out my pocket and send her a picture. But that feels too easy. I hear a train announcement for Liverpool Street. She must still be at the station. She could be at mine in forty minutes.

'No,' I say. 'I really need to see you.'

There's a noise that could be a sigh. 'Shall I come round?'

'Yes, please.'

She agrees and hangs up.

I wait ages for a bus then notice there's one of them yellow signs stuck to the bus stop post, telling me it's closed. I trudge up to the next one, getting crosser with every step. When the bus finally comes, no one sits next to me. I'm like the Gollum of the number 253. I might not stink of old caves, but I've definitely got an ill-favoured look. I message Raych when I'm at the stop before mine and she's already waiting for me outside our block. Azog's wrapping herself round her ankles. Traitor.

Raych smiles. I hadn't noticed before that her and her mum have the same smile. She's wearing Old Skool Vans and her earrings must have cost more than all my clothes put together. Suddenly, I'm feeling – I don't know. Sometimes she makes me feel bad about being me.

She walks behind me up the two flights and waits while I unlock and open the door.

She goes straight into the kitchen. 'I picked up some doughnuts. Shall I get plates?'

If it was me, I'd eat them straight out of the bag. 'I've already got some,' I say.

'Oh,' she says. 'Fair enough.'

I pluck the counter out my pocket and hold it in the palm of my hand. She looks at it and raises her eyebrows.

'We're going to need bigger plates than that.'

My face is no-jokes.

'Sorry,' she says. 'It's from *Jaws*. You know, they're gonna need a bigger boat when they realise the shark's enormous.'

I carry on looking at her.

'For when they catch the shark,' she says. 'We saw it together, remember?'

'Do you know what this is?' I ask.

She picks it out of my hand, then drops it back again. 'Yeah, of course, it's from the fairground. I saved it for you last month when you were ill. I hoped you'd still get to go. Are you giving it back to me now?'

She turns away and opens the cupboard next to the window. She takes out two plates and empties her doughnuts on to them. One doughnut's plain, just sugar on the outside and jam in the middle. The other one's covered in stripy green and pink icing. It looks like it's got minced-up Shrek inside. I want to say that out loud to Raych but why waste good joke energy on her?

I say, 'I want to show you something else.'

'Sure.'

She follows me out of the kitchen and stops. 'Are we seriously invading Silva's room? She's not going to like that!'

'I need you to help me.'

'Right,' Raych says, but still doesn't move.

'You have to come in,' I say.

'I don't feel comfortable doing that.'

'And I don't feel comfortable thinking my sister's not all right and I ain't done everything I can to help her out.'

'I get that, but . . . Okay.' Raych takes one ant-step inside.

'You know Silva. Do you think anything in here's out of place?'

'I don't know her *that* well.' She scans around. 'Not that I can see. But I don't know for sure.'

'That's what *I* thought, so I had to look harder.'

'Right.'

She reverses out pretty quick and we take the two-second journey to my room. It's hard to get in because of the stuff spread across the floor.

'Raych?'

'Becks?'

'I found all this stuff in a box under Silva's bed.'

'Blimey!'

I almost laugh. That word don't sound right in Raych's accent.

'What is it?' she asks.

'It's kind of like a shrine. To some boy she met.'

'Wow! Do you think she's with him now?'

'I don't know. Maybe. I'm trying to work it out.'

'Mmm.'

'What do you mean "mmm"?'

'I know why you're stressed, Becks, but you shouldn't dig through her things. It's wrong.'

She's standing in my room, in my home telling me I'm wrong for worrying about my sister? Maybe when you live in a big house you've got space to be private. There's four of us and a part-time cat in this small place. We've got to fit like Lego. Nothing's gonna stay hidden for ever, especially if you break promises and disappear.

I open my mouth and close it again. I wait a moment.

'Raych, do you know more about this than you're telling me?'

'What do you mean?' She keeps staring at the shrine.

'We've been friends since Year 4, right? I can tell when you're lying to me.'

'I haven't said anything.'

'Not saying counts as lying.' I flash the counter at her again. 'Do you have any idea why *this* was in the shrine box?'

She takes a big breath, bites her lip then takes the counter out my hand. This time she holds on to it.

'You don't know what it's like for her, Becks.'

'You're mad! Of course I know! I live with her. And she was coming round here for years before she moved in.'

'It still doesn't mean you know what it's like for her.'

'And you do?'

'Yes! Because I listen to people!'

'And I don't? Because as long as I remember I've been listening to you complain about all the things your parents want you to do.'

'Yeah, you listen to talking, Becks. But you never stay quiet enough to listen to anything else. Sometimes it's the things people don't say that they want you to hear the most. And sometimes you're only waiting for me to stop talking so you can start talking about yourself.'

Why's she saying this stuff? Raych is my best friend.

I bite back everything I want to say because, yeah, I can listen. I breathe slowly and wait for my stomach to calm down.

'Okay,' I say. 'Tell me what I missed about *my* sister.'

'See? You make it about you. It's about what Silva missed. She missed having someone that was – I don't know – the way she put it was that she missed having someone that was just hers. Logan was hers.'

Logan?

Yeah, Logan, Raych said, the name just rolling off her tongue like he's her own brother. She clocks my face change and swallows hard. Serious, I see her neck move.

128

I step towards her. 'You knew about Logan? And you didn't tell me?'

She steps back and folds her arms. 'See? Still making it about yourself.'

'You knew how stressed I was! But you just . . .'

I want to say something else. Something bad. I have a whole load of bad words saved up for moments like this. I want to use every single one on her. I'm gonna take another step towards her, because our kitchen's small. There's nowhere she can go. She has to pass me to get out the door.

But I clock her face. You don't win all them swimming medals or get top music grades if you give up easy. Raych has steel in her eyes. It's her mum's DNA. She's not gonna tell me nothing if I give her stress.

I move away and cross my arms too. Raych eyes the door, but doesn't move. We stand there bad-eyeing at each other like we're auditioning for *Mean Girls 3*.

'She didn't have anyone for herself?' I say. 'What do you mean?'

'All the wedding stuff was really stressful . . .'

'She hid it well.'

'For God's sake, Becks! Will you listen!'

I look down at my hands. Captain Marvel shoots lasers out hers. I wish she'd shared that gift around.

'Maybe you were too busy picking out your hairstyle to notice,' she says.

Lasers. Ones that zap ex-best friends into radioactive dust.

'Think about it, Becks. It was like she'd gone from having a mum and dad that was just hers, to not having anyone who was hers at all.'

'Justin still treats her like she's special.' Did Raych know how much extra allowance he was giving her? Yeah. Probably. 'And she's got my mum.'

'Yeah, Becks. *Your* mum.'

'Well, I got her dad,' I say. 'And I've got enough dads already. No one asked me if I needed a new one.'

'Becks! Do you want to hear this or not? Are you actually able to stop thinking about yourself?'

Yes, but why should I? I'm never allowed to talk about how I feel. I gave up my big room for Silva, and took the cupboard room. I even let Mum paint over our clouds and kites. Raych used to be the person I could tell stuff to. When did Silva become more important to her?

I keep my voice quiet. 'The Logan guy made her feel special, right?'

Raych nods.

'What else do you know?"

'Nothing.'

I look at the counter she's still holding. 'I don't believe you.'

'I don't feel comfortable . . .'

'I called the police, Raych, because I was so scared something's happened to her. If I can't work out what's going on, I'm gonna have to call the parents off their honeymoon.'

She drops the counter on the table next to the doughnuts.

'We saw him when we were at the fair,' she says. 'That's why we came home early. One minute me and Silva are chatting, the next I thought she was gonna pass out. I thought she'd come down with the bug you had, but then I saw who she was looking at. She had a kind of panic attack and then she wanted to run after him. I made her sit down on a bench with me and she told me all about it. He was there with someone else. He didn't see her. She said she'd known it was all over but seeing him made it more real.'

'You didn't tell me, though.'

'It was confidential, Raych. Do you want me to tell Silva everything you tell me?'

'No, but . . .' *She's not your friend!*

'But, what? Like you said, you live with her. She could tell you herself if she wanted to.'

Yes. She could have. Instead, she left me a note wrapped round some smoothie that didn't tell me nothing.

I say, 'So they're back together? Is that it?'

'Not that I know. Haven't you heard from her at all?'

I almost don't tell her. I want to hold stuff back too. But that's not gonna help.

'She came back last night and left me a note.'

Raych blows out her breath. 'Then you know she's all right.'

I shake my head. 'She won't talk to me, or even answer my messages.'

131

'Becks.' It's not just her smile that's like her mum. Her voice has got a tone in it that's the same too. 'Give her time. She'll be back.'

Then she gives me the Frodo smile. You know the one at the end of *Return of the King* when he's getting on the elf ship to sail away? He turns back to smile at all his hobbit mates who are bawling their eyes out. It's that smile.

'Sorry, Becks. I've got to go. Mum's having a big chucking-out session and I promised to help.'

I stand there while Raych leaves. I have to grip my bedroom door to stop myself grabbing the doughnuts and hurling them out the window. I want to watch the icing splat on her head. But I go back to my room and just sit there with the clues to Silva's secret life around me.

Raych knew about Logan and didn't tell me. That's the last chunk of our friendship floating away for ever. I don't need her. I've got other friends: Hannah, Savannah, Rianna – and . . . China.

The letterbox thumps down. I stick my head out into the hallway to look. White and brown envelopes for Mum and Justin. A leaflet from Morrisons about taking plastic off their fruit and veg, and a letter for me. A proper letter with my full name written on the front. DNA-Dad again.

22

Sorry, Becks. Sorry, sorry, sorry.

I wanted to come home, but there's a plan. I know it will work. I've thought about it for so long. Do you know what went through my mind? My plan is balancing on the edge of a knife. Remember when you made me watch the extended version of *Lord of the Rings* when we both had flu?

See. I'm thinking of you. But I think about him more.

Do you understand, yet?

He used to send me presents. His first gift made me laugh, a roll of zinc oxide tape for the blisters on my feet, with a message saying he'd love me warts and all. The gifts started coming nearly every day. I'm the only one home when the post arrives, so none of you knew. Those were my packages of secrets. He sent mango lip balm for my chapped lips and my favourite orange blossom oil for my diffuser. And then he sent me that picture of Rain.

Oh, Becks, I wish I could have told you about that.

I used to watch Logan play football on the Marshes. I walked through there last month. There was a man trying to fly a kite and two people kicking a ball around while a child swung from a goal crossbar. It made me feel emptier.

I used to love that walk. The wind was so sharp it cut

through my sadness. I'd walk along the canal and breathe in the smoke from the houseboat chimneys before turning away from the cyclists and dog-walkers into the nature reserve. Did you ever see the old machine parts there, Becks? Dad says it used to be a filter bed for the water from the canals. The gravel cleaned the water before it flowed away to the reservoir. He used to point out the stumps of metal and tell me what they used to be. There's a big concrete circle marked into segments. The boundaries are now covered in grass, and weeds poke through where the concrete has cracked.

Before Mum was ill, I used to think that everything had a place. My toys, my books, my clothes. Even the SpongeBob bowl that my first best friend, Mila, bought me as a birthday present had to have its special spot in the dishwasher. Then when it was clean, it had its own home inside the mixing bowl on the dishes shelf. I've always liked to know where things are.

It's the same with my thoughts. I believed that I understood myself by putting them in different mind-rooms. I had school thoughts and Mum thoughts and Dad thoughts and friend thoughts, then when my parents split up, thoughts about you and your mum. Those changed, Becks, in a good way. Believe me.

In my head, each set of thoughts stayed in their own section. I think Mum worried that I was too strict with myself and tried to make everything too clear-cut. She tried to tell me there isn't always a neat answer. I didn't believe her. It was obvious what things were right and what were wrong.

Then she became ill. I couldn't keep my Mum thoughts in their own neat box. They spread out and took over everything. When Dad and I walked round the old filter beds it made me feel better. That concrete circle had been drawn out so perfectly. Every segment looked exactly the same, but there was a mess of grass and weeds around it. Nothing was going to stop the daisies and dandelions breaking through. Dad said they were taking back land that was theirs. I think he was telling me that it was okay for me to be sad, but I don't think he could say those actual words. He was trying to keep his own sadness away from me.

I used to think about Dad and the filter beds when I was going to watch Logan play football. Sometimes I'd imagine that there'd been an apocalypse and that the natural world was claiming back the poisoned land. There are tents in the wooded parts, Becks. I think they belonged to homeless people, but I never saw them. I'd imagine that they were survivors from the apocalypse. The only people left on earth would be them and me and him.

That's selfish, I know. I'm sorry about that too.

I used to sit away from the team. Sometimes they would look over at me and laugh. He said it was because I shaved my head and they weren't used to that in a girl. Now I know it was because they were jealous. They wanted what we had.

I trusted him.

I went to a party, Becks. That's when we started to crumble.

23

Yeah, I opened DNA's new letter.

Yeah, I read it twice, three times, for the bit about him being a changed man.

Yeah, I called his number and I'm on the bus heading south to see him. Meeting him on the other side of the river makes it seem less real, like I'm going through a portal to another world. When I return home to real London, the portal closes and I can forget all about it. DNA's waiting in a cafe in Southwark Cathedral. He reckons it's cheaper than the posh places in Borough Market but not too far from the bus stop. He hopes I don't mind doing the travelling. I can use my pass for free buses, while he has to save every penny.

'I've walked holes into my trainers, Rudy,' he'd said on the phone.

Rudy. Serious? But then I suppose I call him DNA-Dad. I better try not to say that to his face. I managed not to call him *anything* on the phone. I just dialled the number and said, 'Hi, it's Becks'. There was a pause, so I added, 'Your daughter'. Lucky, he's only got one that I know of, so he knew me straight away.

'Oh my gosh, Rudy!' he said. 'It's so lovely to hear your voice.'

He'd sounded like he really meant it. I'd started crying. That's why I'm on a bus going over London Bridge to meet him for the first time since I was eighteen months and, more importantly, the first time since our shared DNA put him in prison.

The river is high and grey like it's made from rain instead of sea. A police boat shoots out from under the bridge heading east. The towers in Canary Wharf poke up into the clouds, like they're trying to hide mysterious experiments.

I stay on the bus until it turns into London Bridge station, then cut under the bridge to the cathedral. Borough Market is busy, even on a cold day like today. I've only been in there once. Mum, Justin, Silva and me went together, like we were a family on holiday, and had a good old look at the stalls. Justin nearly bought an ostrich burger, but Mum said it would be a pity if he didn't like it, because at that price he would still have to eat it. Silva had just looked at her dad in shock. The next day she turned vegan.

DNA-Dad – serious, I have to stop calling him that – is waiting for me outside the cathedral. I slow down as I get closer. I sort of know what he looks like. He sent me a picture in case I end up trying to talk to a stranger. He's a bit like Nick Fury in *Captain Marvel* but with short loxed-up hair and both eyes. I don't know how tall he is, though, or if he's fat or skinny or if he poses himself like a king or an elf. Maybe he'll see me and do a dab like Brainy Hulk in *Endgame*.

I walk towards him. On the bridge behind me, buses are heading back north. I want to be on one.

'Rudy!'

And there he is. DNA-Dad.

He looks – I don't know. He looks like he could be anybody. You know all those stories about twins who've been separated as babies and they meet each other again wearing the same clothes? It's like they've always known what's in each other's head. It shouldn't just be twins. If someone's half of you, you should feel special when you meet up, like you've finally found something you didn't realise was missing. I don't feel that at all. When I see him, he's just a bloke.

He's a bloke who's smiling. His teeth are something special, straight and pure white. Then I remember Rianna telling me about a dealer on her old estate who had perfect teeth too. It was the only thing he could do with his money without bringing too much attention to himself. Is that where the money from the cashboxes went? On dental work? Sure as hell, none of it came to Mum.

Okay, I've got to hold it down. He's here because he says he's changed.

DNA-Dad's light skin, lighter than me, with eyebrows like John Boyega. Or maybe he's just surprised to see me. There's a small mole above his top lip and I realise I've just touched the same place on my face. I ain't got one. I never have. He's wearing jeans and a black T-shirt with a golden fist on it that

139

I can just see under his leather jacket.

He steps towards me, arms up like he's heading for a hug. I have to stop myself stepping back.

'It's been so long,' he says. Then he smiles. 'Though that's not exactly your fault.'

This time I do step back. Because it *is* my fault and he knows it.

He looks confused, then breathes out.

'I mean it,' he says. 'Me going inside isn't your fault. I was the one acting stupid. As soon as the police interviewed me, I admitted what I'd done. It was a relief. I couldn't go on like that. I should thank you.'

I still don't know what to say. Is he happy I sent him to prison?

He raises his arms again, then drops them. 'Shall we go for a walk?'

I've been looking forward to a hot chocolate in the cafe but it might be harder to enjoy if we're staring awkwardly at each other across a table.

'Sure,' I say.

We have to separate to get through the buzz of kids in hi-vis waiting to get into the *Golden Hinde*. A man dressed up as a sailor is ahoying down at them from the boat.

DNA-Dad smiles. 'I've got a boy that age.'

The kids look about seven or eight.

A brother, a DNA-Brother that I know nothing about. I keep my face empty. 'What's his name?'

'Walcott. After the poet, Derek.'

I thought it was after the footballer, Theo. I'm glad I kept quiet about that.

I say, 'Do you see him at all?'

'No.'

We're on the cobbled bit of path. It's noisy – tourists are coming out of the Premier Inn with their luggage trollies, wheels clattering so hard I'm scared they're gonna break off.

'His mum was doing well for herself, working and taking an Open University degree and everything. I think she reckoned she could pull me up with her, but I was just pulling everyone down.'

'You left her?' I say.

'No, she left me. Moved all the way up to Glasgow to be with her folks.'

I don't know if I'm supposed to feel sorry for him. I don't. He touches my shoulder to guide me through a clump of tourists taking pictures of the broken-down old palace.

'But I'm not here to talk about me,' he says. 'What's happening with you?'

Suddenly, there's too much to say and I'm not sure if he's the right person to tell it to.

He's walking beside me again. 'I haven't seen you since you were a baby so I'm probably getting this all wrong. When I was inside, I planned out everything I wanted to say to you when we got to meet.' He touches my shoulder and keeps his hand there this time. '*If* we got to meet. Then I ended up writing it all down in my letters to you. I didn't even know if you got them. Respect to your mum for not dashing them straight in the bin.'

'She wouldn't do that,' I say too quickly.

DNA-Dad laughs. 'I'm not sure I believe you.'

I can't help smiling too. He does know her better than I thought.

We pass under the railway bridge. He digs into his jacket pocket, pulls out some cigarette papers then drops them back in again.

'Bad habit,' he says. 'Especially when you're inside. It costs you a fortune. A Polish bloke I shared a pad with set up his own shop selling . . .' He gives me a sideways look and stops talking. 'Let's go in here.'

He's spotted a Starbucks. I follow him in.

'What do you want?' he asks.

'Hot chocolate, please.'

I find us a table near a window. While he's ordering I check my phone. Nothing from Silva. Nothing from Raych, though I don't know what I'd be expecting. Mum's sent a panorama of a fish market with Justin grinning next to a pile of tentacles.

I look up as DNA-Dad comes back with my drink. A bubble of hot chocolate pops up through the beaker. When I lift off the lid, there's a cocoa powder heart on top.

'They're taking the mick.' He waves a cup of water at me.

'They were trying to tell me I had to buy a bottle if I wanted water. Why? They've got taps, haven't they?'

'Sorry,' I say quietly. I'd forgotten. He probably had less than a fiver on him and he used that to get me this giant hot chocolate.

He rubs his face. 'No, it's me who should be sorry. I need to change my attitude. Adjust back. Yeah.' He sips his water. 'I have to remember I'm not inside no more and it's normal for people to pay silly money for hot drinks.'

Earlier I was given doughnuts and didn't want them. Now there's a big size hot chocolate getting cold in front of me. It's probably gonna turn into ice cream before I drink any.

'Shall we start again?' DNA-Dad says. He stretches out his hand. 'Hi. I'm Benni. I'm your DNA dad.'

I almost fall off my chair. 'My what?'

He looks embarrassed, really embarrassed. 'Okay, not the best joke. But the way we found each other. DNA, yeah?'

Well, it's the way the police found him, but I nod and wonder if I look as embarrassed as he does. If I do, he ain't reading it. He rests his hands on the table, palms up like he's holding a really fat invisible cat.

'I don't suppose you want to call me Dad, do you?'

I keep my eyes on my hot chocolate. 'I don't think . . .'

'Yeah, well. I don't blame you. What about Benni?'

I nod at my drink. I have permission to call DNA-Dad by his first name. That don't seem right, neither, but I can't think of nothing else.

143

'And you don't mind if I call you Ru—'

'Becks. Everyone calls me Becks.'

'Oh. That's what stuck then. Becks.'

He gives my name a really hard 'b' that makes me think of bricks. I wonder if some walls are built so high and strong they can't be climbed over or knocked down.

'Yeah.'

'I need to stop my messing around then and call you by your proper name.'

He looks at me. I look back.

'It's a song,' he says. 'Rudy. "A Message to You."'

I shake my head and he shrugs.

I sip my hot chocolate. They'd forgotten the hot bit.

'Thank you for meeting me,' I say.

'It's what my heart's wanted for so many years, Ru— Becks. I wanted us to find a way to have a proper relationship. I nearly gave up on it all. I just thought that I could never be the father you deserve. Why should you trust me? But the course leader said I shouldn't. He told me I should give you options and be there when you need me.' He nudges my hot chocolate aside. I suppose he wants to see me properly. 'And on the phone it sounded like you needed me.'

My lips are stuck together. My headache's come south of the river to find me. My eyes are straining from trying not to cry.

'What's wrong, Becks?'

He says my name so softly I do start crying. He finds my

144

hand and squeezes it between both of his. Then he lets go, takes a paper serviette and wipes my face. My skin's gonna be full of tear smears.

He hands me the serviette. 'Sorry,' he says. 'I should have asked you first. It's been a long time.' He sighs.

I should tell him it doesn't matter but I don't know if that's true.

'It's about your sister, Silva, right?' Suddenly, he sounds like he's ready for business.

I nod.

'Okay, Becks. Shall we start there?'

I do. I let it all pour out of me until I can't talk no more.

Benni says, 'So you reckon she came back last night to check you're okay?'

'Yes.'

'But you think she's still with this boy Logan?'

'Yes.'

'You think she's in danger?'

It's like the 'do I think she's vulnerable' question the police asked.

'Her mum died a few years ago. I think it was tough for her when her dad married Mum.'

'Your mum's married?'

I bite my lip. I'd said she was on holiday with Justin. I hadn't mentioned it was a honeymoon.

'I never thought she was the marrying type,' he says. 'But then she probably thought the same about me and I've failed

145

at it twice.' He taps his mouth. 'Not saying that your mum will. I hope she doesn't. She deserves happiness.' He finds his phone. 'Which delivery company is it?'

I tell him and he searches for it on his phone.

'They're one of the good ones.' He lays his phone on the table. It's a couple of grades up from mine. 'They take fellows like me that have been away. I'd apply myself if I had a proper driving licence, but I know a couple of guys who work there. Maybe I can ask them to check out stories about this Logan bloke.'

'Yes, please.' *Yes, please? You're asking your just-out-of-jail father to spy for you?*

'And what do you want me to do if I find him?'

'I just want to know that he's not a . . .'

'Psycho?' We say the words together and half smile at each other.

'Have you called the police?'

'Yes. Though not the emergency line.'

'And your mum? And . . . her husband?'

'Not yet. I don't want to interrupt . . .'

He raises his eyebrows. 'Their honeymoon?'

'Yes.'

'Okay, leave this with me. I can put some feelers out. If we don't get no answers by tomorrow, bring her box of stuff round to me and we'll sort through it together. You shouldn't have to deal with this alone.'

His phone alarm goes off and he sighs. 'Got an appointment

with my probation officer. I get into all sorts of shi– crap if I miss it.'

He leans forward and kisses my forehead.

'Stay strong, honey. We'll sort this out together.'

I stand up. I almost leave my hot chocolate on the table, but I know it wasn't cheap. I take a sip. It's too sweet and the cocoa heart feels like sand.

24

Can I ask you for a favour, Becks? Look up the stages of grief. I used to believe that you gradually glide from denial to acceptance, but it doesn't work like that. They don't always come at you one at a time. Sometimes they're a firework sparking out and burning every bit of you.

After Mum died, I didn't think I could feel that deep sadness again, but when me and Logan splintered apart, I was back in darkness. It all washed over me again, anger, denial, depression. I went to college and sat there, silent. When I wasn't at college, I walked and walked.

I thought I had reached acceptance until I saw him on the bus. I haven't, but now I realise that's for a reason. I'm not supposed to accept it. We are not supposed to be apart.

After I left the closed-down restaurant, I walked past the shop where we bought the dress and then on to the pub on the bridge. I had to pick at the scabs so I could heal properly.

I'd been flattered when he asked me to his cousin's party, but I was frightened as well. For a month, it had been just us and I had wanted to keep him close to me. Now I had to show myself to a room full of strangers.

It was a dress-up party, Becks. I had to cosplay. Can you believe that? Every time I saw you, I wanted to tell you. And do you know what was worse? The theme was Marvel Universe.

Oh, Becks! I had no idea. Luckily, Logan did. His idea was perfect and I was going to tell you because you would have been such a help. But I didn't need you in the end.

One Sunday afternoon, Logan took me to the retro stalls and the vintage shops and basements full of clothes and old bookcases and dinner plates. We found the perfect dress in a market in a car park. It was red and strapless. I hid it under my bed. I had to keep checking it was there as I imagined it crawling out to show itself to you, Becks.

The party was in a pub by the canal. After we'd bought the dress, he took me there to see it so I wouldn't be nervous on the night. He wouldn't be able to meet me beforehand as he had promised to help with the preparations.

In the daytime, the street was busy. We walked through the market, weaving between the stalls. The sun was out and every table outside the pub was heavy with drinks, every chair occupied. The canal's towpath was crowded with buggies and dogs, stop-and-start cyclists. I saw a runner knock into a woman with a baby sling. He ran on and she stood there stunned, stroking her baby's forehead. Logan wanted to go down and check the child was okay, but others had already gathered around her. She wasn't hurt, just upset.

The pub is tilted towards the water like it's falling in slow motion. That night, I stood outside, staring along the canal towards the dark curves of the gas holders. Dad says he remembers them when they were working, the lift rising and falling, breathing gas. Now they are still and empty.

What happened next was my fault. I was in a bad mood. Your mum had organised yet another wedding meal try-out that night. She was upset that I didn't want to go because she thought this restaurant was going to be the one. It was hard to find a place that all our different family would enjoy. Do you remember that argument? You took my side and said you could eat for both of us. You thought I was late with college work. If you'd asked me the real reason – I don't know, Becks. Would I have told you?

Dad didn't take my side. He said I was being sulky and letting them down. I should have lied to him and said it was an essay, but that felt wrong. We'd promised after Mum died that we'd be honest with each other. He came into my room and sat on my bed so I had to look at him up close. It hurt because I saw my own face reflected in his and it reminded me how we'd changed. It's like the moment Mum passed away from us, we stopped for a moment too, our breath, our tears, any thoughts going through our heads. If I could have made my hand move to touch my heart, I'm sure it would have stopped too. Whenever Dad and I are together, just the two of us, our faces seem to go back to that moment. We don't have to say anything.

Dad asked me if I was really okay about the wedding. I was surprised, because he'd asked me many times before and I'd thought he believed me. Did Win ask you the same thing, Becks? Did you tell the whole truth? I was never sure if you wanted me to be your real sister. I said I was really happy for him. I am. I don't want him to be alone. I like your mum. And he loves you, Becks.

I was honest and told Dad I was going to a party with a boy.

'A boyfriend?'

'We've been talking for a while.'

'Talking.' He'd laughed. 'So that's what it's called now.' He touched my cheek, frowning. 'Is the party local?'

'In the pub by the canal.'

'London Fields?'

'Yes.'

'Don't walk back through the park late, Silva. Don't walk at all. Get a cab. I can give you some cash. What time *will* you be back?'

'Tomorrow, Dad.'

'Oh.' I saw the embarrassment on his face. 'Okay. Um. Is it an all-night party?'

I felt jealous of you, Becks. You'd never had to tell your mum you were into girls. It always seemed part of you. You can talk to Win about all these things. Dad just sat there, not knowing what to say.

I'd never had a proper boyfriend before. If Mum was here, I could have told her that I never thought that I'd be the one sitting in a sexual health clinic hearing about pills and condoms. I could have asked her what to do. I never thought

I'd like a boy enough to be naked in front of him, not just my body, but all the things in my head. Every time he stroked my wrist or kissed the edges of my lips or wrapped both arms around me so I could bury my face in his neck . . . every time, I knew how much I wanted it to be him.

Dad had made himself look at me. 'I know you're technically an adult and—'

'I'll be okay, Dad.'

He'd kissed my forehead and got up to go, so slowly that I thought he didn't want to leave me at all.

I'd waited until you all left before I started getting ready. You knocked on my door to call 'goodbye', but I didn't come out. I'd bought a wig from Paks in Finsbury Park – the woman behind the counter rushed out to help me. She'd held up virgin hair wigs that looked like they'd just been shorn from teenagers in Brazil. I think she was disappointed with my choice: cheap, synthetic and even for the seconds that I let it touch my head, it made my skin snap. I'd customised the dress, plaiting braid to make straps and decorate the bodice.

I had even tried to make a version of Okoye's neckband from picture wire. You'd have been proud of my efforts. I'd used face paint for Okoye's head tattoos. I wanted you there so much, Becks, laughing and drawing the bits I couldn't reach. You know I've only seen *Black Panther* once. The paint bumped through the stubble of my hair and I think the lines at the back were wobbly. But still, I felt like a warrior.

I scooped up the bag with the wig and spare shoes. When I walked out of the flat, down the steps and on to the street, I could have fought the world.

25

I called China. I didn't mean to. If I had meant to, I wouldn't have, because I'd be talking myself out of it and not getting round to pressing the 'call' button. But on the bus back from seeing DNA, I thought I was gonna explode. I wanted to phone up Mum and spill it all out to her, but I'd already sent her jokes about the tentacles. What was I gonna say in the follow-up? *I hope your sushi was top and by the way, Silva's gone?* Anyway, it's late night in Japan now. Mum wouldn't see it until tomorrow morning and by then, everything might be changed.

I'd scrolled through my contacts, saw China and my finger refused to move. I sent her a text saying 'hi' and she replied straight back. We got a text conversation going and she wanted to know why I had to leave her. I started to send her a message, but my thumbs weren't quick enough to remember everything I wanted to say. My spelling went bad and I'd only just got to the bit about Azog dumping her poo under Silva's bed. I deleted it all and just typed in **Silva's missing** and pressed 'send' quickly because I was getting off the bus.

Then I felt guilty. That's a really heavy message to throw at someone without more words around it, so I phoned her.

She was just about to phone me. Suddenly, I'm walking home from the bus stop telling her everything. She offered to come round. I said yes.

CHINA IS COMING ROUND TO MY FLAT! It's flashing through my brain like my laptop's error message.

I get home and straighten up the place. Funny, I didn't even think about doing that for Raych. I wish she'd stubbed her toe on the cat food tower. I go into my bedroom. I'll have to bring her in here to see the stuff from Silva's box. I put my clothes away and make sure there's no spit stains on the pillowcase. I open all the windows so there's air going through, but all the outside air wants to stay where it is.

I drink some orange juice, not even bothering to pour it into a glass, then remember that I better not serve China out of that carton. I let Azog in, then out, then in again. I put away everything on the drainer. I brush my teeth.

China texts me:

On my way.

I want to turn my head off and on again to fix up.

How long's it gonna take China to get here? It took me just over an hour to get to hers. Some kid made a red London bus on Minecraft and I think of China inside it, sliding along the road towards me. Man, I know those Minecraft buses don't move, but for China I would make it happen. I would fix the landscape so she would whizz through the traffic lights by the park and the next set on New North Road because I'd make them green. I know they've blocked off City Road to fix the gas pipes, so I'd build a ramp so China's bus could leap across them without stopping. That bus wouldn't stop until it arrived at my door.

I try and imagine China in the bus but I don't know where she likes to sit. We've never travelled together. If I was with her, I'd take her to the front at the top. We'd sit side by side, holding hands. Even if no one else could see it, we'd know. Our fingers would be tight together, maybe resting on her lap, maybe mine, maybe snuggled in between us. Maybe we're talking, but maybe we don't have to because we don't need to say nothing. We're just happy being next to each other.

I'd want us to kiss each other. In Minecraft, boxhead China and boxhead me can go in for a big one. But on the front row of the 141? Nah. There's still a few idiot boys who want to smash up girls like me.

I must have been wishing for that bus hard because just when I go into the bathroom to make triple sure I don't look like an orc, the intercom goes. I'd told China to text me when she was near. I go back and check my phone. She did! I damn well missed her message. What if she thinks I'm not here or she's got the wrong place? The intercom bleeps again.

Oh my god! China has come to my home! She's gonna set foot over my threshold, into my space. I have to remember this is not a date. This is a serious thing. This is me and China making plans to find my lost sister.

But—

The intercom bleeps again. I call into it.

'Just coming!'

I shove my key into my pocket and go downstairs to the main door.

China smiles. 'Were you worried I couldn't find my way up?'

I try to reply, but I can't. She looks too good. She's wearing a silver hoodie over black shorts and fishnets and lace-up, clumpy boots like she hustled them from a soldier on her way over. She's wearing the same Panther talon earrings too. There's a small rucksack on her back and she's carrying a case, like the ones make-up artists use. She looks – I don't know – polished. I don't mean flat shiny hair and face contour polish. I don't even know if she's wearing make-up. It's like the sun touched her skin and she's ready to shine for me.

She looks down at my feet and grins. 'You forgot your shoes.'

I look down too. I'm wearing the 'You've Got Seoul' socks that Justin bought me for my thirteenth birthday. Just as well I've never tried to be cool.

I pause like I'm expecting to follow her, then remember it's the other way round. I feel like my head's been turned upside down. Our feet walk in sync up the stairs and though my hand's a bit wobbly, I get my key in the lock first time. That's good because it means I don't look like I'm breaking into someone else's flat.

I wonder what she thinks of our little kitchen. She's got cupboards bigger than this under her sink.

'Nice flat,' she says.

'Thanks.'

She yanks a string bag out of her rucksack and thumps it on to the table. 'I brought this.'

I can see a bottle of ginger beer inside. I wonder if it's the one I'd left behind. She pulls out a plastic box and unclips the lid to show me ribs and rice with another little box of salad.

'Just in case,' she says.

In case of what? It don't matter. She's here.

She pulls out a chair. I sit down opposite her.

'Becks, I'm sorry you couldn't tell me about all this stuff happening to you before.'

'Yeah.' Thinking about it makes my throat hurt.

She stands up. 'Do you want to show me the things you found?'

I stand up too, but turn quickly so we don't end up staring in each other's faces. In China's house, ten steps takes us across the kitchen. In here, you can open our oven door with one hand and my bedroom with the other.

She comes right in. I'm glad I checked for spit stains because the only spare space is on the bed. We go in and step over the stuff on the floor. China crouches on my bed and rests her chin on her hands. I kneel next to her. Her weight on the mattress tips me towards her. I brace myself.

China scans the floor. I realise I've organised the clues in rows like I'm expecting her to give the best one a prize. The box is at the end. She reaches out, hooks the wig off the envelope and looks at me.

'The Okoye one?'

I nod.

'Is it just the wig you've got?'

I lean over and pull the box towards us. I hold up a corner of the red fabric.

She gives me a curious look. 'You think this is part of the casino dress?'

'I can't see anything else in her room that could be.' I think a couple of seconds before saying the next words. 'I searched through Silva's stuff. Just in case.'

She strokes my back. I almost unbrace and fall into her.

'If my brother went missing, I'd do the same.' She stops stroking my back so she can fiddle with the red fabric in the box. 'So you think she cosplayed your favourite character and didn't tell you.'

'It's not a big thing, I know.'

'It is, Becks. When other people love the things you do, it kind of brings you together. She knows you love *Panther*. Maybe she didn't understand all the reasons you do, but she still didn't tell you. I don't think she would do it to hurt

159

you, Becks, so maybe we have to understand what was going through her mind.'

China's hooked into my worry and now she's carrying it with me, it's a little bit lighter.

She picks up the print of the newspaper article. 'This one is . . . ?'

I go over what the coach said to me about Silva being a stalker.

'It doesn't mean it's true,' China says. 'He didn't ask himself enough questions. What did the man actually say to you?'

'He told me the boy was called Logan, though I don't think he meant to. And he said Silva was always coming to watch him play.'

'Sounds to me like she's supporting her man. When me and Poppy were together, she used to come to all my volleyball games.'

When she mentions Poppy, it feels like I've had orange juice flicked in my eye. I blink and try and keep my face straight.

'Becks?'

I realise China's said something else and I've missed it. 'Sorry.'

'I was just saying that Poppy used to play volleyball with us until she sprained her wrist.'

More orange juice. I blink again, but I carry on listening.

'She couldn't play, but she still came. She just liked the

game. She wanted to watch us and feel part of it. We can't always guess people's reasons for doing what they do. Did the coach ever talk to Silva?'

I think hard. 'He said he offered to talk to her about following Logan around, but Logan didn't want him to.'

'Logan didn't want him to . . .' China's face looks like she's bitten into the bad bit of a banana. 'What else did this man say?'

'They'd see Silva coming along the path from the canal and she'd sit far away from everybody.'

'She didn't even sit with them? Nobody talked to her at all? The coach just listened to what the boy said.'

China's anger is like a coat around her.

'I'm sorry,' I say. 'I should have stood up for Silva.'

China's frowning and shaking her head. 'You're sixteen! You shouldn't have to stand up to a grown man! You were doing the best thing, trying to find your sister. That damn coach could have helped you instead of talking rubbish.'

It don't make me feel no better.

She sighs and picks up the roll of tape. 'I know what this is, though. It's zinc tape.'

'Zinc tape?'

'Poppy used it on her wrist when she started playing volleyball again.'

I don't blink at 'Poppy' this time. Now I've heard it three times, I recognise how China's saying it. It's smooth and easy, no little blip before like when you want to hold on to someone's name before passing it on.

She stretches out a strip of tape. 'People tape themselves up when they've hurt themselves.'

I've never hurt myself bad enough to know that. 'I ain't seen Silva limping, or nothing.'

'Maybe it was his. Logan's.'

'Yeah, the coach said he hurt himself at football.'

'Could be that, then, but would he give it to Silva?'

Maybe he's with Silva in the Spiderman Multiverse, stuck to a wall. I keep quiet about that idea.

'Let's leave it for the moment.' China lays the tape down. 'Who's this?' She's holding up the photo in the clip-frame. 'Are those Korean letters? Is he one of them K-pop guys?' She squints at the autograph. 'Rain?'

'Yeah.'

'Why's your sister's got a framed picture of him? Do you think Logan looks like him?'

I don't mean to laugh. 'No. Logan's a white dude.'

She waves at Rain. 'Is she a fan?'

'No! He's meant to be like one of the godfathers of K-pop, but, man! Now and again, some of them groups turn up on a video in blackface . . .'

'Blackface? You serious?'

I feel myself blushing. Mostly because I want to defend them, but I remember my reaction when I saw some of those early days pictures, before they got reminded where

162

they got most of their beats from.

I take the picture and turn it face down. 'He did this video where they're all dressed up like LA gang boys. He whispers in a sista's ear and suddenly her boobs and butt shoot out.'

'Shoot out of what?'

'Her. They shoot out of her. Like they kind of get really big.'

China's face says . . . *and there's a problem with that?* Then she goes serious.

'Your sister's got a picture of this fool. In a frame.'

'Silva hates him. Serious. That's what I don't get. I learned a whole new load of swear words when me and Silva watched that video together.'

'It could have been a present.'

'Huh?'

'If she didn't buy it herself, maybe someone bought it for her. When I say "someone . . ."'

There was only one someone. We were looking at his shrine. Just when I think I'm getting hold of all this in my head, it twist-slides out again. Logan bought Silva a framed, signed photo of Rain. It looks like a real proper ink autograph too. It makes me shiver. I've always thought of Silva as closed in, but she opened all her secrets to Logan. I wonder what she's said about me.

China touches my cheek. I'm suddenly scared that she can feel the acne patch I've got hidden under my NYX Mahogany.

163

She says, 'Are you okay, Becks?'

'I just thought I knew her better.'

'Does she know everything about you?'

'Sort of.'

'Everything?'

I never told her about the boy who called me a name in the lunch queue, or how I cried when I saw the painted-over clouds on my old bedroom wall, or how I used to worry every day that Mum wanted to be with Justin more than me. 'Well, not everything.'

Her finger leaves my skin to pick up the medal. I can't help sneaking a look to check that she hasn't taken the foundation with her. No, it seems like it's still on my face.

She reads the inscription. '"Inspired".'

'Inspired to do what, though?'

'To punch someone. Inspired, it's the name of a boxing club off Holloway Road.'

'Serious?' I've been down that road so many times. I don't know how I managed to miss it. 'How do you know?'

'My brother filmed a promo for them. It was a fundraising thing. They were working with kids who were close to getting thrown out of school, but needed some better equipment.'

'You reckon Logan's into boxing?'

Then another thought hits me and suddenly I see my sister with her face bruised and her eyes all swelled up. Maybe she came back at night because she didn't want me to see how bad she looked. That note was to make me back down.

'We have to call the police, China!'

'Why?'

'He's violent, isn't he?'

'Oh, Becks. Loads of people go boxing. Some of them want to keep fit or learn self-defence. Some of the kids my brother met went there to stop themselves thumping their teacher. Look.'

She shows me the club's website on her phone. It's pretty basic, a menu with half the links not working and a gallery. Two of the photos show the outside of the club from different directions. None of them make it look like a palace. Then there's a picture of the man who runs it. He's a white guy, maybe twenty-seven or twenty-eight, wearing boxing gloves and a cap with the club name on it. It's the same font as the writing on the medal. The caption says 'Kurt Gladdinn, Founder'. He looks like he can't fix his mood for the camera and he's stuck between hardman Kurt and best uncle Kurt.

There's two action pics. The first one's got some women sparring, one white and one black, like the photographer asked for contrast. The other's some boys, two different shades of brown. The last picture is Kurt holding a trophy. I can't read the engraving, but this time he's definitely smiling. I go back and look at the women.

'It's him!' I say.

China gives me a sideways. 'Logan's a girl? Because I think you may have missed out a vital piece of information, Becks.'

'No! Behind them! Next to the lockers! That's him!'

It's like that baby toy, the one where the kid's got to fit the right block into the right-shaped hole. That face slips straight into my delivery man memory space. I zoom in on the picture but he goes all blurry. I shrink it again. We both peer at him. He looks so – so normal. But then I couldn't really remember much about him after he'd pitched up with our groceries that time, and I'd even had a conversation with him.

China says, 'That's the boy causing all this trouble?'

'Yeah. Logan the Legend.'

'Maybe some straight boys have a special smell, or something, that brings all the girls to their yard, because I can't see anything special about this one.'

She shakes her head and her earrings jangle. I reach up and touch the one closest to me. It stops swinging. She takes my fingers, brushes them against her cheek then looks back at the screen. She keeps hold of my hand. I let it fold around her thumb. Then I work out why my lungs are hurting and loosen my throat to let the air through. My head clears.

'Let's go there now, China! We can pick up the 271 to Holloway Road and . . .'

I'm not ready to let go of her yet, but this is more important. That's what my clear head is telling me. I straighten my hand, expecting her to do the same.

China still holds on to me. 'No, Becks.'

'No?'

She shakes her head. 'No.'

'You don't have to come.'

'Becks,' she says quietly. 'Didn't you see? It's closed because of a flood but it looks like they plan to open again tomorrow.'

'I . . . I can't wait that long.'

'You have to, Becks.'

She holds my hand up to her face again. I think she's gonna kiss my fingers and my heart's doing escape room business in my chest. But she lets go of my hand and for a moment it hangs there, then flops to my side like the bones have been taken out. She leans sideways and pulls her case towards her. She flips open the top. The compartments inside are full of nail varnish bottles. There's other stuff too, tweezers and wipes and little packets of shiny shapes. She looks round the room.

'Have you got a small table, or something?'

Mum's got one. I bring it from her and Justin's room.

'Perfect,' China says.

She lifts out the top layer from the case and pulls out a small, pink towel from underneath. She lays it across Mum's table.

'Are you up for it?'

'For what?'

'A treat.'

I notice how good her nails look, extensions glossed up in pink and white, like they know they're only pretending to be natural. The last fingernail on her right is a tiny Trinidad flag.

It looks good on her, but me, I don't do that sort of thing. It's not because it's a fem thing, it's just not a me thing.

'No extensions,' she says. 'You can wipe it off afterwards if you want. And . . .' She flashes up a pic of Janelle Monáe on her phone. The queen's flashing jewels on her fingertips and glitter. 'Where she goes, we have to follow.'

Preach. I hold out my hand and China leads me out the room. Both of us look like the floor's red hot as we hop around trying not to tread on Silva's stuff. We go into the bathroom.

'Fill the sink with warm water,' China says, 'and add something to make it soft.'

She goes back into my room. I drop in the plug and turn on the taps. I pour in a little of Mum's Neal's Yard geranium and orange bath oil. The scent fills the room and I feel guilty. That bougie oil was a wedding present and it looks like I've used half of it in the sink. There ain't even bubbles.

China comes back with a nail brush. She turns off the taps and stirs the water with her finger. She takes one of my hands and then another and gives every nail a little scrub, inside and out. Then she dunks my hand again and pulls out the plug. She takes a towel off the rack and wraps my hands like they're a baby.

'Next stage.' Back to my room again.

When she's checked my hands are properly dry, she takes out some clippers and gives my nails a trim. I feel a bit embarrassed seeing the little white clippings flying around. Next, she smooths everything down with a file, then searches for something else in her case. She pours a little liquid from a bottle on to a cotton pad then dabs it over my cuticles. She takes out a wooden stick and starts prodding them down.

'Can I ask you something?' she says. 'Not about Silva, though.'

I watch her squeeze the skin back on my thumb. 'Yeah,' I say. 'Okay.'

'How do you feel about seeing your dad?'

She's pouring all her attention on to my nails. I answer the side of her head.

'I don't know.'

'So why are you giving him your time? You don't owe him.'

She shifts her hand so my fingers are flat on her palm.

'I suppose I want to see how much of him's in me.'

'Like what?'

'Whether I got his forehead or his nose or his . . .'

'Fingers?' She strokes my littlest one with her thumb.

I have to wait for the feeling to go away before I answer.

'Yeah, fingers. And . . . and there might be things we say the same way or things we both don't like to eat.'

She looks straight into my face. 'Like sweetcorn in salad?'

I look back. 'Yeah. Or cheesy nachos.'

She laughs and the cuticle stick prods too hard. I flinch and China says sorry and strokes the place she hurt. When she stops, I want to tell her that it's still stinging so she can rub some more.

Instead, I say, 'I don't get it. Serious, China, the nachos go all soggy and you end up with cheesy grease round your face. It's nasty.'

She is back nudging my cuticles. 'My mum took me to New York when I was in primary school and we went to see *Toy Story 3* in the cinema. Everyone had these massive trays full of nachos and they were munching all the way through the sad bits. It didn't bother me but it drove my mum wild.'

New York. Damn. I saw *Toy Story 3* on a dodgy DVD that Justin got from his cousin. She looks up. 'I've got a special design for your nails.'

'Cool.'

'Do you want to put some music on?'

'Sure. What do you like?'

'You choose.'

I don't want to choose! What the hell if it's something she really hates? Or a song that knocks out an n-word I'd forgotten about? That could kill the mood. I play safe and find a playlist on my laptop that I made for Mum. She'd said it was okay to add a bit of everything and I'd been careful about content. The first song that comes up is 'Singularity'.

China's lifting little bottles out of her case. She pauses. 'Who's this?'

'BTS. I can switch.'

'No, it's all right. I always thought K-pop was a bit more,

I dunno, pop. This is like 90s new jack swing. But in Korean. And kinda sexy.'

She lines up the bottles, switching them until she's happy with the order.

'Stretch out your hands.'

My hands are right out there like I'm about to start playing piano. She squeezes hand cream into her own hand then rubs it into mine, one hand at a time, into my palm and the back of my hands and between my fingers. The only trace it leaves is the smell. I hold my hand to my nose and sniff. It's like the stuff from the testers in Space NK.

'Good?' She's smiling.

'Yeah. Really good.'

'Time for the base coat.'

I lay my hands flat on the towel. China leans over me so close I could breathe into her ear. There's a tiny mole on her lobe that I always thought was an earring hole.

She says, 'Did you know that a beck is a stream?'

I want to say, 'No, I don't' and it don't matter because my real name's Rudbeckia. I do know what that is. It's a flower that's usually golden with a brown centre. Mum says I'm the other way round. I could tell China that but I don't want to disturb the air. One small breath might blow away the smell of hand cream and China's skin and hair so close to me.

'People usually think that black people are from London, right?' China says. 'When my mum came down here and opened her mouth people looked surprised at her accent.

Even the black people. It's weird. If you've got an accent from the north of Nigeria or Ghana or Jamaica, people accept you. If it's from north England, everyone's raising their eyebrows. In the end she made herself sound like she'd never lived anywhere except London. Though she kept some of her words and taught them to me. Beck was one of them.'

I'm watching her brush the base coat across my nails, two strokes on each finger except for my thumb that gets three. Sometimes I walk past the nail parlours and the stink makes me cough. I see all the people doing the nails have nose masks on. The folks getting their nails done must be able to hold their breath longer than a whale, because that's pure chemicals. Even the base coat tingles, but it soon fades away.

'We have to wait for this to dry,' she says.

I nod.

The next track is Drake's 'God's Plan'. I watch to see how China reacts. Savannah thinks Drake's had his time, but China's mouthing all the words and we sing the bit about loving our bed and our momma together. I wonder how you love someone partly.

'Ready for the next layer?' China says.

She opens a bottle of blue polish. It must have sparkles inside because I start to glitter. Watching China, soft and steady, makes me feel calmer. I'm looking so hard, I don't even notice when she starts to add something to one of my little fingers. Tiny yellow lines, touched up with orange and a brown dot centre. I think it's meant to be a sunflower, but to me it's a rudbeckia. I want to kiss her now. I want to kiss her so much she'll have to get a lawyer to stop me. But she's screwing the top back on the polish and picking up another bottle and squinting at it.

'Top coat,' she says. 'I'm sorry I can't stay too long. We're heading down to Devon first thing tomorrow.'

She's leaving?

And suddenly, I do it. I grab her shoulder and I pull her towards me and kiss her. She's not ready so her lips are making the wrong shape, but then they reform so they're fitting with mine. One of her hands is on the back of my neck, the other's held out still holding the nail polish. I'm kinda hugging her with my wrists because I don't want to smudge her work.

When we stop kissing, I realise that I'm crying again. She hugs me so tight we're like one of those wood carvings you see in the aunties' front rooms, two people together and you can't see where they join. She's stroking my neck and telling me everything will be all right.

Her phone rings. She lets go of me to answer it. It's her mum and I realise that China must have crept out without telling no one. I gather together the nail stuff and put them back in the box. By the time she comes off the phone, it's all packed away. She shakes her head and says, 'Sorry.'

I should say something really deep about not wanting her to go, but all I manage is, 'We didn't get to eat.'

'The ribs are for you,' she says. 'To give you strength.'

China's my strength. As soon as she goes out the door, my strength's gonna go with her. So I walk out with her and she takes my hand as we head down the stairs, out the block and on to the main road where the buses stop. She keeps hold of it, even though an old man at the bus stop is giving us a sneaky look. Then when the bus comes, she kisses me on the lips so everyone can see.

I walk back to the flat alone.

But she's already texting me and I'm texting back. Her energy's coming through the phone and I know that I can do this. I can go to the boxing club by myself. I can find Silva, even if she don't want to be found. I can make everything all right.

I go into the kitchen and peel the lids off the food, careful so I don't mash up my nails, all blue and glittery, like water. A beck. Then the golden flower, tiny and perfect. I hadn't realised how hungry I was, but the ribs and salad don't last no time. The ginger beer is perfect to wash it down.

China messages me to say she's home safe and has to ditch her phone to spend some time with her mum. I hope *my* mum's having a good time. She deserves this break. Then I go and put the latch on the door. If Silva wants to get in, she'll have to message me first.

I go back into my room. Azog is sitting in the shrine box. I sigh and lift her out. The red fabric gets caught around her and something metal drops on to the carpet. I plop Azog down. The thing that's fallen out is a key, a cheap one on a thin silver ring. It looks like a swimming locker key. I take a picture for China. Then I go back on to the Inspired website, and find Logan. He's in the background, and in the background behind him – yeah. I've remembered right. Lockers.

26

I was still a warrior when I waited outside the pub for Logan to come down and meet me. I could hear the music and the voices leaking through the open windows. I should have been nervous, but I was filled with energy. Warrior energy. You know what I mean, Becks!

But I still held the anger from earlier. I should have left it behind in my bedroom.

He came towards me out of the pub, smiling. He was wearing a suit and carrying a briefcase. He'd written 'Everett Ross' on it in black Sharpie, so everyone knew who he was supposed to be. He'd tried to brush his hair to look like Martin Freeman, but I think only I noticed. But it wasn't about him, he'd said. It was about me.

He asked me to show him my costume. I was wearing a scarf to hide my Okoye head tattoos and a long coat. I took them off and his smile shifted.

'You cut up the dress, Silva. Why?'

I'd showed him the picture of Okoye's casino dress on my phone. He'd looked from the screen to me.

'But you didn't ask me first?'

'I didn't think you mind.'

'It's just that we chose that dress together and it felt

176

special.'

'It's still special. Even more special. More like the real thing.' I held up the bag. 'Wig or no wig?'

'It doesn't really matter. The dress looked good as it was. You didn't need to do nothing to it.'

He walked back into the pub with me following.

The air in the upstairs bar was scratchy with perfume and hairspray and heavy with alcohol and dancers' heat. Everyone had dressed up but I didn't know who people were supposed to be. I missed you again, Becks. You would have known them all.

A girl in a gold helmet and blue tunic stopped by us. Her sleeves were padded out to look like she was full of muscles.

'Good Thanos,' Logan said.

She'd looked him up and down. 'Who are you supposed to be?'

He held up the briefcase.

'Of course,' she'd said. 'Another white boy that needs fixing.' She'd tapped my arm. Her fingers were lost in a massive glove. 'If you're Okoye, aren't you supposed to have a wig?'

I took it out of my bag and put it on.

'Good,' she said. 'A little advice, Okoye. Keep trying to be someone different. It might help.'

She wasn't looking at me, though. Her eyes were on Logan. I tucked my arm into his.

'And another thing, Logan.' She was looking at me again. 'Congratulations on the new Avenger.'

She weaved away towards the bar.

'I'm your new Avenger?' I'd asked.

'Yeah. You are.'

'I don't understand why she congratulated you.'

'We went out a while back. I don't know. She was trying to be funny.'

I held him tighter and looked over the crowd for her, but she had gone.

'Does she want you back?' I'd asked. 'She'd looked at you like . . . Like you were hers.'

He wasn't anybody's. He'd said it, and laughed.

The drinks were cocktails decorated with Infinity Stones. I only know that because I'd wanted to know why the ice was different colours. I imagined you shaking your head slowly at me and telling me what they were. Mind, power, reality, soul, space and time.

How do you hold someone's soul? I wish I knew.

The music was from the 80s and 90s, songs I'd heard Mum and Dad play when I was little. We danced and he stayed close to me. I'd thought I'd be introduced to people but he knew I was shy and just us being together was enough.

When he left me to find more drinks, his brother came over. It was like he was waiting for the moment. He wasn't in a costume, just jeans and a T-shirt. He asked my name and how I met Logan. I didn't want to answer because he spoke like he had a right to be told. I saw him for what he was, Becks, ready to smash his way between us.

He held out his hand for me to shake and said he was sorry he wasn't good at small talk. His name was Kurt and I could see the family resemblance, but he was taller, his nose twisted and there was a cut above his eyebrow. I told him my name. I said we'd met at work. I'd looked over his shoulder to try and find Logan, but it was just strangers and superheroes.

'Work?' He laughed. 'Which job?'

'The one he has now.'

'Right.'

He stood there, watching my face. 'What has my brother told you about—'

Logan appeared. He thumped the drinks on to a table and stepped up close to his brother.

'You didn't say you were coming!'

'You didn't say you were bringing a new guest.'

Kurt grabbed Logan's arm and pulled him out of the door. For a few seconds, I stood there, heart beating, as the party carried on around me. 'Mr Blue Sky' blared out and there was a cheer and everyone started singing along. A circle formed around a dancer that was dressed like a tree. I'd wished I was part of all this.

But that's why I needed Logan. When I'm with him, the shadows fall back to the edges. The loneliness twists in on itself until it almost disappears. If I'm torn from him, I know that all that badness will creep back.

I took a sip of the drink. It tasted like Night Nurse.

The song finished and I was still there, alone. I could see a guy looking at me from across the bar wearing a gold helmet with curved horns. Were there devils in the Marvel Universe? Are you shaking your head at me again, Becks? I didn't know, though. He was trying hard to meet my eye. He was also wearing a gold chest-plate that was so much wider than him that it almost made me smile. I don't think he would have minded me asking who he was dressed as, but he wasn't the one I wanted.

I went to look for Logan, my heels clattering on the stairs as I ran out. His brother was sitting alone by the canal. I watched him finish drinking a bottle of beer and throw it spinning through the air. It landed with a splash in the dark water. As he stood up, he saw me.

'He's gone.'

'Without me?'

He moved around me and stood by the pub door. 'He shouldn't have come. Sorry.'

'Did you make him leave me?'

He stood there a moment, with his hand on the door. 'I made him remember where his responsibilities are.'

'His responsibilities?' They were with me. I knew that.

'If you really want to know, pass by the boxing club. It's called Inspired, just off Holloway Road.' He turned away then back again.

'Can you get home all right?'

I managed to nod my head and walk away.

Do you know that feeling, Becks? Like your guts have been hooked out through your mouth and squeezed to a mulch in front of you? That was me.

I was sitting by the bus stop watching as the buses paused then moved on. But Logan found me! He put his arms around me and told me how sorry he was. His brother was a bully and hated anyone being happy. He understood if I wanted to end it, but if we could talk – he wanted to talk. He wanted to be honest. He wanted me to understand who he really was.

We could walk our separate ways, there or then, or I could go with him as we'd planned. It was my choice.

27

Yes, it was my choice.

All of this is my choice.

What happens next is my choice. I don't want to hurt you, Becks. I don't want you to think badly of me, but please tell me you understand. You want someone so much that every molecule of your body is reaching out to them. But imagine, Becks, that every molecule of their body is reaching out to you as well. Would you give that up?

The wall here is cold against my back. There are shadows, real shadows, but I'm not ready for brightness yet. Early this morning, I pushed my nose into the pillow. I tried to remember sweat and leaking showers and leather. There was nothing.

After Logan found me at the bus stop, my choice was to go back with him. How could I come home when Dad was expecting me to stay out until morning? How could I face all your questions and sad smiles for me? But also, Becks, I wanted to be with him so much. We were supposed to go back to his flat as his sister was meant to be going away with his niece. But the baby was ill so they'd stayed home. Logan said they wouldn't want to be disturbed.

Becks, I'm not romantic. I didn't expect four-poster beds

and champagne and the world crumbling away around me. I know that sex can hurt and be messy and awkward. There was no pressure, Becks, I swear.

We took a cab and walked through the park. It had taken a while for him to find his keys. The park had still been busy and I was frightened that anyone who passed would turn their attention on us. We crept into a cold, dark building, my flat shoes slapping against the slippery floor, my heels in my hand. No four-poster, but an airbed and sleeping bags and the smell of sweat and damp leather in an empty boxing gym.

He kissed me and – I don't know how much I want to tell you. It's private and between me and him. We were careful, Becks. We've just found each other. I want it to be just the two of us for a while. It did hurt at first and he kept his eyes closed. Is that normal? I don't know. Did he want me to be someone else? The girl who'd congratulated him earlier? I'd turned my head and saw my red dress, a dark shadow pooled on the floor by the mattress.

Afterwards, we lay awake and listened to a man calling for his dog outside the window. That's when he told me that his mother hadn't moved to Durham. She died just after his dad. Logan and his sister had inherited the flat in London. He said he hadn't told me about his mother before because it would be like he was trying to make his life harder than mine. They hadn't been close, but he missed her. His brother was jealous because she'd only left the flat to him and his sister. He knows he doesn't always do the right thing, but he knew I was right. We were right.

We . . . we tangled together again, and this time our eyes were open and I felt my heart jump.

We left the gym early, before his brother arrived. He found me an old sweatshirt in his locker, but I gave it back to him at the bus stop. The smell was wrong for me. He waited until the bus came and kissed me goodbye.

Even at five in the morning, the bus was busy. There were people changing shifts at the hospitals and council workers heading to a depot. An older woman across the aisle from me was deep into her Bible. On the top deck, a group were shouting songs at each other. A bottle rolled across the floor upstairs then banged down the stairs at the back. I looked out of the window and saw a young black guy with a white girl on his back, trying to race the bus at the traffic light. That will be me and Logan one day. In front of me, a Rasta guy in a hi-vis saw them, sucked his teeth and started to tell his white workmate how Jesus's name is used to scam the black man. The white man tried to meet my eye then thought better of it. In that light, he probably couldn't work out what side I'd be on.

Whose side was I on? I was on Logan's and he was on mine. Becks, you don't need anyone. You are your own force. Me? I do. On that bus home, it was the first time I felt that I belonged. I was part of something.

I got off by the main road and walked through the estate.

A delivery van was parked outside the newsagent and a jogger flitted past me. A cat was slinking by Mr Phan's window, but it was too big and ginger to be yours. I looked up at our sitting room window. The curtains hadn't been drawn and I could see a hint of brightness. The light in the hallway had been left on. I hoped the latch was off as I didn't want to wake anyone up.

But – I was finally equal, Becks. Dad and your mum had each other. You have everyone, your friends and all the girls that see you as the wonderful person you are. Me, I had Logan.

And then, he left me. Completely.

28

China. She's filling up my head. That should be good, right? But, man! My stupid dream turned her into a robot in boxing gloves leaping out a stream to punch me.

First thing I do when I wake up is check my nails, just in case I thrashed around and damaged my rudbeckia. A dot of blue on one of the thumbs is missing, but my flower is still golden and whole. It's like the totems in *Inception*. Now I see it I know I'm properly awake.

Azog's fallen asleep on the pillow next to me. Silva's gonna go mad if she finds out there's been a cat's butt where her head lays itself down. If she finds out? She *is* gonna find out. She sure as hell found out that I was sleeping in here. When I find her I'm gonna tell her. This used to be my room. If Silva don't want it, me and my cat will have it back. And I'm gonna make her hear about every second of every moment of crap that's gone down since she abandoned me. And I don't just mean Azog's crap, neither.

Inspired Boxing Club is only one bus ride away. The answers are waiting for me right there in the mouth of Kurt Gladdinn, Founder. If man don't tell me where my sister's got to, I'm gonna call the police. Or Mum and Justin. No, both.

My phone's going off somewhere. My heart pops. It's China. Last night, she said she wanted to be the first person to talk to me this morning. My girl's keeping her promise.

My girl. CHINA IS MY GIRL.

Isn't she?

My phone's fallen down the side of the bed and the ringing stops. I dig it out. It's only quarter past seven. When all this is done, my holiday is gonna start proper. Though if it is China, I won't mind. She promised to set her alarm specially. I stare at the screen. It's not her. She left me a couple of messages around 6.30. Mum has too. It's DNA-Dad who wants to talk.

I read China's messages. They give me strength.

Then I read Mum's. They give me questions. She's not asked me nothing about Silva. Are the parents getting the Silva texts that should be coming to me?

Time to phone DNA.

'Hi,' I say. 'It's Becks.'

'Good morning, honey. Did I wake you up?'

'No.'

'Another early riser. I never used to be, but, man, when they lock you up, you have no idea how much that regime is gonna mess with your body clock.'

'Sorry, did you want . . .'

'Yeah, Becks, sorry. Can I buy you breakfast?'

'I . . . I would like to, but I have to do something.'

'This boy, Logan. I think I've got news on him. I don't

187

want to talk over the phone. I can jump on the overground and meet you in Highbury in half an hour.'

My stomach bumps. 'If it's about Logan and you can tell me now, that would really . . .'

'Highbury, is that good for you?'

It's on the way to Inspired. It could work out, though I don't appreciate the fact that he's only known me two minutes and he's already laying down rules.

'Yeah,' I say. 'All right.'

I feed Azog, stroking her back while she yams down her chicken pâté special. Then I let her out and gather together what I need – the locker key, the medal – the tape? No, I leave that. I'm not planning on hurting myself badly or sticking myself to a ceiling.

As I open our block door, I see Azog pattering away towards Mr Phan. I reckon those two are proper buddies and they're both too shamed to let me know. I cross the main road and wait at the bus stop. It's quieter because of the holidays and the bus comes quick. China calls me, but it feels different talking to her when other people can hear us. So our conversation is short and afterwards I feel empty. I don't think DNA-Dad's breakfast is gonna fill that gap.

I see him from the bus. He's waiting outside Highbury station smoking a roll-up and looking at the sky. I wonder what it's like for him after being locked up for so long. Savannah's uncle was in prison for a couple of months. She said he'd come round her house and sit in the garden for

188

hours because when he was inside, he was only allowed out his cell for a couple of hours a day. He wanted to be somewhere with no walls, no smells.

I should feel sorry for DNA-Dad. He's making an effort, so I should too. As I walk towards him, he sees me coming. He's finished his roll-up and I can see the butt by his feet. He smiles and reaches towards me like he wants to hug me again. I let him.

We go into the McDonald's. There's more staff than customers, but I reckon the place is gonna fill up soon. I mean, when have you ever seen a McDonald's that ain't busting with custom? DNA wants to order from the counter instead of the touch screen. He says it's gonna take him a while to get used to that type of technology. He's still enjoying speaking to someone who ain't in another cell or paid to rehabilitate him. I choose pancakes; he asks for a double sausage McMuffin and a chocolate doughnut for himself and orange juice for both of us. Then he adds a bacon roll on top of that.

He plonks the tray down on a table far away from the door. I want to say, 'So, tell me what you found out', but I wait for him to work on the bacon roll. Half of it goes in the first mouthful.

When he finishes chewing, he says, 'There were some bruthas on my wing who were converting to Islam.' For a moment, I think one of them must know Logan but he shakes his head and finishes up with the roll. 'I try and tell them how much they're gonna miss bacon. They told me it was worth it.'

He wipes his mouth with a paper napkin. I realise he's brought a whole heap with him from the counter.

If I was with my girls, I might have flipped the pancake in two, picked it up and dipped it in the syrup with my fingers. Instead I use the fork to slice it politely. He squashes the muffin down flat and cheese slice flops over the edge. He scoops it up with his finger and licks it off.

'After five years of prison nosh, I'm not wasting nothing!'

I chew my pancake and he takes a bite of muffin.

I say, 'Did you find out something about Logan then?'

I hope I don't sound rude, but he can't leave me hanging like this. The muffin's disappearing and there ain't many bites left. Time's short man. I can't wait for it all to go. It's like the locker key's poked in the back of my neck and slowly winding me up.

'Ah, yes.' He cracks open one orange juice bottle and hands it to me. I take a sip even though it mucks with the taste of the pancakes. His throat must just open wide because he gulps down his juice in one go. He drops the bottle on to the tray and it rolls to the end, bouncing off the scrunched-up napkins. He sits back like Gimli after a good feast. I almost expect him to pull out a pouch of pipe-weed.

'There's a lot of drivers pass through that depot,' he says. 'Some of them can't take the hours and don't stay long. Some of them, the boys I know, they're happy to have the job and don't mind the evenings and the weekends. It keeps them out of trouble.'

I fork in more pancake and chew quicker, like it's a spell for speeding up time.

'And they know Logan?' I say.

'One of the boys does. Or did. One day Logan's there, next day, he's gone.'

'What happened?'

'Man likes women way too much.' It was funny hearing DNA-Da— Benni talk like boys at school, but with a different accent creeping round the edges. He must have been like China's mum, changing his voice to fit in to London. Maybe there are words from Gloucestershire he knows that he could have taught me if we'd been a family for long enough. 'He'd see a girl he likes and write a message for her on the back of the receipt and see what happened.'

You are the most beautiful.

'And it always worked?'

Benni pulls the chocolate doughnut apart. I think half might be meant for me, but it's got dents from Benni's fingerprints and the insides are oozing out.

'I don't know any man who's gonna be honest about how many girls say no to him. But my bruv says this Logan just loved girls. Logan the Legend! Proper loved them. Any time one of those girls answered him, he glowed like those pictures of Jesus. The problem was, the glow faded quick and soon he

191

was looking around to top up.'

Nothing I hadn't worked out for myself. 'Anything else?'

'He got into some stress with some girl on holiday.'

Stress with a girl? I've heard boys use that to defend all sorts of nastiness. 'Like what?'

'She wanted to carry on when he came home. My bruv said this girl even tried to move to England to be with him.'

'Poor girl.'

He looks at me, the chunk of doughnut in his fingers ready to drop in his mouth. 'I suppose so. Don't worry, I won't let no boy treat you like that.'

'They won't.'

'Good.'

I could have told him then. *There's a good reason, Benni, why no boy's gonna treat me like that.* But I don't owe him no explanations. It's none of his business what kind of sexual I turned out to be.

'In the end the delivery place gave him the boot.'

'Because of the holiday girl?'

'I think one girl he tried to hook was younger than she looked and her dad complained to the company.'

'Is he . . . did your friend think he's dangerous?'

'Seems not. A smooth operator, not much to look at, but girls seem to like him. Yeah, pretty harmless, I'd say.'

'What do you think the girls would say? The ones he dumped?' I remember how bad I'd felt about Glinda even though we were never gonna be together. 'It don't feel harmless when people leave you. It hurts.'

Benni glances round McDonald's as if he wants to find someone who feels sorry for him. When he's done a full circle, he comes back to me. 'Things are complicated sometimes.'

'How? How are they complicated?'

We both know I'm not still talking about Logan.

He leans forward over the leftover doughnut mess. 'I know this sounds harsh, but I didn't really want to have a kid, but I was scared I'd lose your mum if I refused. When you were born, I thought you were the best thing that had ever happened to me. I was – I don't know – proud of myself for doing the right thing for once.'

'You still left, though.'

'I wasn't good enough for you.'

He looks me in the eye when he says it, as if that's meant to make it okay. I want to ask him why he didn't work on getting better, because he must have still been pretty rubbish when he had his other children too.

I stand up and try and brush pancake sugar from my lap. It sticks to my hands.

'I've got to go.'

Benni stands up. 'I've mucked it up again, haven't I?' He almost looks like he's ready to cry. 'I really want to give you something back, something for all the years we've missed out.' He tries a smile on me. 'Please don't go. Please.'

I sit down again, even though a girl with a cross toddler in

193

an Elsa costume was ready to grab our seat. The key feels like it's twisted another notch in my neck.

'I should ask you more about yourself. How you're doing at school, if you've got any interests, if you've got a boyfriend.'

I think of China and her hand on my neck and the way we just had to shift a little so our lips fitted.

'I haven't got a boyfriend,' I say.

He laughs. 'Of course not. You're way too young. I'm proud of you for being sensible.'

I take a deep breath. Coming out to my biological father in breakfast-time McDonald's wasn't part of my plan this morning. Maybe I should have read more of those blogs about how to tell your parents you're a lesbian, even if none of them were written for black girls with a dad in jail.

'There are never gonna be boyfriends.'

'Don't be too hasty! Not all boys are wastemen.'

'. . . because I don't like boys.'

'Oh.' He looks down at his fingers. He's got chocolate doughnut filling under his nails. 'Right. Well, there's nothing wrong with that.' He's got that look on his face like I should be grateful that he doesn't mind. 'Nothing wrong at all.'

'Yeah,' I say. 'I'm gonna wash my hands.'

'I'll wait for you.'

'No,' I shake my head. 'I'll be all right. Like I've always been.'

The expression on his face is making me feel bad, even though I ain't done nothing. So I turn away and walk

194

towards the toilets. This time of the morning, they shouldn't look too much like Mordor.

After I scrub away the sugar, I splash water over my face and then realise they've only got one of those crap hand dryers, the ones where an ant coughs stronger than the air flow. I can't go back for toilet paper to dry myself because all the stalls are occupied. I wipe my face on my sleeve and come out slowly, scanning the tables and chairs in case DNA-Dad is still there. But he's gone. He always was gonna go. That's what he does.

And then I see Silva. I have to blink and check again. I've been thinking of her so much, I could have beamed her out of my brain. But she's still there, standing by the door. I should run over to her, but my body's buffering. I got the energy in me, but I'm not going nowhere.

Our eyes meet. She's so shocked she looks like she's gonna fall over. She steadies herself, turns away and she's gone. I move, wriggling my way through the queues to get to her, but hungry people don't shift easy. When I finally get on to the street, she's disappeared.

'Are you all right?' DNA is standing outside, another roll-up between his fingers. He tries to hide it behind his back.

'My sister! Silva! I just saw her!'

I look up and down the street and he does the same, even though he doesn't know what she looks like. She must have been standing right next to him. I take out my phone and call

195

her. Of course, she doesn't answer.

Call back! End call.

Call back! End call.

Call back! End call.

Each time it rings until it hits messages. I leave one.

Silva's still alive! She don't look like no boxer's used her for a punchbag, neither. She saw me, but she ran away. That pancake's churning, like my stomach's too small for it.

DNA-Dad says, 'I wasn't gonna leave you, Becks.'

I shrug. I don't mean to be disrespectful, but I don't know what to say. I've done all right without him so far and I've got more important things to think about now.

'And I really don't care,' he says.

What?

'About you being . . . into girls.'

I'm still not gonna say thank you.

'I just want you to be happy.'

Well, right now, I'm not.

'I've got Logan's home address, if that helps.'

He drops it all casual but I can see him watching me.

'My boy gave me a call. He's just bumped into one of the drivers who used to give Logan a lift home after late shifts. Logan lives with his sister, not far from here.'

'Cool.' I'm still not gonna say thank you.

'We could go now if you want?'

'"We"?'

'I'm not letting you go by yourself.'

He starts walking off. All I can do is follow, a few steps behind in case my rage burns scorch marks down his back.

Logan lives off the Holloway Road. I must have passed his street on the bus as many times as I've gone past the boxing club. We pass the big library on the corner. Mum told me she used to bring me to toddler sessions here when she had no money. Apparently, I once had a big screaming tantrum because the librarian didn't read *So Much!* with the same voices Mum did.

DNA-Dad turns round. He's smiling.

'I brought you to a baby thing here once,' he says. 'Your mum says you were a horror, but you were all right for me.'

When he smiles, I see how he must have worked his charm on Mum, and all the other mums too. A part of me wishes I remembered doing things with him, but then, he's the one who left before I could build them memories.

I say, 'You don't have to come with me.'

'I don't want to cramp your style, Becks, or look like I'm babysitting you, but some of these blocks round here . . . When I was in Pentonville,' he swept his arm around, 'it sounded like this place was always a bit hot. I can't have you coming here by yourself.'

'I've been coming around here for years.' By 'coming around', I meant going to kids theatre stuff at Jacksons Lane and a picnic in Waterlow Park. Oh, and the McDonald's.

'To this estate?'

I shake my head.

'It's this way,' he says.

I follow him past a closed-down petrol station into a side road, posh houses on one side, blocks on another. I wonder how much those rich people pay to look out their window into a sitting room like ours. The communal door don't have a lock, even though there's a swipe card panel. DNA pushes the door open wide and strides in – yeah, just like Aragon returning from dead to Rohan. Except, I ain't been waiting for no king to return. I don't want no king.

I catch up with him. 'What number?'

He's got his foot on the first stair. 'I know where it is.'

'But you ain't told me.'

Something in my voice makes him stop. 'What's the matter?'

'I don't want you to do this for me.'

'I'm not doing any . . .' He looks at his foot on the stair. 'Yeah. Right.' He takes it off. 'You're not going into a stranger's gaff by yourself. I can't let that happen.'

Although his foot's back on the ground floor, he's still blocking the way to the stairs. And I still don't know which flat's Logan's.

I say, 'What if you can wait on the landing? If his sister sees you at the door, she might not answer.'

He raises his eyebrows and suddenly I realise that's one thing that I got off him. Eyebrows that don't need contour nor pencil, but are racing each other to meet in the middle. DNA's have almost reached.

He says, 'You mean she's not going to answer the door to some strange black man she's never seen before?'

My face goes hot. Hopefully he don't know how to read me properly yet, because maybe that was what I was deep down thinking. What would I do if I saw him through our spy hole? Knowing me, open the door like I do to everyone else.

'Point taken,' he says. 'I'll wait on the landing. Close by, though.'

He starts up the stairs again with me still behind him. We stop by a fire door on the second floor.

'Two more floors,' he says. 'Number twenty-seven's on the fourth.'

I come out on to the landing, puffing. It's barely a landing, just three flats. There's a little metal plate screwed to the wall that tells me which way to go for twenty-seven, even though I can see it from the top of the stairs. I look back at DNA. Man can't hide nowhere, so he just goes up a few more stairs so he ain't so obvious.

Really, I want him to knock instead of me. Serious. I don't know what the hell I'm gonna say when the door opens, but suddenly I wish it wasn't me saying it. I want China standing next to me, holding my hand.

Is it Logan or his sister who's gonna answer? Logan might recognise me through the spy hole and pretend he's not in. I mean, last time I embarrassed the hell out of him. And he knows I'm Silva's sister. Then what do I do? Well, I can't do nothing unless I knock. Silva might even be in there, with him. I take a big breath but not so big that DNA's gonna notice my back moving. I stretch up my spine to make me a little taller, lift the letterbox and knock.

The door flies open and a girl's standing there. 'What?'

I reckon she's about nineteen and as furious as the sun. She frowns. She's got the same wide forehead as her brother. Her hair looks like it's growing out black with a red ombre starting halfway down. It's a face that's either gonna fit right in or make itself known. She's the kind of girl that I don't want to be my enemy. I try and look past her into the flat, just in case, I don't know . . . Maybe Logan was lounged back on the sofa, playing *Creed*? All I can see is a *Frozen* rucksack and a wooden xylophone. Man, she must have started young. Though now I sound like my mother, even though her oldest sister had her first baby when she was fifteen.

'I . . . I was looking for Logan.'

'Jesus, the idiot needs to pay me for this. He's not here.'

'It's just my sister's looking for him and I wanted to find him in case she's with him.'

The girl looks me up and down. 'Your sister? Which one is she?'

Which *one*?

'She's tall and . . .'

'Bald?'

'Yes. Sort of.'

200

'Came around earlier. If he's gonna hand out our address he should be here dealing with who comes knocking.'

'Sorry. Silva was here?'

Her eyes seem to focus on me properly. 'If your sister's a bald, black girl, yeah. If not, I don't know. But tell you what.' She pokes her own chest. 'This sister's looking for him too. I'm fed up with all this crap.'

'What did Silva want? Did she say?'

She sighs. 'She wanted Logan. Like all of them do. At least she wasn't a shouter. We've had one of them before. Seriously, I need to go.'

She closes the door.

DNA falls into step beside me as we go downstairs.

'Helpful?' he asks.

'Silva was here.'

'I heard. Where are we going next?'

We?

29

Logan wouldn't respond to my texts. Logan wouldn't answer my calls. I couldn't eat. Your mum was trying to cook all the things I liked but I couldn't touch them. I did feel guilty, Becks. Everyone's heads were full of the wedding. Even Dad had a to-do list, and a week before, he still had masses he had to do. You tried to get me to help, but I just pushed the chair against my bedroom door to stop you bursting in. Dad even organised another appointment with the counsellor. He thought it was a bereavement blip. It was. I had lost Logan.

I had to get up, go to college, try and push words together for my essays. I had to damn well smile every time our parents talked about their vows. I had to put on that dress and stand and clap as they slipped a wedding band on to each other's fingers. I had to watch them dancing and staring into each other's eyes with you whooping next to me.

I want Dad to be happy.

I want to be happy too.

Hour after hour, I stared at my phone. Hour after hour, I tried to work it through my head, wondering how I could make myself better so he would want me again. Each time, I was more convinced he was frightened. He knew we belonged together; he'd realise it in the end. I thought about how far I would go to have him back. The hole inside me was so big, my skin was going to be sucked through my bones.

At home, everyone talks – you, Win, Dad. Even your damn cat meows more than any cat I know. Sometimes I think Dad pays the counsellor to listen to me because he doesn't have time any more. Logan listened to me, Becks. He'd lean forward to make sure he heard every word, so he'd know everything about me. It was like he took me apart then filled in the spaces where the gaps were. I was angry at myself for feeling that way, then even more angry that I wasn't doing anything to change things.

Go backwards in your memories, Becks. Think of a time when things happened around you, bad things that you couldn't change. I never told you how I found out about Mum. I had come home from school and Dad was sitting beside her on the sofa. My parents were always polite to each other after Dad left, but when he arrived to collect me, he usually never came in. He certainly never ever sat down. But they were there, holding hands. Even that was different, though. It wasn't the way they used to, when they still loved each other. In the old pictures of them, it was like they were holding hands with their whole bodies.

They both looked up at me as I came through the door. Mum said she had some news. They'd moved apart for me to sit in between them, but I couldn't move from where I was standing. Why do adults think children don't know what's going on? Sometimes we understand even if we can't put our thoughts into words. I knew my mum's moods. I knew when things hurt her inside and out. I just stood by the door until Mum came over to me and told me not to be scared. I *was* scared and it never stopped.

I was scared that I had lost Logan for good, but I knew I could change that. I followed him after football one day. I waited until he was alone and caught up with him by the road at the edges of the Marshes.

He was surprised to see me. I think he was glad that I wasn't giving up so easily. I called his name, but he carried on walking. I ran to catch up with him and told him that I understood. Since his mother had died, he'd been left empty. He was frightened that he was betraying her by filling the gap with a different love. I knew.

We walked through a park and sat on the bench near the children's playground. We watched a toddler on the beach volleyball pit jabbing the sand with a plastic fork. A young guy held a little boy up to help him swing across the monkey bars.

I said, 'Do you think he's a dad or a big brother?'

'Maybe he's an uncle giving his sister a rest. That's where I should be now, Silva. Helping out.'

'But you're not. You're here with me.'

I'd laid my hand on his. I'd told him how much I missed him and then – I'd asked him to come back to our flat. I said it was important. We could put everything right. I'd wanted to remind him how close we could be, not in a park or cafe or crowded against each other at a party. Just him and me alone.

I watched the dad, or brother, or uncle, help the child swing back, the little one's feet nearly catching the man's head. He didn't even flinch, just carried on calling encouragement until the little boy reached the end. The toddler in the volleyball sandpit had been joined by two little girls doing handstands. As their feet thumped down, the sand billowed up into the toddler's eyes and he started crying. His mum bent down next to him, pulled out a pack of wipes and swabbed at the sand crust on his face.

'I really missed you, Logan. Please?'

The mother grabbed the buggy, slotted her child in and wheeled him away. The plastic fork dropped to the grass.

Logan's body was turning towards me. His hand was still beneath mine.

I said, 'Remember that first time we saw each other? Remember how you felt? I know you lost your job because of me. Make it worth it.'

His hand twitched but he didn't pull it away. 'How do you know about that?'

'Your brother told me. I know drivers aren't allowed to date customers. I looked it up. You did. I meant more.'

He tried to tell me it didn't matter now. I shouldn't worry about him. I wasn't worrying. I was thinking about everything he had done for me.

'You let me come and watch you play football even though some of the others must have teased you about me. I know your coach hated me, but I still came.'

He tried to tell me that he shouldn't have asked me to do that. But he *had* asked and I had wanted to be close.

'You invited me to a party full of your friends.' I remembered his face when I'd shown him my costume. 'I shouldn't have cut up the dress. I should have trusted you.'

I curled my fingers between his.

He said, 'Silva, I don't think this can work.'

'Yes, it can.' I stood up. The playground had emptied out. 'If you come back with me now, it's like we're starting over. We'll remember how we felt when we saw each other for the first time. Please, Logan?'

I knew that our parents were out looking for honeymoon clothes. Dad had said that he was happy to wear jeans and trainers, but your mum booked that posh restaurant in Tokyo to celebrate and she wanted them both to look good. You were hanging out at Raych's after school. The flat would be empty.

Logan stood up. 'Okay.'

We'd crossed the road, still holding hands. I could hear the children from the school around the corner. It must have been afternoon playtime. Mr Phan was outside watering his window boxes and the dry cleaners had wedged their door open so hot chemicals coiled around me as we walked past.

'I'm glad we're back together,' I said.

We went through the security doors and up to the flat. He kissed me, pressing me against the door. It should have been romantic, but the latch dug into my back and his sports bag knocked against our legs. He let it drop to the floor. I managed to wedge my hands up against his chest.

He'd stepped back. 'I haven't got much time, Silva.'

We went into my bedroom and sat down on my bed. The mattress bent us towards each other, but he still wasn't looking at me. His gaze moved from wall to wall. This wasn't what he'd imagined, he said. He'd thought I was an arty type, or maybe a scientist and there'd be strange posters on my walls, double helixes or Picasso, or something.

Him being here and seeing my world made me love him even more.

He'd stood up again and looked at my shelves. I thought he'd ask about the photo of me and Mum, especially after he told me about his own mother.

'What happened to my picture?'

All our snaps were on our phones. I didn't know what he meant.

'The K-pop guy, remember? I got you one with an autograph. Did you take it down when we split up?'

I should have said yes. I should have said that it hurt too much to see it knowing how he'd been to so much trouble to find it. But stupid, stupid me, I was honest.

'It was a brilliant present, but me and Becks weren't into Rain. He did a dodgy video and . . .'

He was sort of smiling. 'You didn't like my present? I bought it for you. It was meant to be special.'

'I know, but—'

'You said you liked that Korean stuff.'

'It *was* special. I know. I'm sorry.' And I was. I'd been selfish. Other boys wouldn't have tried so hard to please me. I'd got it wrong.

I went over to him and pulled him towards me, my arms around him, my chin resting on his shoulder. We moved back towards the bed and lay down. I held him to me, wanting to find our closeness. I tried to kiss him but he stared ahead as if I wasn't there. Suddenly, I heard the front door open and a thump in the hallway. It was you, Becks! You'd tripped over the sports bag. I sat up as my bedroom door flew open.

'Why the hell did you leave that—?' Your mouth fell open like a cartoon. You swore and slammed my door shut again. Then I heard your door bang and your music blasted out, that funky Nigerian stuff that Savannah got you into.

'That's my sister, Becks,' I'd said. 'I'm sorry.'

He remembered you. I suppose he would, wouldn't he? Then he said something about asking your permission before he bought presents for me next time.

I was losing him, Becks. There wouldn't be a next time.

I put my arms back around him. 'I didn't mean to hurt you. I wasn't thinking.'

He moved away. 'I shouldn't have come here with you.'

I'd tried to brace myself, but it was like a hand slamming right through me to the other side. 'What do you mean?'

'I don't want to be with you, Silva.'

'I'll put the picture on the shelf, Logan! I promise!'

'It's not about the picture, Silva.'

He told me I didn't understand. He had to go. I heard the front door shut and your music thud through the walls. Later, I made myself get up and leave too. I walked around our estate to try and make the hurting stop.

It wouldn't though, Becks. It wouldn't.

30

DNA-Dad don't want to listen. There ain't no 'we'. It's me. And it's him. We're separate. What does he expect me to do – turn into an obedient daughter because he passed on Logan's address? I don't want him to follow me to the boxing club. Doesn't he understand that you can't clear off for fifteen years then claim your place as Big Man Dada without any questions? I don't need his protection and I'm starting to wish I hadn't involved him at all.

He's following me along Holloway Road and I'm checking my phone and ignoring him. China's sending me quotes. It's like she's found every song in the universe that tells me to girl up. She says she's putting together a playlist for me so I can have musical encouragement. It's just as well I've got limitless data because I'm gonna be playing it on loop for ever.

She tells me I shouldn't get side-tracked because I saw Silva. Yeah, it means that I can stop worrying about her being kidnapped, but if she ran away from me, she must still need my help. I think of China's story about when Poppy kept coming to volleyball even after she sprained her wrist. You don't always know the reasons why people do what they do. I won't really understand Silva's actions until we get to talk and she sure as hell didn't want to talk to me today.

I start to think of what I'm gonna say to Kurt Gladdinn, Founder of Inspired. I've got a problem – everything makes my sister sound crazy. I glance across at DNA. He's talking quietly on his phone. I pop in my earbuds. I feel like I'm in a film or TV series and I want to find music to match. I'm not up for Busan zombies or K-drama love songs. I scroll through and stop on the soundtrack to *The Handmaiden*. Yep. That's the one. Maybe China hasn't seen that film yet and won't mind watching it with me.

I come to a junction with a steep hill. My map says I have to drag myself halfway up and then walk through the park to the club. DNA is still by my side.

I say, 'You're not coming in with me.'

He lifts his hands. 'Okay! I get it! I can't anyway. I've got to make an appointment. I might even be getting my own place. But call me if you need anything, okay?'

I nod and watch him walk away.

The building's like one of those cafes that Mum complains about, where it looks cheap but a cup of tea costs more than a box of a hundred tea bags in Lidl. The windows are open and I can hear thuds against the punchbags, with heavy beat music beneath it. Maybe they've got a class going on or something, though the punches don't match the beat.

Stop thinking too much, Becks. The front door's open. It's inviting me. I make my feet say yes.

The foyer's got that smell. It's sort of a gym smell, but it also reminds me of the couple of years Mum made me go Brownies. It was in a church hall in Stoke Newington and in the end it had to close down because the pipes kept bursting and flooding it. The floor started getting rotten and there was mould around the radiators. The dirty water smell wouldn't go away.

Just as I'm standing there, a guy comes out the main hall towards me. He's wearing a blue T-shirt and matching baseball cap with 'Inspired' on them. I wonder how I could have imagined that Inspired could be anything else but the club. He looks surprised to see me. I'm surprised to see him too because he's the same guy I'd seen on the website. Kurt Gladdinn, Founder.

He smiles at me. 'Can I help you?'

'I . . . I . . .'

'You're not seeing us at our best today, but I can give you some information about our classes. We've got a few for your age group. There's a couple of spaces left on the girls-only, and just one on the mixed. The mixed is more circuit training, some light sparring, but all supervised.'

'It's not about a course. It's . . .'

There's a shout behind him and he looks around. Then it's back to the punching and the music.

'Someone's gone missing,' I say. 'And I think you can help me.'

I take out the medal and the locker key and show him. 'I found these and I think they're from here.'

He looks down at them. 'Who are you, may I ask?'

'My name's Becks.'

'And you know the owner . . . of these items?' He sounds tired.

'They're my sister Silva's. Well, sort of. I want to check out who gave them to her first. That's why I came to ask you.'

'Ask me what?'

'If you know who did.'

He blows out his cheeks like it's the end of the day and he just wants to put on his coat and go home.

'Please,' I say. 'My mum and my sister's dad got married a couple of months ago, but they've only just managed to take their honeymoon. I'm really worried. Silva went to the airport with our parents. She was supposed to come back to be with me and – well – she hasn't. I've seen her, but I don't think she's all right.'

He's frowning. I don't blame him. That was a real mix-up of words.

'What's your sister called again?'

'Silva.'

He nods. 'I thought that's what you said. It's not the sort of name you forget.'

'You know her?'

'She and my brother . . . Yes. I know her. I was hoping she'd be over him by now.'

'She isn't.'

'How old are you?'

213

Why do adults always do that crap? They start to say something deep then get embarrassed and ask you your age, like they're scared you can't take it. They've got no idea what we can take.

I make myself stay polite. 'I'm sixteen.'

'I don't think I should be talking to you. Haven't you got parents who can sort this out?'

'Yes, but they're in Japan. On their honeymoon. They've saved for ages. I'm gonna have to make them come home unless I find her soon.'

He looks at me for a moment, then says, 'Let's go into my office.'

The gym is like its website, kind of working but a bit shabby, though that's how I've always thought boxing gyms should look like. A tall girl's holding up pads while her mate punches the crap out of them. They must have been doing all that punching I heard from outside.

We pass by the lockers I saw on the website and straight away I want to try my key in every one, but Kurt's holding the door of his office open for me. It says 'Manager' on it. It should say 'Founder'. There's a small desk inside with a laptop and bundles of flyers scattered across it. He unfolds two camping chairs that are leaning against a mini-fridge and waves his hand for me to sit down. He takes his chair to the other side of the desk from me. He's left the door a bit open so the *doof-doof* thump of music is in the room with us.

I lay the medal and the key next to the flyers. 'I don't

know if the key's from here, but I was really hoping you could help me.'

He picks up the medal. The ribbon's twisted so it does a little spin.

'This is certainly ours. We've given out a hell of a lot of medals.' He looks past the medal at me. 'It's called positive affirmation. A kid does something good, for once, and you praise them so much that they want to do it again.'

'I think this one belonged to someone called Logan.' I wait for him to react, but he's keeping poker-face. 'He's white and he used to drive—'

'I know who it was awarded to.' Kurt's voice is so quiet, I have to lean forward to hear him better. 'These were from early days, when we had to do everything cheap. Even our medals. So only a few kids got these ones. Logan came third in one of our first tournaments.'

'So you know him?'

'He's my brother.'

Oh? I stare at him. I can't see his forehead because of the cap, so I got no idea if it's wide like the others. But why would he lie? It makes sense. He holds up one of the flyers. It's got a picture of the inside of the club and there's Logan again, gloves up, about to wallop a punchbag.

'That's him,' I say. 'He delivered our groceries.'

'One of many jobs,' Kurt says. 'He's not very good at sticking with things.'

'Or girls.'

'Yeah,' Kurt says. 'Or girls.'

'Do you think Silva's with him?'

He shook his head. 'I'm pretty sure she isn't. To be frank, normally he would have moved on to someone else by now, but he's got a few personal issues he has to sort out.'

'And Silva's not one of them?'

He kind of laughs though I don't think what I said was funny.

'I spoke to him this morning. He never mentioned it. I think he's . . . I know this sounds harsh. I think he's forgotten about her. That's how he works. It's everything or nothing. Your sister should do the same with him.'

Like it's that easy for her? If it was, I wouldn't be here.

I keep polite Becks on duty.

'She kept a box of things under her bed, things that your brother gave her or, I don't know, stuff that they did together. It was like he was everything to her. The weird thing was, she still didn't tell none of us about him, even when she cosplayed my favourite character.'

'Sorry?'

'Okoye, from *Black Panther*. She's in a casino in Busan in Korea and she's . . .'

'Wearing a red dress.'

I nod. 'You know?'

'It was a party. I was there.'

He doesn't say nothing else.

'Silva's mum died,' I say. 'When she was thirteen. My

mum loves her, but it's not the same. All the things I remember from when I was little with Mum, she doesn't have that. I think – Logan listened to her. Nobody had really listened to her before.'

I don't know why I'm telling him this. I think I'm just working it all out for myself. Kurt's looking even more embarrassed, but he should. If my sister behaved like Logan, I'd move out of London and change my name.

'I'm sorry that you can't find Silva,' he says. 'I really am. I don't know what to suggest, but I don't think it's anything to do with Logan.'

'Yes, it is! He started this! She was minding her own business and he sent her a damn note!'

I don't want to, but I have to say something to make him help me. So I tell him about the receipt and my sister being the most beautiful and the football coach who thought Silva was a stalker but adding in what China said, about the coach never bothering to find out Silva's side. I tell him how I heard from a couple of places that Logan was always picking up girls and how he's lost his last job because of it. I tell him how Silva stopped eating for a while and how none of us knew why and that even when she was sad she looked happy at our parents' wedding. I don't tell him how I wished I was a better sister, but I'm pretty sure he understands.

'Even if she's not with him,' I say, 'he's sure as hell got something to do with it.'

Kurt rubs his face so hard it leaves a blotch on his cheek.

'It's always me who has to clean up his damn mess!'

Polite Becks stops me telling him that I seem to be doing a lot of cleaning up myself right now.

He says, 'I saw her at my cousin's party. I don't really party any more, but I'd heard Logan had a new girl and I went with gallant ideas of warning her off, but what do you say? "My little brother's a total dick, go now?" I could see what he meant to her and the last thing I wanted was public humiliation. I told her where I'd be if she needed me, because I knew she would, when things took their inevitable course.'

'What do you mean?'

'Logan loves love.' Both Kurt's cheeks are turning the colour of the blotch. 'He loves it when people fall heavy for him. It makes him feel like – I don't know – a big man. And the thing is, he really means it. He's really into his girlfriends and he'll do anything to make them happy. He'll find out what they're into – theatre, films, zoos, whatever – and he makes pretty sure the girl knows how much trouble he's taken.'

Pity he didn't find out more about Rain.

'Then when the girls are really into him, he drops them. It's like job done.'

So my sister's a load of shopping he can dump on the doorstep and then walk away from.

Kurt glances down at the locker key and for some reason, I slap my hand over it.

He says, 'You got this from Silva, right?'

'What is it?'

'It's for Logan's locker. Silva came here, not long after the party. She wanted . . . I think she just wanted to talk, but things were kicking off. She told me she'd left something in the locker so I gave her the key.'

My phone's sounding off in my pocket. I take it out and glance at it. I look at Kurt, then down at the phone again.

'It's Silva,' I say.

'Good timing. I'll leave you to it.' He squeezes past me and heads back to the workout area.

I turn and run out the gym, away from the music trying to hear her properly.

'Silva? Where are you? Why did you run off earlier. I—'

'I'm at home, Becks. Where are you?' Her voice sounds tight.

'I'm at a boxing club looking for you and—'

'You need to come back! It's Azog. She won't wake up.'

'Azog?'

'Quick, Becks! Please!'

I run out through the park. I try and call Silva again, but she's not answering. Something sharp digs into my palm. I'm still holding the locker key. I dash it into my pocket and sprint. That's my bus. I need to run harder. I need to catch it.

31

There is not much more to tell you, Becks. Or not much that I can put into words. I didn't forget about that double helix. I chalked one on my wall, white on white, so that only I knew it was there. I wanted to paint two thick red ribbons weaving across each other turning sideways, edge on so they've nearly disappeared. I imagined them moving, twisting around, wide and heavy and hurting. My mother's death, of course that hurt. No matter how long I look for her, no matter how much I think I see her, she'll never be with me again. I just have to deal with that ribbon always flickering away, sometimes in full sight, sometimes edge on. But how could losing him hurt like that? The ribbon should have flickered then fallen apart.

I saw him twice afterwards.

The first time I was at the fair, not long after he walked out of our flat. You had been pointing out the poster for weeks, Becks. You said it hadn't been around our way for a while since a girl died on the ghost train a few years ago. You love having your stomach thrown all ways. I'm not such a fan, but bumper cars and candyfloss remind me of good times.

You were supposed to go with Raych, except the night

before you came down with tonsillitis. You were burning hot and still trying to stagger out of your bed and put on your clothes. Dad and Win made you stay home. It had taken Raych ages to talk her mum out of making her go to swimming practice so in the end, I'd gone with her instead.

It's not that me and Raych didn't know each other. I'll never forget those early days, when I used to stay with Dad at your mum's over the weekend. It would be me, you and Raych synchronising our moves to BTS, though now I think about it, you always preferred the girls in Red Velvet.

Then we grow up and suddenly our paths shoot off in different directions. You and Raych stayed with K-pop, I followed Mum to wherever she was going until I couldn't follow any more.

Raych and I bought enough counters for four rides, to begin with. We started on the swings that flare out as the ride spins, swooping out above the trees. I let Raych pull me on to the twister. More spinning, both of us squashed together into the corner of the carriage. We topped up our blood sugar with candyfloss before the giant swing boats flung my stomach up in the air but didn't catch it again. I was so pleased I went, Becks. I don't know if I was happy, but I was lighter. And for our last ride?

Raych let me choose. I wanted the bumper cars. We headed across the fairground and stood in the crowd of families, waiting. It had been so many years since I'd been in a bumper car. Mum was the mad driver in our family and she was the one who'd take me on, teaching me her sneaky little back bump moves as soon as I could reach the wheel. She was always good at getting a dodgem too, streaking out from the side and jumping into a car. She almost got into a fight once because she was lifting me in while an angry racist granddad was still getting out.

Raych and I were standing there, plotting our strategy. Was it worth racing the punk kid and her girlfriend? Nope. They would fight me to the death. What about the hen party? They were powerful in their high heels, but we might get ahead of a couple of them. I turned to nudge Raych and that's when I saw Logan. I couldn't breathe. My heart was beating so hard, I could feel the ripples across my face. Raych had to take me to sit down.

But that's when I saw what was at stake. It should have been the end.

The following week, I went to see Kurt at the boxing club. He had promised he would be there for me if I needed him. I needed him then. I had stood on the edges of the park, trapped in a cage of traffic fumes, willing myself to move closer. I walked around the club twice, building up my courage.

The windows were open and I could hear the thump of the punches. Did I imagine the funky sweat smell seeping between the bricks? As I circled the building for the third time, I made myself slow, made myself stop by the open door, made myself go in. My mind flashed back to the night

222

of the party, Logan telling me to mind the step, me waiting with my gold shoes in my hand, shivering while he tried to find the right keys to open the door.

We had walked through the building in darkness, letting the streetlights in the park guide our way to his brother's office. Logan knew he kept a mattress and pump here from when Kurt and his ex-girlfriend had gone through a bad patch and he'd needed somewhere else to stay. I can tell you now, Becks, I *had* been frightened. Perhaps I was disappointed too. There was a girl at school whose first time was on a beach lounger in Barbados. Another who did it on her friend's parents' bed with a boy she'd just met at a party in Homerton. I had streetlights instead of candles. An inflatable mattress instead of a four-poster. But I've heard of far worse stories than that.

This daytime visit was so different. The sounds and smell of the place were pulsing around me. I saw Kurt straight away even though he was in a tracksuit with the hood pulled low over his brow. I imagined the energy rolling off him smelling like a loud whistle blown for too long. He was standing by two boys who looked Turkish, brothers, maybe. They had paused mid-spar, listening to him intently, one ready to punch, one holding his defences. Kurt looked up at me.

'One minute,' he said.

I nodded.

He lifted his own arms to demonstrate what the boys

should be doing, shoulders turned, fists clenched, bouncing from one foot to another.

'Remember where the power is,' he said.

He looked at me again, frowned and then I saw his face change. He came towards me, softening his tread and relaxing his arms. He stroked the hood away from his face. His hair had been shorn short like mine.

'Hello, again,' he said. 'I didn't expect to see you here.'

Did he know you'd abandoned me? What did he expect?

I said, 'I was . . . I just wondered . . .'

He shook his head. 'He's not here. He doesn't really come any more.' He'd touched my shoulder. 'Let's go outside.'

We moved from the hot, damp air of the club to the grit of the traffic fumes.

'I'm sorry about the party,' he said. 'I should have just let things go.'

He squinted against the sunshine. 'How long have you and Logan been together?'

His eyes were asking different questions, trying to root into me without using words.

'We met just before Christmas.'

He nodded. I think he was waiting for me to say more.

'But it's over,' I said.

I tried to take a breath, but it jumped in my throat. I pushed my lips together, trying to kill the prickling in my eyes.

He studied my face. 'Right. I'm sorry. Look, I know it

hurts, but that's the best thing. Logan is . . . he's my brother but— he wants people to love him and then he runs away. It's sick.' He laughed. 'And I don't mean that in a good way, neither.'

One of the Turkish boys exploded out of the door. 'He did it deliberate, man!' He wiped blood from the side of his nose. 'Look! See!'

His brother followed, one glove on, the other hand waving in the air. 'You should've moved your head! I was going easy!'

The younger one lurched forward, gloves raised. Kurt jumped between them.

'Don't even think about it, lads! You want a lifetime ban? You just carry on!'

The young one pulled away, swearing. He jabbed a glove towards his brother. 'Man's a dick!'

He stormed back inside, his brother behind him.

'That's why you get bust up, man! You got idiot mouth!'

'I need to sort this out.' Kurt followed them.

I waited a second, then went after Kurt. I did want his sympathy, yes. But I think I wanted more than that. I needed to hear from him why I should never think of Logan again. Kurt, of all people, should know why.

The younger boy picked up the glove he must have thrown into the ring, wriggled his hand into it and held it beneath his chin as he strapped it up. The other boy strutted past a row of lockers towards what must be the changing rooms.

Kurt watched him for a couple of seconds then turned back and seemed to notice me again.

'I'm sorry, Silva. I really am. But honestly, it hurts me to say that you're best out of it. His life is complicated.'

I know, I wanted to shout. *Tell me the truth!* But instead I said, 'How?'

He looked around. 'I don't discuss family business in public.'

We went back into his office. I kept my eyes looking down because I didn't want to linger on the cupboard where he kept the mattress and the pump and the sleeping bags. The trees outside the window hid the streetlamp. Did he know that in the dark it blinked through the leaves, scattering the office floor with shadows?

'We came here,' I said. 'After the party.'

'Did you? That's a low, even for him.'

I had to look away. I didn't want him to know that I'd felt the mattress shifting beneath me with the coldness of the floor seeping through.

'Why did you come to see me today, Silva?' he said.

So you can make me stop thinking about him. But it was worse. The thought of Logan was burning through me. 'I . . . I left something here. After the party. I wondered if I could get it back.'

'Right.' Kurt stared at me for a moment then turned his back to me and pulled open the drawer of a filing cabinet. He emptied a key out of an envelope.

There was a shriek from the gym and another loud string of swear words. English and yes, that was Turkish.

'Jesus!' Kurt dropped the key on the desk and ran out. 'You want a ban? Is that what you telling me? Because that's what you're gonna get!'

There was another thump outside and a yell.

He poked his head around the door. 'Get into the changing rooms! Both of you!' He looked back at me. 'It's the top row, third from the left. Just leave the key on the desk.'

The lockers were different colours as if they'd been found in different places. Logan's was a tarnished dark blue and the lock looked loose and scratched. It took two attempts to open it.

I could hear shouting in the changing room. Kurt was winning the argument.

I flicked the locker door open. There were my gold shoes from the party. Logan had kept them. My first thought, Becks, was that he still wanted me. It flared out before I could stop it. I tried to cool it with other thoughts. Perhaps Logan kept trophies. Perhaps there were other things in the locker from other girls. Suddenly, I needed to know. I pulled out my shoes. I saw the dark sweatshirt he'd tried to lend me shoved at the back of the locker. I left it where it was. I noticed a flash of silver and dark green underneath. I pulled out the end. It was a tatty old school tie. A big, brown envelope was jammed at the side. I took it out, shook it. I wanted to look inside, but it was sealed. Not fully, but just enough. Did I

227

want Kurt to come and find me pawing through his brother's personal stuff?

Except – Logan's address was written on the front. I would never need it. Ever. Because it was over.

It should have been over.

But that thought, Becks, about him still wanting me – it had grown. It was like a fog surrounding me that I couldn't quite push through. When I moved, it moved with me.

As I was about to close the door, I saw a photograph stuck on the inside of it. I almost took it, but I knew it was there for a reason. I locked the door and slipped the key into my pocket. The fog thickened and I wished I could draw it round me like a cloak.

32

Did Azog get hit by something? We've got idiot boys on our estate who used to race up and down on stolen mopeds, but now they know the CCTV's working, they've quietened down. Sometimes a mad driver shoots down our road, not realising the end's blocked off to cars, then they reverse and shoot back the other way, trying to style it off.

Is this what's happened? Azog got bashed?

Nah. Silva would have said that.

And, damn! She's a street cat. She knows better. I'm sure I've seen her look both ways before she crosses the road.

I message China. She gets back to me straight away.

Don't worry, hun. I've checked some things out for you. Cats can faint like humans if there's not enough oxygen in their blood. Specially older cats. Do you know how old Azog is?

I don't, do I? She's not even really mine. I kept seeing her outside the newsagent looking hungry so I started buying her food and bringing her upstairs. It was soon after Mum told me Justin was moving in, so I argued that him and the cat could be the new ones together. Mum was so loved up she didn't complain too much.

And it was Justin who gave Azog her name. And he hates the Hobbit films! He thinks they're too long and the dwarf–elf love story thing wasn't what Tolkien intended. But I can forgive him for that. Azog the Defiler is the best cat name ever.

And now Silva says Azog's not moving.

But . . . she was all right when I saw her earlier. She ate a whole bowl of hard food with beef chunks in gravy to follow it up.

Silva hates my cat. Maybe she came back, took one sniff in her room and knew what happened. But she wouldn't hurt her, would she? I don't know anymore.

I wish this bus would move quicker. There's a whole stretch of clear road ahead and it's like the driver's using his legs to run the bus instead of the engine. I've just seen a woman walking one of them tiny short-leg dogs outside. They just strolled right past my window and are heading for the distance.

Jesus! Hurry up!

Okay, I'm gonna ring for the next stop and run the rest of the way. I text Silva to ask how my cat is.

No change, Becks. No change at all.

I run up the steps and my hand is shaking so much I can't get the key in the lock first time.

My poor, poor cat. Whatever money I've got is gonna go towards fixing her.

No double lock, so Silva is definitely here. I open the door and the only sounds I can hear are the ones in my own body from running so hard.

'Azog? Silva?' I run into my bedroom. 'Azog!'

My cat's lying there, all still next to Silva on my bed. I pick Azog up. I look at Silva. I don't understand. Azog's breathing normally.

'What's wrong with her? Did she faint? Was that it?'

I scratch Azog's neck. Her eyes are still closed but she stretches her head out towards me. And she's purring. The cat I thought was dead is purring! I look at Silva again. Here she is, my missing sister, looking not nearly sorry enough for what she's put me through. Azog wriggles out of my arms and jumps on to the ground. That is a cat who ain't come anywhere near death.

Azog lands on an envelope. It's the one the wig was in. I realise that the things from Silva's shrine are still laid out on my bedroom floor. My face goes hot. My face is a traitor, man, because if she hadn't disappeared, I wouldn't have gone looking. Now, I'm here because she lied about my cat.

I say, 'Was there anything wrong with her at all, Silva?'

Silva shakes her head.

'What the hell is this about? I would have come anyway. All you had to do was call me.'

I can't cry no more. My tear ducts must be crust up with

dry salt. Instead, I start shouting. Didn't she understand? I'd thought she'd been abducted or kidnapped or beaten up! I'd been looking everywhere for her! I had to deal with that stupid coach calling her a stalker and almost damn well believed it myself! I nearly called Mum back from her honeymoon! I even called the police!

Then I stop, because there's nothing else. Yeah, my body *can* cry a bit more. I wipe my face with my sleeve. I want Silva to hug me, but she just sits there.

'You're not even sorry?' I say.

'I'm sorry I wasn't here for you, Becks.'

What? That's it? I want to shout but my energy's left me. 'Is he worth it?'

Silva stands up. 'Yes. He is.' She taps the shrine box with her toe. 'You had no right to go digging around under my bed, Becks.'

'You went off with the delivery man and left me! Don't make this my fault!'

She won't even look at me. Silva, who's supposed to be my older sister and in charge of me, don't care at all.

'There were more things in the box, Becks. What have you done with them? The medal, where is it?'

'This?' I take it out of my pocket and hold it out to her. 'That's why I was at the boxing club.'

'And?'

'I know what this is about, Silva. He's called Logan. I went down to the marshes and found out you used to watch him

232

play football and . . . and you went to a party. You were Okoye. You didn't even tell me.'

'You've really been going through my stuff, Becks.'

'Because I thought something bad had happened to you!'

'I'm fine. Things with Logan are fine.'

Fine? 'You're back together?'

Silva smiles at me, the first time since I came in. It's a weird smile mixed with something else. It's like I'm watching her through those old-school cardboard 3-D glasses with red and green plastic 'lenses'. If I squint, maybe I'll see what she really feels.

She says, 'How are things with China?'

'China?'

'You were going to see her the other night.'

'Yeah, but . . . how d'you know?'

She don't say nothing.

'You came over when I was out and left that note. How did you know I wouldn't be here?'

She moves round me and out the bedroom. 'Becks, there's things I need to sort out. I promise you'll know everything soon.'

'Where are you going? I thought you'd come back!'

'Not yet. But you don't have to worry. You know I'm okay now.'

'I'm not! You made me think my cat was dead! And guess what, Silva? My other dad got in touch. I was having breakfast with him this morning. That's why I was in

McDonald's when I saw you.'

'Oh.' She blinks and looks away for a second.

I carry on. 'He told me some interesting stuff. One of his mates worked with Logan at the delivery place. Do you want to hear what I found out?'

Suddenly, she looks sad. 'Oh, Becks. I've been so selfish, haven't I?'

'Er. Yeah.'

'Look,' she says. 'I'm going to make us some smoothie and then we'll talk, all right?'

'Yeah,' I say. 'All right.'

She goes out the bedroom into the hallway and through the front door. For a second I sit there like my brain's frozen. Through the front door? Maybe she's gone to get something for our drinks. No, our cupboards are full of stuff. Then I race to the door. It's too late. She's double-locked it from the outside.

Silva has locked me in.

33

So, Becks, what happens next?

This is the day *it* happens. This is the day Logan and I are together again.

That picture I'd seen in Logan's locker closed me down. I was so confused. I'd always believed that me and him should be together but he was pulling away so hard we would snap. I felt stretched. The shadows weren't only surrounding me, they were slipping into me. I was losing myself like I was becoming a shadow too.

Then I saw him on the bus. As it drove away, I knew I had a decision to make. Was I ready to lose him for good? No. If I was, I would have thrown away the box under my bed. Do you know how many times I bundled everything into a bin bag, ready to shove down the chute? Each time, my heart had banged so hard that I'd thought I was having a heart attack. I couldn't do it. These are my totems. They remind me of what is real. Oh, Becks. If it wasn't for you making me watch *Inception* all those times, I wouldn't know what a totem was!

I didn't think I would be writing this. I thought I would be gone already, but you threw me, Becks. I should have known that. Other girls your age would just celebrate their freedom.

You looked for me. I'm sorry. I hope you read this and understand.

And look around you, Becks. Can you see? This is who me and Logan are. *She* doesn't deserve him. *She* doesn't really want him. *She* doesn't really need him. I do.

I went to his flat first, early this morning. His sister wasn't happy to see me. She said he wasn't there. I had to believe she was telling the truth. He'd told me once that most of the drivers had a McDonald's habit. His favourite meal was breakfast. So that's where I went.

You should have seen your face when you saw me, Becks. But I imagine mine was the same. You know McDonald's is one of those places that everyone seems to understand, except me. Do you remember when I asked you about it? There are so many places to eat in London. Why go there? You told me that you have to move with the right crew to get McDonald's. It also helped if you've been going there since you were a baby. Mum definitely didn't take me to McDonald's. Dad didn't neither, even when he was with Win, because he knew how strongly Mum hated it.

I'd walked in and there was food all around, smells trapped in boxes and cardboard cups. Bagels and pancakes and hash browns and coffee. Piles of wrappers and sugar spilled across the closest table.

I saw that girl first. Then I saw you. Now I know why you were there, but I'd thought you knew everything. I thought you were going to stop me. I had to get out.

Maybe seeing you was fate, fate telling me to stop, to come home, to forget Logan.

I won't forget him. I won't let myself. Good memories wriggle away too easily. Not this time.

I have photos of my mum and there are things I remember. Most of that seems to be sickness, though I know Mum was so much more. I have the tree we planted after she died and my aunty in Canada who wants me to come and stay. But most of all there is space where she should be.

Dad was right. I should have taken some of Mum's old clothes when we moved out. Mum had offered me her jumper, a pale blue one with silver beads around the neckline. Grandma knitted it for her to celebrate my birth. The first time I put it on after she died, I thought I'd feel like I was inside her hug. It was big and soft and smelt of fabric softener and, I think, faint onions from a meal cooked long ago. But I didn't smell Mum. The hospital 'mum' had taken over everything. It brought back all those other smells, the endless coffee Dad bought from Costa and the lavender oil Mum dripped across her pillow and the sour smell of skin when a plaster's ripped away.

A few days after Mum's funeral, her best friends came around to sort out her flat. They'd agreed it with Mum before she died. I knew them all from the early days after Dad moved out. Mum had said that no matter how many times she'd told them the break-up was mutual, they were furious with him. When they came to organise Mum's things, Dad and I went to the cinema. I know it sounds strange, but we could both sit in the dark thinking our own thoughts while a morning show of *Whale Rider* played out on the screen. When we returned to the house, the wardrobes were empty and Mum's bedroom smelt of women's breath and dampness. They'd been crying. I'd wished I'd stayed with them.

How can I make good memories, Becks, when only the sludgy stuff stays in my head? I found the answer. It's when someone loves the whole of you and you love the whole of them back.

I went to the flat to wait for you. I wish I could remember to say 'home', even after all these years. I still see my old tiny house as home. You never saw it. It was wedged between loads of other houses, at the top of a hill. We had a miniature front garden which Mum said must never ever be paved over. She filled it with pots of roses and lavender and geraniums to attract the bees. I don't know what's happened to it now.

I walked up the stairs to the flat. The cleaning fluid was so heavy and sweet I could taste it. A boy in a Nike cap was just leaving the flat next door. He brushed past me without saying anything, not caring if I belonged there or not. As I opened the door, your cat seemed to materialise from the air and stroll in beside me. It looked up at me as if it was challenging me.

The kitchen was almost tidy. There was a half-empty

bottle of ginger beer on the table and plastic containers waiting to be washed up in the sink. Nothing had changed in the sitting room, but your bedroom door was open. You had taken my box. The lid was propped up against it. My totems had been taken out and laid in rows across the carpet.

I was angry, Becks. So mad! You went into my room and snooped through my precious things! How dare you! But, if you didn't come home for days, would I do the same? Perhaps.

What did those totems tell you?

Everything in that box told its story so easily to me. What did they say to you? I noticed that you'd put the receipts in a different bag. I wonder if Dad's ever going to wear his Abercrombie and Fitch wedding shirt again. The receipts are a bit bent too. I can see you holding them just a little too tight, your face scrunched up the way it always does when you're thinking hard.

I know you saw the story about the football team. I'd found it after the party when I'd missed him so much, when I was trying to find anything about him. You were so bold, Becks, that you marched right down to the marshes to ask questions.

What did you make of Rain? Perhaps that was easiest. You would have known I hadn't bought it for myself.

Your cat came in and leapt on to the bed. She settled down with one paw hanging over the edge as if she expected me to pat her head. She waved her tail at your model of

Okoye from *Black Panther*. How could I ever have thought I'd be a warrior queen like her? I looked back at the floor, at the envelope with the wig in it. How soon did you know? Did you wonder why I tore up the dress? I was so angry with myself for ruining it, I couldn't bear to look at it. Did you look for the shoes, Becks? I dumped them in a charity bin after I left the gym.

I couldn't see the medal. Now I know that you took it and it led you to the boxing club. (Did Kurt tell you everything? I don't think he did, or you would have spat it back to me earlier.) Logan didn't want me to buy him a birthday present so we agreed to swap something special – not something new, but something with a story that no one else would understand. I gave him the school tie from my primary school. I told him that ties weren't compulsory, but I wanted one so Mum could knot it for me every morning. Sometimes she'd knot Dad's too, if he was going to a meeting to ask people for money for his projects. When she died, I used to sleep with it in the pillowcase beneath my cheek. And then I gave the tie to him.

The medal was from Logan's only boxing competition. Kurt made him go to the club in the early days to stop him being thrown out of school. He told me he enjoyed it more than he admitted to his brother. Kurt was the big brother who was always right, always telling him what he should do without listening to what he had to say. He entered Logan for the beginner's contest. It was the best of five rounds.

Logan came third out of sixteen.

That was my tie in the locker, next to my shoes. Three weeks ago, I'd gone to the boxing club because I wanted to make myself hate Logan. But my heart understood that Logan wanted to keep his memories of me.

This morning I pulled the scraps of my torn dress out of the box and shook it. I shook and shook and shook. I picked up everything on the carpet and looked underneath. I went into my room and searched under my bed, sweeping my hand across the darkness. I checked the shelves and under my pillow.

The locker key was gone. You had the medal *and* the key. That was too much. I imagined you heading to the boxing club and talking to Kurt. Perhaps you would work out what I planned to do next.

The cat shifted on my bed. Its paw patted my skin. It was asleep, but so still it looked dead. So, I phoned you, Becks.

I'm so, so sorry.

I have to act quickly. I know you won't be stuck there for long. I know you're calling me and I will answer, but not yet.

34

Man! There are words that get used for girls and I don't ever use none of them, but right now my brain's putting together new words to call my sister. I'm so damn stupid. Like when she said she was gonna make a smoothie why didn't I get it? She didn't even ask what we've got to make it from. And it's the way she said it, all nice and calm, telling me to clear up while she strolled off. And locked me in.

Locked. Me. In! Serious, if you filled a 38 bus full of wastemen cussing each other out and you carried them to Victoria station and then back again to east London, you still wouldn't hear enough cuss words in all them hours to match the number coming out of my mouth right now.

I try my key in the lock, just in case. I don't understand how this crap works, unlock and lock up easily on the outside but not moving a single millimetre on the inside, even if I use two hands to try and push it. I want to force it, but I'm careful in case the key snaps. That happened to Mum once and the cost of the locksmith meant we were eating cheap tinned chilli with baked potatoes for the next two weeks.

I sit down by the front door, right where the delivery woman left our shopping. It feels like there's a dragon twisting awake inside me and I need to wait for it to cool down. Deep breath, Becks.

What can I do? I can call the police or the fire brigade. Then they're gonna call social services because my sister locked me in. Also, they may go and arrest Silva. Of course, right now that would make me very happy, but I don't think that's gonna do Silva no good. And I don't want to call Mum and Justin to tell them that the girl's in a police cell.

I could call a locksmith again, but they need paying. Mum's topped up my account for emergencies, but not by that much.

I dig for my phone in my pocket. I call Silva. It rings and rings until it hits messages. I try again and again. I leave a message telling her exactly how I feel. Then another one with some more thoughts. I don't suppose she's gonna listen to it anytime soon but it makes me feel a little bit better.

Then I message China. I guess she's chilling out with her family, walking along the beach, maybe taking a swim, if that's her kind of thing. I don't know if it is. There's so much we've got to find out about each other, if I ever get out of here.

China phones me straight away. She'd been making herself some brunch, but she'd kept her phone close in case. I want to ask her how close, like whether it was anywhere next to her skin. I shake my head. I need to focus. Just hearing her voice sends the dragon to deep sleep again. There's just a few little snorts making my stomach burn. She asks me if anyone else has got a key. I think. Savannah! Of course! Her mum said it was a good idea I kept a key there after I kept pitching up on her doorstep after school because I'd left mine at home.

I ring off from China and phone Savannah. It goes to messages straight away, like she's on a tube. I send messages, Whatsapp, Insta, plain old SMS. Whichever way she sees her notifications, she's gonna be getting plenty from me. I need to decide how long to give her. What if she's on a really long journey, like from one of those Essex stations along the Central line to Ealing? What if she's lost her phone and she's never gonna get my messages?

Half an hour. That's her limit. Then . . . then what?

Smaug's big, bad grandma is starting to puff fire inside me again. Okay, what else can I do? I can pass my keys through the letterbox for someone to open the door from outside. The postman, she ain't been yet. I'll call through to her when I hear the letterbox flap. Though, what if we don't get any post today?

Rianna, she can come. Or even DNA-Dad. After this morning, he might be ready to put things right. If I called him now, he'd come straight away. It's bad enough meeting up with him without telling Mum, but letting him walk across her carpets and see her kitchen . . . I feel like I'm betraying her just by thinking of it.

But this is an emergency.

Half an hour. That's how long I'll wait for Savannah to call back. No, it's only twenty-three minutes left now.

What am I gonna do when I get out? Silva don't look like she's in danger. She's the one causing the stress. Though . . . if I believe that, it means that football coach was right about her, and Logan's as innocent as baby Jesus. That don't feel right, neither. The boy gets off on girls falling in love with him. It's like he took one look at my sister and knew he could reel her in.

Break ups make folk do bad things. Even Mum didn't behave that well about DNA. She cheered when he was put in prison. I mean, real life loud cheering. She never usually talked about him. She told me when I was older that she kept silent because she couldn't think of anything good to say and didn't want to disrespect him in front of me. (Of course, she doesn't know I heard her on the phone to some of her friends. This flat's small. Sound carries. When she started on about my father, her voice got louder. It didn't happen much. It was usually when she'd tried to get him to pay up his child support.) After she cheered, she looked over at me, and gave me a guilt smile, but didn't say sorry. She knew she shouldn't have been celebrating his prison sentence in front of me. There was I feeling officially part-criminal and Mum was just grinning. Even she was pushed to do something not good because someone she loved had let her down.

So, in spite of this locked-in crap, I'm gonna carry on believing that Logan was the one who started it. I'm gonna believe that Silva really loved Logan. And I'm gonna believe what Kurt said. Logan was always gonna be in it for the short term, making her fall for him, then move on. And I'm gonna try really damn hard to believe what Raych said, that I was too busy talking to stop and listen to what was really going on for Silva.

And do you know what the other thing is I'm gonna believe? Mum should have made an Indestructible Duvet Cover for Silva to stop all of Logan's weird voodoo mucking up her head.

I look at those clues across the floor. I pick up the green plastic counter. Raych and Silva went to the fair together. Raych knew about Logan way before I did. Was that really all she knew? Just that? I can't believe it. I think harder.

Maybe me and Raych's friendship had been fading for a while, but after she went to the fair with Silva, it changed. We didn't message as much. When we did, there didn't seem much to say no more. Maybe she was saving her best conversation for Silva. Like . . .

Like, how did Silva know I went to China's the other night? Raych was the only one I told about that. Me and Raych seriously need to talk.

I call her. I'm almost surprised that she picks up.

'What's going on, Raych?'

'For me, or everyone in the world, Becks?'

'I'm seriously not in the mood. Is Silva with you?'

She gives a little laugh. 'Why would she be with me?'

'Because . . .' I slap my hands against my face. Maybe all that K-pop's turned my brain into fluff. 'Because she ain't been sleeping here, so where *could* she be? Whose sister's got a handy free flat, Raych?'

'She's not with me, Becks.'

'I'm not asking you if Silva's with you right now. I'm asking if you let her stay in Melissa's flat.'

'I've got to go. I'm really busy.'

'Did she tell you that she came home and locked me in?'

A little silence, the really empty type like the microphone's been muted. 'That's weird. Maybe it was just an accident. You know, automatically locking the door after herself. You always said she was hot on security.'

'Yeah, so hot she accidentally locked me in. I can't get out.'

'God. I don't know what to say.'

'You could say that you're coming straight round to help me.'

'I can't though, Becks. Like I said, I'm busy.'

I'm holding my phone so tight, I expect the battery to shoot out the end. 'I'm locked in, Raych! I need to get out! I need to stop my sister doing something weird!'

'I'm across the other side of London. I'd take ages to get to you. There must be someone else who's got a door key. And there's the fire bri—'

I hang up. She ain't gonna come, that's for sure. And the other thing I know for sure is that she's lying. I heard the announcement for the 11.32 Stansted Express in the background while she was telling me she was too far away.

Raych ain't across the other side of London. She's at an overground station. I google the Stansted Express stops to be sure. Funny enough, it stops at Tottenham Hale station, the closest one to Melissa's flat. She could be with me in forty minutes.

So, right.

Silva's locked me in.

Raych don't want to come and let me out. She's near her sister's place, but she's lying. And she didn't come straight out and deny that Silva's staying there. Something's happening, but I don't know what. Melissa's flat, that *must* be where Silva's been hanging out. And all this time Raych knew.

I call Savannah again. It's not quite half an hour, but close. It goes to messages. Another try. Still messages. I swear so hard and long I'm sure Mum can hear me in Japan. I feel my cheeks flush. I drop my phone on to the rug and I notice my nails again and think of China's fingers, so steady as she strokes on the blue and the tiny, gold petals of my flower. Some of that calmness curls back through my nails, into my skin and into me. I take a deep breath and send Savannah a text. I also text Rianna. She gets back to me straight away. She's in Southend with her aunties but can send her brother round if I need it. I tell her to hold back. I'll use up the brother favour if I'm really stuck.

I'm okay. I've got options. Mum and Justin won't come back and find my angry skeleton. I'm gonna give Savannah three more minutes to get back to me and then I'm gonna make a call. I don't want to do it, but the man owes me.

35

So yeah, I make the call and I wait. Azog sits on my lap and reaches out her paw so it's on my shoulder. I kiss her forehead and feel her eyebrows tickle my nose. She's purring and it calms me down. My sister's gone rogue and my ex-best friend's a liar, but at least my cat don't hate me and she's alive.

The intercom goes and I press unlock and wait. When I hear a knock on the door, I drop my key through the letterbox and, at last, the door opens. Me and Kurt look at each other. He must have run out of the gym as soon as I called because there's a sweaty patch across his chest.

'Thank you,' I say. 'I really appreciate it.'

'Yeah. It's not something I get asked to do every day.'

He stays outside. It seems rude not to invite him in, but it would be awkward for him to be in my flat with me. I think he gets that because he doesn't move.

'Have you checked on your brother?' I ask.

'Yeah.'

'And he's definitely not with Silva?'

'He's definitely not with Silva. He's got a solicitor's appointment.'

'A solicitor?'

'It's a personal matter. Nothing illegal.'

'Silva seemed to think they're together.'

He sighs. 'No. Logan's not with your sister. Look, I'm in a dodgy parking place and I need to get back. Can I drop you anywhere?'

I don't know what to do now. Maybe I should just relax. Silva's not dead and Logan's not with her. I probably can even take a good guess where she's been staying. So why did she lock me in? She could have schmoozed me with smoothie and gone about her business.

I say, 'The last time she saw you, she went into Logan's locker, right?'

'Yes.' He looks a little embarrassed. 'I could have been a bit, I don't know, kinder.'

'What's in there?'

'You didn't have a look?'

'Silva called me, remember? That's why I had to run out. She told me something was wrong with my cat because she knew I'd rush home. Then she locked me in. The thing is, she'd kept the locker key so I thought there might be something in there to help me work out what she's up to.'

Now he looks even more embarrassed. 'She said they went to the boxing club after the party and left something behind.'

'But you don't know what?'

'I've been tempted to take a snoop in there, but the brotherly relationship is already in a pit. I was planning to clear it out next month anyway. We're getting busier and need more lockers.'

I wonder if China's brother's promo video helped. I almost smile thinking about it.

Kurt carries on talking. 'I know there used to be—' Then he goes red. 'There used to be a photo on the inside of the locker door.'

I'm wondering what kind of picture is making a grown man glow as hard as Sauron's eye. 'Of Logan?' I ask.

'Yeah.'

'And another girl?'

'Yeah.'

'Doing what?'

'Nothing! Just a picture.'

'And you think Silva saw it?'

'Maybe. I don't know. Logan might have moved it, but he hasn't come down in ages. Well, not in the day, anyway. We always end up arguing.'

'Is it all right if I come back to the gym with you? I can take whatever Silva left in the locker and check out what else is in there.'

I grab a bag from the kitchen for Silva's stuff, stick my phone in my pocket and follow Kurt out the flat. I double lock from the outside, of course.

Kurt's van is outside the newsagent. Man's lucky he didn't get a ticket. Maybe he parked up in the quantum realm. He moves a big toolbox for me to sit down on the passenger seat.

The back's full of gym equipment, a bag of small cones and some spades.

'There's a charity that help folk who can't manage their gardens,' he says. 'I volunteer there. Most of it's fighting weeds, because even when you put in flowers folk often forget to water them. But not always.'

I peek at the flower decorating my little fingernail.

We pull out on to the main road.

I say, 'Why did you set up the boxing club?'

'I suppose it was for people like me. Or the person I was when I was young. Not just me, but Logan too. You could have dipped our behinds in concrete, but we still weren't going to sit in a classroom long enough to learn anything. Our dad was in prison for a bit, not long, but long enough for me and Logan to take the piss. And long enough for Mum to start divorcing him. Vicks is the only one of us who's got her head screwed on.'

'Is that your sister?'

'Victoria. Yes.'

'She must have had the baby quite young.'

'Baby?' He glances across at me, then back at the road. I deserve that. Most folk don't want reminding if their sister's pregnant at school, even if things turned out right.

Traffic's snarled up round Highbury, all the longer for us to sit there, awkward.

I say, 'Logan lives with your sister, right?'

'My parents moved to Spain three years ago, but wanted

to keep a place in London, just in case. They don't charge no rent.'

I hear something in his voice. Kurt ain't happy with that arrangement.

I say, 'Do you visit your parents much?'

'I went last year, but it's hard to get away when you've got a business.'

Yeah, I remember Justin saying that too.

The gym meets us outside. Well, water from it does, dripping out from under the door and down the step. Kurt swears, jabs his key in the lock like he's trying to kill it and knees open the door. I almost expect to see Noah waving hello as he goes by on his ark. The flood's not bad as it could be, but it's still more water than anyone wants on their floor.

Kurt steams into the changing room. I hear him shout, 'Bastards!'

He comes out holding a wad of sopping green paper towel.

'I couldn't leave anyone here unsupervised so I asked them to get dressed and come back later. So the little . . .' He holds up the towel and it drips over his foot. 'They turned on the taps and showers and blocked up the plugs. Banned, man, the whole lot of them.' He drops the towel on the floor. It makes a splat. 'I knew I should have got them push in and hold showers, but after a good workout . . . You want a proper flow, not two cold drops then nothing. I should have known better.' He sighs. 'Sorry, I'm going to have to clear this up. The place hasn't even dried up from the burst pipe last week.'

I nod. 'Can I still check out the locker?'

'Yeah, yeah. Of course. It's two rows along, third from the left, beneath the Nicola Adams poster. Do you know who she is?'

I nod hard. Of course I do. I even asked the stylist to braid my hair like hers for the wedding, the style where she's holding up her gold Olympic medal. The stylist didn't think it was flash enough and added her own touches. Those are the bits that are fuzzing out now.

Kurt opens a cupboard and takes out a mop and bucket. I follow him round the corner to the lockers. I see Nicola. She's smiling at me and I smile back. You *have* to smile at Nicola. I take the key out my pocket and slide it into the lock. I wiggle it and when I try and pull it out, the whole door opens.

The first thing I see is the photo stuck on the inside of the locker door. Gosh. It's Logan with my sister, not some other girl. They're out having something to eat and I recognise one of the dresses she bought on Fonthill Road. Seeing them together – I don't know why I feel shocked. Of course I know they were lovey but seeing it – him taking the picture of them both, her grinning like I've never seen her grin before. My sister was happy then, so damn happy, and I'd never even noticed. How did Silva feel when she saw it? Maybe she thought he kept it there because he still cared about her. Why wouldn't she want to be happy like that again?

Then I see some shoes, high gold things that I can never imagine Silva in. Even for the wedding, she wore brogues with the bodycon. I take them out and drop them in my bag. There's a sweatshirt shoved in the back. I pull it out. I don't know, is it Silva's or Logan's? It's plain, washed-out dark blue and could fit Silva. I sniff it. Then I look around in case anyone saw me doing that. You can't live with a mother who sniffs shirt armpits all your life without picking up habits. The sweatshirt's kind of like nose-cinema, a mix-up of smells that maybe only Silva could sort out. There's red and black smudges over the inside of the collar. Lipstick? Mascara? Then I look down at the shoes and laugh. Did my sister have a go at drawing on Okoye's head tattoos? Maybe she brought spare shoes and a sweatshirt for after the party and smeared her tattoos when she was getting warm. It's either that or some other girl's make-up. I'm gonna presume it's Silva's and take it too.

Under that's a school tie. Now, that's a bit weird, but I'm not gonna judge. I'm probably gonna burn mine when I'm done with school. From what Kurt was saying, Logan didn't spend much time in school neither. Maybe he shoved it in there and forgot about it. Anyway, I'm leaving that. Let Kurt decide.

The last thing is an envelope, a thin A4 brown one. Logan's

address is written on the front. I wonder why he didn't take this one home. It's rude to open other people's post. I don't need to look. It's nothing to do with me or Silva. And, come on, Mum could have snuck a peek at that first letter from DNA, but she didn't. Like my food tech teacher says, I need to exercise discipline.

I turn the envelope over. It's sealed, but loose sealed, like it's been opened and the flap's been pressed back against the last bit of glue.

I stand back from the locker and look around for Kurt. I can't see him, but I can hear swearing as he empties his bucket in one of the changing room toilets. Then I grab the envelope and empty it into the locker. I keep the sweatshirt nearby in case I need a quick cover up. A page of paper flops out, and some pictures. I mean serious, do I want to check out Logan's private snaps? I flip one over. It's Logan with his arm round a girl. She's cute looking with a fluffy afro and wicked lashes. I check out another. It's them in some posh garden somewhere. I can't tell if it's behind a house or in a park. Then – is that the Royal Albert Hall? They're grinning, in a queue outside.

O-kay, what's the issue? I check over the note. It's written in gold pen and I kind of have to skim over a bit because I'm blushing so hot. I don't need that much detail. I quickly get the issue, though. Our cutie – she's signed herself as 'Cara' – was only sixteen when Logan passed her a 'beautiful' note. Cara wasn't happy when he dumped her and moved on. If he didn't come back to her, she was ready to tell her dad that her boyfriend was four years older than her and picked her up when he was delivering their groceries. Seems like she was true to her word from what DNA said:

I think one girl he tried to hook was younger than she looked and her dad complained to the company.

I want to feel sorry for Logan, but I'm struggling.

I slide Cara's letter and pics back into the envelope. That's definitely staying here. I take another look at the photo of Silva and Logan on the inside of the locker door. That's coming with me. He don't deserve her. I pull it off and it comes away with a sticky click. There's another photo beneath it.

Oh. This is for real, right? Yeah, because . . . Why the hell would you fake it?

It's Logan. Of course it is. Man likes to mug for a shot, especially when he's with a girl. He's with a girl here, but I can't see no smile. They're in a courtyard somewhere, between two big vases of white flowers. Logan's wearing a suit. She's wearing a dress, long and white with sleeves made of netting.

Is it a . . . ?

I know it is. I've looked through enough magazines with Mum to recognise it when I see it. It's a wedding. And it's not just that it's a wedding. Our girl's pregnant. Big time pregnant, like the baby's gonna bust out and offer to hold the ring.

I stare at the girl. She looks like she's got a good dose of different ethnic genes, just like us. Justin once took one of those online ancestry tests where you spit in a tube and send it away. His results showed him split between nearly twenty different countries, none of him more than 15 per cent. This girl with Logan looks a bit like Justin, though there's a greasy spot across her face from where Silva's photo was stuck on top of it. She's smiling though, like she's made of love.

'Ah.' Kurt's voice makes me jump. 'That's the photo I meant earlier.'

'Logan got a wife?'

'Wife' shouldn't sound like a cuss word, not least because my mum's just become one. But seeing that picture . . . Then the one with my happy sister. 'And he's a daddy?'

Kurt balances his mop against the wall. He jerks his head towards his office and I follow him in. He opens a cabinet beneath his desk and pulls out a photo album.

'Mum made up one for all of us.'

I flip open the cover. The first photo's an old white couple, though they're both suntanned right up. I squint at them. There's a hint-of-Kurt look. They must be Kurt and Logan's parents. A grumpy baby's sitting on the woman's lap. It's wearing a vest with 'Born To Run' across the chest and a hat that looks like a Christmas pudding. I wonder if my grandma's got any of those style time-bombs of me in her albums.

I turn the page. I'm looking at a meal in a restaurant. Logan's parents are there, holding up a glass of wine for the camera. The girl's there, next to Logan. They're both giving camera smiles, the ones that are lips-only. I recognise Vicky holding up a bottle of beer. She ain't got a baby and she don't look close to having one. I feel a bit embarrassed for even thinking it.

'What's their names?' I ask.

'His daughter's called Vanessa. Her Mum is Isabel.'

'He's not exactly grinning in his wedding picture, is he?'

'No, but at least he didn't run away. My parents moved out to Majorca three years ago. There was no mortgage left on their flat in London and they had enough savings to lay down a deposit on a small bar. They took in language students for extra money. Isabel's from the Philippines and came over to improve her Spanish. She also just happened to be there when my brother was between jobs and helping the parents redecorate the bar.'

I turn another page. It's baby Vanessa again, a bit older and sprawled across her grandparents' laps. She looks much happier. Maybe she prefers to chill in a vest and nappy. The picture opposite is one of them official wedding portraits, Logan and Isabel, cheek by cheek. He's managed a smile for this one. Hers is ten times bigger.

I look from him to her. I just don't get it.

Kurt laughs like he read my mind. 'I never used to understand what girls saw, until I saw him with Isabel. He gave her attention. Not just opening doors and easy stuff like that. He was really interested in her.'

I flip through more pages. Pictures of the baby when she was small and wrinkly in Logan's arms. Man, the boy's terrified. At least in my baby picture with DNA, he don't look like he thinks he's gonna drop me if he breathes too hard. DNA even cracks a smile. The photos with Isabel and her daughter, she looks pretty scared too.

I say the words again. 'He's got a wife and a baby. And he's still chasing after my sister. What the hell's that about? And . . . the baby . . . ? Where's she?'

'She's here in London. Isabel's parents weren't – shall we say – happy with the situation. They're very religious and they'd saved up to send their daughter over to learn Spanish, not to—' He coughs. 'Not to learn whatever Logan was teaching. When my parents found out she was pregnant, they managed to get her a work permit. Her dad's an accountant and she's pretty sharp with a spreadsheet, but Mum and Dad sure as hell weren't going to pay for a baby-sitter when their son was kicking his heels over here in England in a rent-free flat.'

'Why did he come back?'

'Because he didn't like Mum and Dad breathing down his neck. He was supposed to be sorting out residency for Isabel, but, well – he saw himself as a free man again.'

I turn the page of the album.

A nasty thought's wriggling its way to the front. 'If the baby's with Logan over here, that means your parents made Isabel give her up.'

'No. My parents are tough, but not that tough. Vanessa was with her mum for a while. Logan went over at Christmas and brought her back. The plan was that she'd get to know her dad better. He was supposed to pay Vicky to help out with childcare while he looked for a job. Isabel comes over to see her whenever she can and she wants to move here full time. It's not easy, though. Logan needs to get a job. Not just get one, he damn well needs to keep one, if he's any chance of getting her citizenship.'

'If he's meant to be supporting his wife and baby, what's with my sister? He came back with his child and he's still chasing up girls! Your brother must be a total dick.'

I clap my hand over my mouth. Kurt just laughs, though not like he's enjoying the joke.

'Yes. A dick. That's about right. The wedding was really just for show to keep Isabel's parents happy. I must admit, I pushed Logan into it a bit too. Vanessa didn't ask to be born. The least he can do is step up to the plate and be a decent father. He'd have probably been happy for Isabel to go back to the Philippines and take his daughter with her. But then, maybe five, ten years' time, what? Say she's gonna come and look for him and ask him difficult questions. Or, even more miraculous, Logan grows a conscience and wants to know what happened to his child. Then what? And . . .' I look at Kurt. 'I didn't want to lose my niece. Just a minute.'

He's fiddling with his phone. I think about DNA-Da— Benni not taking no for an answer when I didn't want him to come with me. His promise to be my safety net. Then I think about all his younger kids who've probably got a whole load of questions of their own to ask him. There ain't no easy answers, any time.

'Here,' Kurt says, holding up his phone. 'That's her now.'

Man, she's like Boo from *Monsters Inc*, even with the little side bunches. Except, this Boo's dressed like Elsa from Frozen.

I suddenly remember a cross toddler in an Elsa costume at McDonald's in Highbury, one who looked just like this.

Kurt grins. 'It's her favourite outfit. I bought it for her.'

'She's lovely,' I say. 'Really cute. It's just . . .'

He frowns. 'What?'

'Nothing. She's gorgeous. She reminds me of someone.'

He's grinning again. 'She's why I need Logan to sort out his crap.'

'Yeah. Sure.'

He looks at his phone like he's ready to kiss it.

'I better go, Kurt. Thanks again for rescuing me.'

'Sure. And I'm sorry about the way Logan's treated your sister. Really sorry.'

So am I.

36

I would love to live here, Becks. So would you. You would feel like a superhero with the world beneath you. You can see new buildings growing out of the rubble of an old industrial estate. The cranes reach so high. They have red lights on their tips so at night they look like angry stars. A mad, red universe.

I will miss you. I will miss Dad and I will miss your mum. I can't stay. It will be too difficult. Moving to yours was supposed to be a fresh start, but it couldn't be. Everything that was supposed to be new could never make up for what I had lost.

Becks, do you know everything now? It's easy when you have a name.

Logan Gladdinn. Look it up.

A girl called Isabel posted a picture of her and Logan on their wedding day.

The girl called Isabel has posted pictures of a baby called Vanessa.

The girl called Isabel posts in English and Tagalog.

Rhoda and Anthony Gladdinn have a bar in Majorca called Dirty Vodka. They have pictures in their gallery, including a wedding. I recognise the two people getting married.

Rhoda Gladdinn is on Facebook and posts picture of her granddaughter, Vanessa. She was really upset when Vanessa came to stay in England with her dad.

So, Logan is married. He has a child. His mother isn't dead.

I'm glad I know this. Now it all makes sense. He lied about his mother to help him understand what I was feeling. It was his way of making us equal. And he's married? Of course, he thought he was doing the right thing. He's a good person, but the fact that he was with me proves it wasn't the right thing. He was unhappy. He was making Isabel unhappy.

Is he trying to be a father? If he was, he would already be working, earning money, to make sure the family can stay here. A father doesn't have to share your DNA, that's what you're always saying, Becks. She will meet someone else who will be a better husband and father. She doesn't need him.

I do.

37

Two things are stressing me now. First, I must have been looking straight at Isabel and Vanessa, but a light brown baby dressed like Elsa is hardly a novelty in Highbury McDonald's, is it? Second thing. Silva wasn't there by accident and it wasn't me she was looking at. It was them. I popped up in her vision, unexpected. She must have thought I was there deliberately, and I was gonna tell them something. Or warn them, I don't know. But it was enough for her to pretend my Azog was dead and lock me in.

And there's a third thing. You know them apps where you can hail a cab? The satellite pings your location to the driver and where you want to go and then in a few minutes' time, the car just rolls up. They're a great idea. None of this sticking your arm out and looking hopeful, because no black cab's gonna stop for a sixteen year old who don't look like they've got no money. But they're only a great idea if a birth accident gives you parents that got money and set up an account for you. Mine don't.

I think about phoning DNA to see if he's got anything set up on his flash new upgrade. Except, he told me it's a hand-me-down from an old mate, pay as you go because he could never be accepted for contract. He says he's used to dealing in cash. Especially the cash that came in security boxes, I didn't say. I'm learning.

China messages me just as I'm standing by the bus stop trying to work out if it's quicker if I jog. I've been texting her with updates. She sends me the password to her taxi account. I tell her that it's bad manners to finesse your . . . your girl, so quickly.

Jokes, hun. You don't finesse a girl who's giving you something for free. They built a vibranium monorail down Holloway Road yet? Take my password, honey, and get there quick xxx

Four minutes later, Amad pulls up in his Prius and I'm messaging all my thanks.

The ride seems to take longer than walking because of the roadworks outside the station. My leg's jiggling like it's hearing the best music and can't wait for the rest of my body to catch up.

My phone rings. It's Raych.

She says, 'Hi.'

It's only two letters, but man, I don't even want to waste one letter on her.

She says, 'Are you there, Becks?'

'Am I where?' My tone makes Amad glance back in his mirror at me. 'Locked up in my flat like an idiot? Or on my way to your sister's flat? That's where Silva is, right?

267

You knew all this time.'

'I want to explain.'

'Explain what? Why you lied to me?'

'Yes.'

I didn't expect her to be so honest.

'We've been friends for a long time, Becks. I don't want to give all that up.'

'I don't care what you want.'

'I'm outside Logan's flat,' she says. 'Meet me there as soon as you can.'

'You know where he lives?'

'He and Isabel and Vanessa were with me earlier.'

'You know about them too?'

'Meet me, Becks. I'll explain it all.'

I look out the window. All I can see is buses, none of them moving.

'I'm coming,' I say.

Amad's not happy that I'm getting out, but I tell him he can carry on to the address and charge the full fare. I run down Holloway Road and see Raych sitting on the wall by the closed-down petrol station. She smiles when she sees me. I'm not wasting mouth-muscle energy on her to smile back.

'What's going on, Raych?'

She's looking at the pavement. 'I was only trying to help.'

'Help who? You lied to me! You knew how mad I was going trying to work out what was happening. I even reported her missing!'

'I tried to tell you!'

'Tell me what? I was – intense? I didn't listen enough? That's not telling me. That's blasting me when I've already been blasting myself.'

Now she meets my eye. 'I brought that note round. I thought it would help.'

There must be some invisible angel pulling me back because the devil on my shoulder is screaming at me to push her off that damn wall. Mash up her bougie top in the heap of old chips behind her. Watch her hop around trying to wipe London street spit out her hair. I step back.

'It was you? You who crept into my flat when I was asleep? Or man, did you think I was gonna be spending the night at China's and no one was in?' For a second, I imagined sitting up in Silva's bed the moment Raych walked through the bedroom door. The girl's heart would have stopped. 'You know, I wondered why Silva fetched my duvet and covered me up instead of shoving me off her damn bed.'

'Would you rather I left you to freeze?'

And if her heart *had* stopped? Right now, I wouldn't have been mourning. 'Man, you really wanted to help Silva out, didn't you?'

'Only because you wouldn't.'

'What? She never asked! She never told me!'

'And would you have helped her if she did ask?'

'No! And I can't see nothing wrong with that! Why did you?'

'If you'd seen her at the fair, Becks. If . . .'

'When she saw Logan?'

'Yeah . . . and . . .'

'He was with his family, wasn't he? His wife and his kid.'

She's staring at the pavement again. She must really like the chicken box by the lamp post because she can't take her eyes off it.

'Raych, you're not doing much explaining.'

'Okay!' She stands up so she's face to face with me. 'How come I get that bitch, Melissa, for a sister and you get Silva? Melissa gets everything she wants without doing anything for it. Me, I've had to do Mum's bloody flute and guitar and swimming and Mandarin and all I get for that is time off to see my friends. And only that if I ask hard enough. All Melissa has to do . . .' She pulls the corner of her mouth down. 'Put on a sad face and my parents throw money at her. They even bought her a flat, for god's sake! I asked them if I can stay there if I go to uni in London, but they're going to sell it when the market improves.'

When the market improves? Man, what language is this? The market could dance better than BTS and learn to cure cancer but there'd still be no chance of me owning no place in London. She thinks I'm gonna be sorry that her parents ain't wrapping up a flat in bows for her?

'You've got Silva,' she says. 'She's kind and, I don't know, delicate. She's gone through so much and I want things to be right for her. She was having a good time at the fair, Becks.

She was telling me how her mum was this really scary dodgem driver and how she'd let Silva take the wheel. Yes, Logan was with the girl and the baby. Seriously, Silva's face changed so much, I almost thought she'd seen her mum's ghost.'

'She didn't know nothing about them before?'

'He'd told her he lived with his sister and baby niece. There was no way she could have been his sister, though. You and me, we live in families where we're all different colours. God, the amount of times Mum got asked if I was really her daughter. So, I don't make assumptions about who's family and who isn't. But the girl, she looked east Asian and dark. The baby – you remember Boo from *Monsters Inc*?'

I catch myself before I shout 'Yes!' I'm not gonna big up our shared past, because this girl's like a stranger.

'The baby looked like that,' Raych says quietly. 'It was definitely the girl's and the way it clung to Logan, I was pretty sure it was his too.'

'Did he see Silva?'

'I don't think so. They were in those spinning teacup things. When they slowed down, there was a massive crowd trying to get on and we couldn't see them any more.'

'And afterwards Silva told you everything.' I keep my voice blank, although there's every type of hurt spinning up inside me. She told Raych everything and hid everything from me. Man.

'They'd split up by then. It was still raw for her, like she couldn't believe it. She didn't want to think about him

271

any more, but she couldn't stop. She went to see his brother at the gym. She wanted him to persuade her that Logan didn't want her. I think he nearly did, but then she saw a photo. It's Logan and her and they're happy. It was like she became more convinced that they should be together. She said she'd wait, no matter how long it took. How could he really want to be with the other girl and the child if he'd never mentioned them? Other days, though, she'd be really down, and thought it was all over.

'Then she saw Logan on the bus when she was coming back from taking your parents to the airport. He saw her too and she knew that he felt the same way as her.'

'Right,' I say. Raych's eyes are almost shining like she's been infected by Logan's Jesus glow too. 'You didn't believe her, did you?'

'That is why she didn't tell you!' Raych's eyes flash. More Captain Marvel than Jesus now. 'She needed to talk so I met her at Melissa's. She was already upset from the airport. She just wanted some time out.'

'She could have messaged me.'

'You can look after yourself, Becks.'

'Yes!' Yes, but . . . I don't always want to. And I just wanted to know that my sister was safe. I feel my phone vibrate. I take it out and check. It's China. Strength.

'She wanted someone to listen to her and believe her,' Raych says. 'And, do you know what? I do. I want to think that one day you're going to find . . . You've watched all them

K-dramas. What about the one where the girl has to pull the invisible sword out of the god-warrior and then marry him? You told me you cried loads at the end of that one.'

'That stuff's not true.'

'It might be. Not the invisible sword bit, of course. But, you know, what if someone really loves you and you love them back? You both know it, but all these things try and stop you.'

'Things? Like someone you've married? And a baby daughter?' My phone vibrates again. I take a deep breath. 'Raych, what's happening now? What's she planning?'

Raych shrugs. 'They're going to meet up and sort stuff out.'

I step towards her. 'Raych! Tell me!'

She shoots me a look. That looks says that if there was a sword stuck through *my* ribcage, she'd shove it in deeper instead of trying to pull it out.

'It's pointless,' she says.

Have I done a psychic take over? Seconds ago, she was saying the opposite.

'Pointless? You said she's doing the right thing!'

'See, you're still not listening, Becks. It's pointless thinking that Isabel can stay here.'

'What do you mean?'

'I managed to get them a session with my dad. He does free advice twice a month. Silva sent a message to Logan. We chose our words carefully. She said she'd found out his true

273

situation and was sorry he didn't think he could tell her. If he needed help, her friend had a dad who was a lawyer. She hinted that she was still a little bit into him too. He replied pretty damn quick!'

'Yeah. I bet he did!'

Raych ignored me. 'There's always a massive queue for the free sessions, but I sneaked them in. They needed to know the reality. Well, Isabel did. Staying here is tough and it costs a fortune. Logan hasn't even got a job.'

'Was she put off?'

Raych laughed. 'I think she knew it already. She'd reckoned that her parents could help with money. Now she knows exactly how much help they have to give.'

'You're vexed you didn't scare her off?' Raych's face has still got half a laugh on it. 'Seriously, Raych, you were gonna make sure that baby was taken away from her daddy?'

'For God's sake, Becks. You of all people should know that the father you're born from isn't always the best one to bring you up!'

My mouth opens and snaps shut again.

'But if you must know, Isabel wasn't scared off. So it was on to plan B. I asked Isabel if she really wanted to stay with Logan's sister every time she came over to visit. It's not exactly private. I said I knew someone who might have somewhere cheap to rent. Isabel wasn't that bothered, but Logan was seriously up for a low-rent flat of his very own. He really liked the idea of privacy.'

'I don't get it. Your folks were gonna rent Melissa's flat to him?'

'Of course not! I just wanted Logan and his so-called wife to go round and have a look.'

I stare at Raych's forehead so long that she has to look up.

'So they're on their way to your sister's flat now?'

'Yes, Becks.' She sits down on the wall. 'I paid for a cab, so they're probably there already.'

I turn away then stop. 'You called me here to take up my time, right?'

'I promised Silva I'd help.'

'Where's Melissa's flat, Raych?'

'Why should I tell you?'

'In case instead of going there, I head to your mum's and tell her what's been going on in the flat. I mean, she thought you were organising a tidy up, but maybe . . .'

'124 Bernie Grant Heights.'

'Message me the address.'

She takes out her phone.

'You're still going to be too late,' she says.

That's when the angel lets go of me. I shove her. She screams and topples backwards. I run off towards the station. Yeah, Raych, you can chuck out that T-shirt, but man, you're gonna have to swim in shampoo to get rid of all the nastiness that's sticking to your hair.

38

I race back to the bus stop, then remember how the traffic keeps backing up round here. I keep on running until I reach the station. I try and catch my breath. Kurt's already messaged me. He says that some strange girl dropped Vanessa with Vicky but Logan's not answering or picking up. I text Kurt Melissa's address, slam my card on the ticket reader and I'm down the quick side of the escalator, through the tunnel and on the platform. It's the direction that ain't busy and there's two minutes until the next train.

Man, it's a dentist's two minutes. It's when you're sat in the chair and the drill's coming towards your mouth and you're sure it's spinning in slow motion just to give you longer to feel scared. You know you're gonna feel every single turn when it grinds into your broken filling. Two long, long minutes.

The train comes. I slump on to one of the fold-down seats. All that running wasn't good for my system. I once did one of them 'create your own superhero name' quizzes online. I wanted to be a sleek, black panther streaking through London and biting villains. The name it gave me when I entered my adjectives, animal and nationality was Cougar-Woman. When I told Mum, she made a really funny face and checked the parental guidance settings.

It's only three stops, bumping and clattering so loud I still can't sort out my proper thoughts.

Isabel and Logan, man, they're on their way to the flat or already there. Silva's waiting for them. I don't give no stuffs about Logan, but Isabel . . . she's stuck living in Spain. She don't know no one there apart from her baby's family, but she can't even have her baby with her because she's got to work. If Logan wasn't gonna stay with her, she wants to follow him here. But she can't stay here unless she's married and he's supporting her. I don't know how she carries on believing that.

Maybe her parents will have her back now she's married. But is that what she wants? To never see her husband again? Yeah! The first thing I want to do when I see her is yell, 'Do it, girl! Leave him!' But that's not gonna be that helpful. She's got a right to do what she thinks is best for Vanessa, and if it's moving far away from home and making that tool of a husband fulfil his daddy duties, then, why not? When them fathers try and start from fresh when you're sixteen, it can be too late.

But what if she don't want to believe her man's a tool? What if she's been closing her eyes to the things he's been doing that can hurt her? It's not as if he's keeping it secret. Man, he took my sister to a family party. Even if Silva was in cosplay, no one's gonna mistake her for Filipino, are they? Did he want Kurt to tell Isabel about Silva? Nah! Kurt wants the family together. Man thinks his own brother's a tool.

Man, what would I do if I was Isabel? I'd be vicious. I'd book me and my child on the first plane back to the Philippines and block Logan and anyone who knows him from seeing her again. I might even change our names. My angel's definitely left me for good.

The train stops and the doors open. I'm so full of thoughts, I almost forget to get off until I glance up and see the station name on the tiles. I jump out, just as the doors are closing. I bet Cougar-Woman can't do that.

When I come out of the station, I'm confused. This place looks like it's been invaded by the giant were-worms from *The Battle of the Five Armies*. Random chunks have been taken out the road everywhere and everything's being knocked down and rebuilt, even the station. There's probably a troop of stinking goblins about to burst out through a pipe.

I follow some arrows, then realise that someone's having a joke because I land back at the station. I try again using my phone maps and end up in a new-looking estate. I think they tried to cram as many people on to this little piece of land as they could, even more than where I live. It's all tall blocks, close together. Everyone must be able to see whether their neighbours prefer KP sauce, ketchup or siracha. I walk past a gym and a Tesco's and one of them coffee shops that Mum complains about, trying to work out where I should go.

The blocks are new and clean looking, with balconies that look like them see-through wrappings round Quality Streets.

I check the address that Raych sent me and wonder if she made it up. If that Judgement Day my grandma's always preaching is real, then I sure know what way I'm heading, because thinking about Raych falling off that wall couldn't make me happier. I damn well hope she has to cut the chunks of goo out of her hair. Finally, I see a guy emptying the bins and he tells me where to go. It's the last block, next to a car park and kids' playground. Everything is bright and new and empty. I'm used to the hustle round my estate. How can so many people live here but not be here?

Bernie Grant Heights is fresh and feels like an upgrade. No one in these places has to stare into their neighbours' kitchen windows. The main view is gonna be over the canal and some marshes. The door panel hasn't got no smudges on it. No one's eating barbeque sauce then pushing buttons in this place. I wipe my hand on my jeans and press the numbers for Melissa's flat. Nothing. Then I press them again. Then I remember to press 'Enter'. No one answers. I try different mixes of numbers and there's nothing. Eventually, a Deliveroo guy comes out. He holds the door open for me to go in.

I check the board that tells me what numbers are on what floor and realise that I've got to go to the very top. Of course. Melissa was always gonna get the flat with a view. I stab the lift button and yeah, even that's not on my side. I have to wait. It should give me time to think about what I'm gonna say. Has the lift already delivered up Isabel and Logan to my sister? Am I really too late? When the lift door opens,

I almost expect to see Isabel inside it crying, but it's empty and I step in.

I stopped taking the lift on our block long ago, after Justin had to be rescued. He'd had a load of filming gear that was too heavy to carry up the stairs. Even the fire fighter who got him out was impressed with his equipment. This lift's quick. I bet they've got their own engineer who oils the engines every morning. The smell inside ain't the council heavy-duty pink stuff that kills your nostrils when you step inside.

The lift stops. It don't even shake first. The doors slide open for me.

Melissa's flat is opposite. The front door looks heavy-duty. I stand by the lift and hold my breath.

My phone vibrates. I look down, expecting it's China. It's not. It's DNA. He wants to know where I am. I ignore him and walk towards Melissa's door. My phone rings. It's him.

'Becks? Where are you?'

'I'm all right.' I try not to whisper and make him suspicious.

'I didn't ask that. Where are you?'

'Nowhere. Sorry. I need to go.'

'Don't do anything that's gonna put you in danger, girl. Becks? Becks!'

'I won't.'

'Is that a promise?'

'Yeah. Sure.'

'Becks . . .' I hang up.

And now I'm feeling vexed and a bit like I want him here after all, just next to me while I knock on the door. I want him in the place where Raych should be, or Silva. But Silva's on the other side of the door and I'm the last person she wants to see.

39

I knock. I don't do it gentle, because if I wait too long for an answer, my brain might make me walk away. I keep knocking and almost shout 'fire' because they say that's what you're supposed to do when you want people's attention.

The door flies open. It's her. Isabel. She looks like a painting with a frame round her. She's the same height as me and we're almost nose to nose. I don't know what to say.

'Who is it?' A man's voice. Logan. The damn cause of all this.

'Excuse me,' I say, because it seems rude to just push past her. 'My sister's in there.'

'Your sister?' She don't sound surprised, like most people do. She sounds angry as hell. 'You're here to help her take away my husband?'

'No. I want my sister back. Your husband's yours.'

Yours, but why? Dump him, Isabel!

For a moment she looks like she's not gonna move, but then she lets me pass. I'm in a small hallway, the same size as ours, though ours has to accommodate four people. There aren't no piles of shoes nor camera stands in the way. I notice the intercom phone hanging off its cradle. They wouldn't have heard me buzzing. Isabel walks ahead. I can't hear no

282

more voices. I'm not sure if that's good or bad.

We go into the sitting room. There's a glass coffee table with nothing but a big exercise book and a pen on it and a wall of windows to show off the view. One of them's wide open so the sun's shining through like it's heaven. I can hear the rumble from the building site below and the trains pulling into the station. It's all pale walls and silver lights and grey furniture.

But Silva and Raych have added their own touches. If that box under Silva's bed was a Logan shrine, this is the man's temple. Some print shop guy must be taking all his children, grandparents and cousins on holiday to Hawaii with the money they've made from Silva. Logan is everywhere. Blown-up pictures stuck on the wall, small pictures clipped to string tied between a window catch and the light fitting. Mum used to hang up Christmas cards like that. I'm staring at a damn army of Logans. The biggest picture, right in the middle of the wall, is a copy of that one from the restaurant, him with my sister, looking so happy.

I look from that picture to Silva. She's sitting on a sofa under the window. She's calm, man! Like she's gonna wave her hand and make us all do what she wants.

'Silva? What the hell?'

'Becks?' she says. Then she gives me that Frodo smile. 'It's okay.'

'I don't think so!'

I glance at Isabel. She's standing in the centre of the room, surrounded by her husband's face. Her expression ain't saying nothing. Suddenly, I think she's a whole lot tougher than I'd imagined.

And where is he? The man that no girl can resist. He's sitting in an armchair under one of his own big faces. Even here, when he's in the same room as me, when he's damn well everywhere, I still do not get it! He's the man in the red shirt who gets killed in *Star Trek*. No one should ever remember him. He's got that stunned look on his real face, like he got zapped by Kirk's phaser first.

I kneel in front of Silva. 'Shall we go home?'

She looks really confused. 'Why?'

'Because this is . . .' I don't know what's the right word. '. . . He's nothing. You're worth more.'

Isabel makes a noise, then says, 'Yes, Logan. Let's go.'

He doesn't move. I almost reckon I can hear the gurgle sound as his thoughts slosh around whatever brain slime's inside his head.

I look at him. 'Serious, man, go.'

He nods. 'Yeah.' And stands up.

'I know what I'm worth,' Silva says. 'He's the one who showed me. Your flat isn't home, Becks. I don't fit there. I tried, but I'm like the spare no one needs.'

'You're not . . .' I shut my mouth. I think about what Raych said. Silva's kind and delicate. I know that. But *I've* never told her she's kind. *I* never thought about what her delicate was. After she stopped the K-pop thing with me, I

284

just thought she wanted to go her own way. I didn't think she needed anything. I didn't think she needed me to ask.

'I'll be a better sister,' I say.

'You're great, Becks. It's not you I need.'

I just got Okoye's spear straight through the heart.

She looks up at Logan. He don't meet her eye.

'Not him, though,' I say. 'You don't need him, Silva.'

Silva says nothing. Nor does idiot-boy, Logan. He's loving this love.

'What about your dad? *He* loves you.'

'You can love people without needing them.' Her eyes are still on Logan.

'Let's go!' Isabel pulls at his arm. 'This girl is mad!'

'Don't call my sister mad!' Though Silva's not doing anything to change Isabel's mind.

Isabel won't hear me, anyway. She's got one heavy reality filter on. She only sees what she wants to. She only hears what she wants. Exactly the same thing my sister's doing.

Logan don't want to be pulled anywhere by Isabel. He shakes her off and leans against the far wall. I wish this was like Nebbercracker's place in *Monster House* and it would swallow him right up.

Silva stands and goes over to the window and looks out.

'I've always wanted you to see this view, Becks. I thought you'd feel like a superhero or a wizard in a tower.'

Okay. It's not all Logan. There's been space in her head for me. That's good.

'I'm here now,' I say. 'I missed you, Silva. I was thinking about all these things we used to do and, I don't know, we don't do nothing together now.'

She doesn't look round.

'Remember how I told you about Glinda? You were the only person who knew, the only person I could tell. Even Mum didn't know!'

'There's a reason why wizards and superheroes are only in films. No one comes to rescue you in real life. Well . . .' She turns away from the window. It's like I'm just a hole where a Becks should be because her eyes pass by me without stopping. 'Not in the way you think they will.'

And yeah, she's looking at Logan again.

'Logan! We have to get Vanessa.' Isabel goes over to him and grabs his hand.

Logan smiles. I don't know who that smile is even meant for.

Isabel takes out her phone. 'I'm going to call your brother.'

Logan's hand flips up and knocks the phone from her hand. It thumps to the floor. Lucky that posh carpet kept it whole. Isabel slowly bends down and picks it up. Then she's right in Logan's face, nose to nose. Man, she may have needed to improve her Spanish, but her English cussing is perfect. He shifts away from her, like she's not there.

'See? He wants to be with me,' Silva says.

Isabel wipes her mouth like she's got cuss words still stuck to her lips. 'I am his wife. You are just . . .' She flutters her hand. 'One of the others.'

One of the others? Isabel knows about other girls for sure? And she's sticking with this boy who can't keep his trousers on?

Someone has to stop this. Looks like it's got to be me. I yank a picture off the string. Logan playing football. *Rip*.

And another one, Silva and Logan drinking coffee. *Rip*.

Logan playing football again. *Rip, rip!*

I scrunch them up and drop them on the floor. Silva and Logan by the canal. Logan and Silva, Silva and Logan. Yank, rip, drop.

I reach for another one. Okoye Silva. Man, she got it so right. Does she know how beautiful she looked? The red dress – she took time copying the original! I didn't know she could do stuff like that. Gold shoes, and that harsh wig on top of her head. I barely notice him in his suit next to her, because she's the one who's shining, not him. My warrior sister.

I glance at her over by the window with the light behind her, then back at the photo. I don't tear this one up. I drop it face down on the sofa. Ripped-up paper's scattered all over the carpet, but no one's bothering with me. It's like I'm in the quantum realm with Kurt's van.

'Time to go, Silva!' I say it really loud.

'Yeah.' Logan sort of shakes himself like a dog. 'Time to go.'

Isabel moves towards the door. 'So come on, Logan!'

God. She still wants him. Why? The girl's got choices. Okay, not good ones. She's gonna be busting numbers for Logan's parents in Spain while her baby's in England with her drop-trousers daddy. Or she could be heading back to the Philippines with Vanessa. I don't know what her family's got to say about things there, but the English family won't get much of a look-in with the baby. So what?

They shouldn't have such a tool for a son.

Then I remember Kurt's grin as he showed me the picture on his phone of Vanessa in her Elsa costume.

I don't know nothing about DNA's parents. That's a whole set of grandparents I'm missing. Uncles and aunties too. It's not that I need more family, but I do wish I knew what they looked like. Mum don't even know which country his dad came from. She reckons he's never wanted contact with his birth parents. They were actually married, but his mum put him in care because she didn't want him. Plain and simple. He was the second one, born darker than the rest, and her husband started asking questions. She took her baby son into the doctor's surgery and left him in his basket on the magazine table. You want to hurt someone's life? Man, that's the way to start.

So maybe Isabel's asked herself the question Vanessa's gonna ask when she's older. Who's the other half of me? And because of that, Isabel's staying strong.

'Isabel?' Silva's reaching in her pocket. She takes out an envelope. 'How much money do you need? There's a thousand pounds here. It's enough for you and Vanessa to leave England with some money left over. You could rent—'

Isabel spins round. 'You think money can buy me?'

'I'm trying to help you,' Silva says. 'He doesn't want you. He wants me.'

'No, he doesn't, mad girl!' Isabel holds out her hand and touches her wedding ring. 'If he wanted you, you'd have this. He's ready to change, he told me. For Vanessa's sake.'

'Your ring didn't stop him being with me!' Silva points to the pictures on the wall. Edge to edge, grinning Logans. I should have torn them ones down first. 'You were already married, then.'

Isabel takes one step forward and spits in my sister's face. My stomach jumps. I'm not squeamish. I've cleaned up the mangled mouse Azog left in the middle of the kitchen and even my own mum's sick, when she caught norovirus. But dribble, damn. It's globbed on Silva's cheek. She wipes it away with her shoulder sleeve and I think of it soaking through to her skin. Her body's all tensed up.

I should do something. But . . .

I've seen girls this way at school, all their beef been stewing for a few months and now properly cooked. You know they're ready to go for each other, chins stuck out, hands all squeezed-up fists. And the mouths that've been running full time suddenly shut down. You want to call the teacher because you know there's gonna be blood, but at the same time you want to stay and see the action.

289

I don't want Silva getting hurt, Isabel neither. Especially when the boy who started it is just kicking back enjoying the show.

'Logan!' I shout. 'You need to stop this.'

'Yeah,' he says. 'I do.'

He comes over, looks at Isabel, shakes his head and then goes and stands next to Silva. The. Wasteman. Goes. And cuddles up to my sister.

'I tried, Is,' he says. 'I really tried. You know I didn't want any of that married stuff. I only did it so your folks wouldn't be down on you.'

'But you did it,' Isabel says quietly. 'And you can't get out that easy. Remember, your parents will only let you stay in your flat with Vicky if you look after Vanessa. Where are you going to live with . . .' She waves her hand at Silva. 'On the street?'

'I've saved enough for both of us,' Silva says. 'We can find somewhere together.'

Hell, how much allowance *was* Justin giving her? I suppose she wasn't spending much. She didn't go out or buy many clothes. She was just in her room all the time. *And don't forget, you never knocked on the door to ask her why.*

Isabel puts her hand on Logan's arm. 'Vanessa's your daughter, Logan. Please don't desert her.'

He looks down at her hand. 'I told you I'd be crap at this. I told you not to . . . You didn't have to have her. I can't be a dad.'

290

That was it for me. 'It's too damn late for that! You *are* her dad, even if you did try to make out she was your sister's.'

There's a silence.

Oh.

Isabel's face is travelling through so many moods and none of them look like good places to stay. She jerks her hand away from Logan's arm.

'You said Vanessa was Vicky's?'

Logan's face is moving fast too, but twitching, like all it can manage is short trips. 'Yeah. I did say that. It doesn't matter. She's just a baby. She doesn't care.'

'I do.' Her fist moves quick.

Silva!

A thud.

A crunch.

A scream.

Then so much blood.

40

I saw it coming. Like I said, I've seen girls coiled up and ready to spring. I know what happens next. Savannah acts all proper now, but in Year 8, my girl was a fighter. I'd seen how her shoulders would hunch back like they'd been strapped together. Her arms would bend, like they were scooping up strength, her fists ready. But I know Savannah well. I saw the scaredness behind her eyes, mainly because she knew what her mum was gonna say when the school called. But she would smile it off because she was standing in front of her enemy and couldn't go backwards.

Isabel was coiled, but man, she didn't look scared. She looked like her skin was gonna crack and pure anger shoot out. If I stood in her way, I would have lost my skin too. When she lifted her fist, the sun caught her wedding ring.

I grabbed Silva and we both fell backwards on to the sofa.

Logan was too busy feeling proud of himself to see what was coming his way. Why should I care? What *was* coming was Isabel's wedding ring, top speed at his nose. He staggered back and hit the back of his head against the wall, lost balance and slid to the floor with blood pouring out of his nose. He touched it, looked at it and tried to stand up. His head must have been woozy, because he wobbled back down.

All Isabel's anger must have flashed out with the punch. She was crying now, heavy sobs. Whatever makes you cry that hard ain't never gonna be properly fixed. Silva scrabbles off the sofa and I think she's rushing to comfort Isabel, but she's bending over Logan. Even now!

I say, 'Just leave him!'

'Go and get some tissue, Becks.'

I shake my head. I don't care if he bleeds his brains out. It wouldn't take long with him.

Silva strokes Logan's hair then runs off to the bathroom. Isabel walks towards Logan and crouches down next to him. I think she's gonna punch him. If I was a much better person, I'd try and stop her. I don't and she don't punch him, neither. She just looks up at me.

'She can have him,' Isabel says. She turns to Logan. 'Don't worry. You don't have to be a daddy any more.'

Silva runs in with a wad of toilet paper. The two girls stand there for a second looking at each other. Silva takes the money out of her pocket and offers it to Isabel. Isabel takes it. Good. The girl's gonna need that money to survive. She opens the envelope, pulls out a handful of notes then shoves them back in again. She drops the envelope on to Logan's chest. She don't look back at any of us when she walks out. That heavy front door slams shut.

I want to run after and tell her that she did the right thing.

293

I want to know if I can help her, but things sure ain't finished up here yet.

Silva kneels down by Logan. He snatches the tissue from her hand and presses it to his nose. His other hand grips the cash prize.

And that's it. Silva won.

Won what, though? Logan ain't no trophy. He is the cheap medal. I saw his eyes glint when Silva showed that money. If she ever wants it back, she's gonna have to jemmy those notes out of his cold, dead hands. Respect to Isabel that he still is alive. I don't think I could have held back like she did. Man denied his own baby so he could pick up more girls. Gosh.

And my sister? She's fussing over him like Mary Seacole healing a sick soldier.

And what next, Silva? You think this boy's gonna stick with you? You think 'together' is gonna last as far as the station? You helped him drop his wife and baby. He's probably already got the next girl lined up to take your place!

She deserves the grief.

I take my phone out my pocket. There's fourteen messages from China. I'm gonna save them for later. I look at my sparkly blue nails and my tiny flower gripping my phone and think about what she would say if she was here.

Are you going to be like that football coach, Becks? Having an opinion about Silva when you didn't ask her any questions?

I suppose I always knew the question I should have asked

her. I didn't. I couldn't. I was scared that it would hurt *me* too much.

This is what I should have said to my sister –

Silva, how much do you miss your mum?

41

I leave Silva with Logan's nose and I go out into the hallway. I call DNA. 'I . . . need your help.'

'Are you okay?'

'Yes, I'm fine.'

'You said that before. Are you sure you're not in any danger?'

'I'm sure.' I look through the door at Silva. 'But I just . . . if there's any way you can help me. I really need it.'

'The thing is, it's a bit difficult at the moment. I have an appointment over in south London.'

'You said you'd be my safety net.'

'Yes. I did.'

'And I ain't got nothing but you, right now.'

'No?'

'Please.'

Please!

'Okay, honey, tell me. What do you need?'

I tell him everything, though it's jumping round so much in my head, I don't know if it even makes sense.

'And where's Isabel now?' he asks.

'Vanessa's with Vicky. I think Isabel must be heading back there. She's really upset.'

'Yeah. She must be.'

'Do you think you can find her?'

'Me? I'm not sure it's gonna help much if I pitch up at Vicky's flat. Remember, she might not even let me in.'

Yeah. I remember. I rub my cheek to break up the blush.

'And everyone's gonna be proper upset already,' he says, 'without some stranger adding their bit.'

He's right. 'Raych helped Silva.' *Raych who used to be my right hand girl*. 'Can you go to her place and get her mum? Raych's mum is fierce but if she knows her daughter helped cause this stress, she'll help sort it out.'

'You think she'll open the door to me?'

'I'll send over some pictures from inside Melissa's flat as proof.'

'Okay, Becks. Send over the address too.'

I go back into the sitting room. Silva's still dabbing at the blood. I want Logan to hear this. I want him to know his brother's coming for him.

I find the number and press 'call'. 'Kurt? It's Becks again.'

'Kurt?' Logan's pulling himself up.

I speak quickly. Kurt's gonna drop everything and come right round.

'You called my brother?' Logan's voice sounds squashed and I want to laugh. He's standing in a sun spot. The fallout from his mash-up nose makes him look like he's been baptised in blood. 'You've got no fucking right!'

Silva stands up too. Maybe she's gonna cuss him for

swearing at me. But no, her reality filter is running on warp drive.

'We better hurry then, Logan, before he gets here.'

He looks at her. Honest, if I didn't see it for myself, I swear to God I wouldn't have believed it. The man looks real, proper surprised.

'We?'

'It's just us now,' she says. 'You and me.'

'I . . .' He backs away. 'I think we need to wait until things are sorted out. It's just a bit complicated. You saw. I need to make things right with my family. For Vanessa. My mum's never gonna forgive me if she can't see the kid again. It would be cruel to do that to her.'

Silva's shaking her head. 'It's all sorted out. Isabel's gone. You're free.'

'Yeah. But there's still gonna be issues. I don't want you to deal with that, Silva. It wouldn't be fair on you.'

I step in front of Silva. 'Then maybe give her back her money until you sort your issues, yeah?'

He grips the envelope tighter. 'It's got nothing to do with *you*, has it, Silva?'

He's looking over my shoulder.

She says, 'It's okay, Becks.'

'No. It's not.' I try and grab the envelope from him.

He pushes me. Those are hands that carried heavy bags of shopping up and down stairs and along balconies. Those hands are strong. That push would have started Black

Widow's heart back up after she dropped off the cliff in Vormir. I fly backwards. I feel the breeze behind me from the open window as I topple. I open my mouth, but nothing. There's no point. It would just get lost in the air.

My back hits the sill. I jerk forward. Silva's got hold of me. My sister's got strong hands too.

42

The cat's waiting outside the front door of the block when we arrive back. Becks says Azog usually takes the short cut over downstairs' window boxes, but it's like she's here especially for us. She struts past both of us like she's leading a procession. A procession of what?

'Warrior sisters,' Becks whispers.

I touch her hand. I want to agree, but nothing has been won. Not for me.

I step into the hallway and breathe in. I smell blood, his blood. The sharpness of sweat from a hot day. The meaty fug of cat food. And beneath that are the smells I know, bleach, morning bath bubbles, orange juice, chips. I breathe out again. I bury my nose in my sleeve and breathe in hard. Yes, I can smell his skin there. I want to keep my face buried but both our phones go off at the same time. Dad's calling me. It must be Win talking to Becks. They're booking flights to come straight back. Dad's sorry he hasn't been there for me. I never thought he wasn't, but he says he made things easy for himself. He made himself believe that I wanted to be left alone.

He asks me about Logan. My words feel like bubbles inside a bubble, bouncing together, pushing at the sides to be free. Maybe the skin will stretch thinner and thinner until the words stream out, but for now, they're trapped.

How *can* I describe him?

When I was little, Mum used a pin to dislodge splinters from my finger. She would heat it over the gas jet on the cooker or dip it in boiling water to kill off germs first. Just then I'd want to run away because I never knew what would hurt more, keeping the splinter or letting her take it out. Did I want the sudden sharp pain or a throbbing ache that wouldn't go away? Mum used to tell me that if I kept the splinter, it could go septic and my finger would go green, so I'd let her squeeze back the skin, slide the pin next to the spike of wood or thorn and ease it out. She would kiss it and rub in antiseptic cream and everything would be all right.

I don't know how to remove Logan. After all that's happened, it just feels that he's dug in deeper. I don't think he will ever shift. I don't know if I want him to.

I make myself think about Isabel and the baby. Raych's mum went to Vicky's to help calm everything down. Kurt ended up there too, just in time for Logan to arrive.

We waited at Melissa's flat until her mum made it over. I watched Becks clear up the torn photos and take Logan down from the wall. Logan took so much of me with him that I couldn't move. I thought Raych's mum was going to faint when she saw the blood over the carpet, but she didn't say anything much. She handed me the envelope of money she'd taken back from Logan and brought us home.

301

Becks is stroking my shoulder and asking if I'm all right.

I lied to you, Becks.

I was ready to abandon you, Becks.

I feel guilty, but . . . if there's just the smallest chance that I could be with him now, I would do the same again.

There's a pain behind my eyes. Perhaps that's where the splinter is, sharp and permanent.

Becks goes into the kitchen.

'Tea or smoothie?' she says.

I make myself smile for her. 'Both?'

43

Me and China are in the back of the car and we're holding hands. Justin's vexed because he feels like a cab driver, but I promised him I'm on his side if he gets stopped. He's now my legal stepdad so I have to keep him sweet. And as China reminds me, what he's doing today *is* pretty sweet too.

Not as sweet as her, though, but she kind of knocks that back. She says she's doing this because I want her here and if I want her here, she wants to be here too. She's designed special matching nails for us, in gold and blue and red and black. Wakanda plus Rudbeckia plus Becks. I say that the red and yellow can represent China's flag too, but she says that she's not named after the country. Her mum called her that because she wants her to be handled with care. She is.

Justin finds a parking space and I can feel my heart beating hard. China squeezes my hand tighter and kisses me on the cheek. Justin checks that we've got our passports and we follow him across the tarmac to reception. I read the list of clothes I'm not allowed to wear. I don't support no football team. My belly top's in the wash. I've got a little rip behind the knee of my jeans and I hope that don't cause no problem. I reckon it's the serious chopped-up denim they're banning, the ones that's string and holes.

At each check, my heart's beating harder as my photo's taken, and then my fingerprints, and then I go through the body scanner. Each time, I'm scared I'll be thrown out or that I've got something with me I shouldn't have, even though me and China could probably pass an exam on the list of stuff that's prohibited because we studied it so hard. At last, we join the queue to go into the visits hall.

Justin's with us because we're not old enough to come by ourselves and he didn't want to put Mum through it. Silva said she'll escort us next time, though that depends. Benni says prisoners are passed round the country on pretty short notice. South London's easy enough for us to get to. Suffolk may be tougher. Even so, Silva says she'll still come.

Benni's waiting for us in the visits hall. I thought it was gonna be old school with four chairs nailed to the floor round a table, but this isn't so bad. The chairs are still nailed but they're on a bendy spring, so you can move them and they're in groups.

He's in prison sweats. He'd warned me about his lack of style. He'd also drawn a picture of the visits hall, though the real thing don't look nothing like it. It's better, kind of like my school assembly hall when it's set up for the quiz night. He stands up, smiling, and shakes hands with China and Justin. Me and him don't know quite what to do with each other, so we kiss each other's cheek. I see him look sideways at a prison guard, but it's all right.

There's a snack bar at the end of the hall and Justin takes

our orders and goes and joins the queue.

'Thanks for coming,' Benni says.

'Thank you,' I say. 'For everything.'

I've already said that in my letters to him, but I wanted to say it out loud. I'd tried to say sorry too, but he won't accept it. He says that it wasn't a choice. I was more important than an appointment with his probation officer. That's where he should have been in south London. Instead, he'd been knocking on Raych's mum's door. He couldn't even phone the probation place because he'd spent the last of his credit calling Mum in Japan to tell her what had been going on. He knew he'd be called back to prison and he wanted her to be there for me. Two days later, Mum and Justin were home, cross because I hadn't called them earlier.

Kurt told me that Isabel's gonna go back to the Philippines with Vanessa. He's not happy, but he can understand why. She's promised, though, that him and his parents can visit them any time. Logan's gone back to Spain for a bit to help with the Dirty Vodka. After this, he gets a free holiday in Spain with a fresh pool of trusting girls to fish for. Kurt's sure his parents aren't gonna go easy on Logan, though. Still, I want to think of all the girls he's mucked up meeting together to plot against him. Yeah! Revengers assemble.

At least, there's only three weeks left of Benni's sentence. Then he gets another go trying to make it in the big, bad world outside. I say I'll do anything I can to help him, though I don't know what I can do. He's probably thinking the same,

305

because he don't say nothing. Justin comes back with tea and chocolate, crisps and flapjacks and we lay out our feast. There's so much it can hardly fit on the table.

Justin starts talking about a band he was listening to on the in-flight entertainment coming back from Japan. Benni looks like he's eaten all the chocolate in one go and the sugar's just hit him. His eyes get bright and he leans forward and he's chatting away about how he loves that band and don't know anyone else who does. There's a gig in Camden a few weeks after he gets out. Next minute, Justin's planning to get them both tickets.

China grins at me. I want to put my arm round her but I don't know if I can. This place is buzzing now and I'm not sure how most of them are gonna feel about two girls together. China strokes my cheek and brings her lips close to my ears.

'It's okay, Becks. Everything's gonna be all right.'

'How do you know?'

'Have you forgotten? We're warriors, Becks. You, me and Silva, together we can conquer anything.'

I say, 'Even the choreo to BTS's "Danger"?'

She nods her head. 'Yes. Anything.'

44

I've filled my notebook. I started writing it for Becks. I was going to leave it when Logan and I went away. She will never see it now, of course. My counsellor asked me to keep this journal to help me make sense of my feelings. She wasn't sure if I should use the same notebook, but now we agree that it was a good idea. I can flick back through the pages and finally see how far I've come.

It has taken three months, but today I was ready. Becks and China were there too.

'Okoye, Shuri and Ayo,' Becks said. 'Mess with us and die!'

Becks and China held the rubbish bag open for me.

Rain hit the bag first. I unclipped him from his frame and studied the signature. It was a proper unique signed autograph. If it was a cheap lie, that would have been easier. Logan had tried, really tried. I had to do it, though, tear through the tough card until Rain's face fell apart and his name looked like dark marks. The frame clinked in afterwards.

Becks laughed. 'Good riddance.'

China nudged her. 'Shush.'

The printed-out football article tore easily. The fold lines were already there. I threw them on top of the frame.

Next, the red fabric. That's all that was left over after I cut up the neckline for Okoye's dress. I don't know why I kept it, or that wig. Those aren't happy memories. I should have thrown them down the chute with the rest of the dress and the face paints. Both have become rubbish now.

It was time for the receipts.

The wad was too thick to tear together. I crumpled them and ripped a few and shoved them into the bag, except that first one. You are the most beautiful. That needed special treatment. Becks passed me the scissors from the tidy on my desk and I chopped. It fell in shards like soft glass. They were swept into the bag and muddled with the rest.

The zinc tape. For blisters from shoes I would never wear again. Into the bag, followed by the fairground counter. I heard it bounce off the side of Rain's frame.

Becks gave me back the medal. She said Kurt was going to clear out the locker. I wonder what happened to my tie. It was the twin to the medal. If one's thrown away, the other should be too. I wanted to hold the medal to my nose to see if there was some imprint of him in the ribbon. I didn't.

I started to tie the top of the rubbish bag into a knot.

'Just a moment,' Becks said.

She and China left me.

'Got to set up the video,' China called from the sitting room.

It's a BTS choreo. 'Danger'. Becks has been trying to get me to have a go for weeks, but today we're doing it. She returned a minute later with a cloth bag.

'These are yours too,' she said.

I opened it and looked inside. My golden shoes from the party. I felt a little stab of hurt. It radiated out, then faded. The counsellor says that I may always be tender and always feel grief. I may not heal fully, but at least I know that I can heal at all. I took them out and held them up. I was about to drop them into the rubbish bag.

'No you don't,' Becks said. 'I can drop them at the Crisis shop.'

Under the shoes, there was a photograph. It was me and Logan at the restaurant. A waiter had taken it. We're looking at each other and smiling.

'I wasn't sure if I should give it to you,' Becks said. 'But it's not mine to keep. When I look at it, I sort of understand. He really made you happy, didn't he?'

I nodded. 'I went back to the restaurant but it's boarded up. They're going to knock it down and turn it into flats.'

I wanted to be brave and drop the picture into the rubbish. I wanted to do it with sass and a smile, just for Becks's sake. I couldn't. I put it down next to me. There was one more thing in the bag.

I started to say, 'This isn't mine . . .'

I took it out and held it to my face. No, that blue sweatshirt wasn't mine, but as I stretched it out in front of me, my head filled with *him*. I pressed my face deeper into the folds. There were stories rippling through those threads. Deodorant? Aftershave? Faint traces of showers and parties. Underneath that, his body, his skin and sweat and the dampness of the boxing club. And then, me. Orange, and mango and rosemary sunk into the fibres of the red dress from the oils I burn in my diffuser, printed on to the inside of the sweatshirt when I pulled it on. Waxy face paint from the wobbly tattoos on my head. Then other perfumes, other soaps. Smells that weren't mine, weren't his. They were the history of all the girls who had kept themselves warm with this sweatshirt before me.

I drop it on to the carpet. I'm crying and Becks is next to me. Her arms are around me, and the aching splinter between my eyes slowly starts to shift.

And that's it. Well, that's it for now. There's only one thing left for me to do. Join Becks and China, and dance.

Acknowledgements

My beautiful J, 사랑해. You answer questions way beyond the duty of any daughter from queer nail art to K-Pop suicides.

Cheers, little bruv Lee, for lock expertise and to Fen Coles for being my reader and reminding me about Janelle.

Thank you, Caroline Sheldon, my agent, for patience, encouragement, food and wine – and the back up team, Felicity, Georgia and Jade.

Michelle Brackenborough, at Hachette, you always spark joy with your original, beautiful and wonderfully detailed cover designs. I'm so lucky. And gratitude to the editors – on lead vocals, Polly Lyall-Grant with back up from Sophie Wilson, Rachel Boden and Ruth Girmatsion.

I would not dare ignore my brutally honest but eternally supportive Free Lunchers – Nathalie Abi-Ezzi, Katherine Davey, Jenny Downham, Anna Owen and Elly Shepherd.

Savita Kalhan and Muhammad Khan, thank you for – well – you know!

Librarians, teachers and bloggers – without you my books would sit sadly on shelves. (And a special callout to Ella, in Barnet, Charlie Morris and Laura and Faith.)

And the certainly incomplete roll call of friends who are

the framework for my life, but also let me talk at them when I haven't seen anyone for days. Nathalie Batchelor, Sarah Broadley, Sheryl Burton, Fen Coles, Jane Elson, Jo De Guia, Lucy Donohoe, Kathy Evans, Jo Franklin, Flo Headlam, Jo Heygate, Catherine Johnson, Miranda Macaulay, Pauline Madden, Kerry Mason, Odina Nzegwu, Mel Ramdarshan Bold, Emma Roberts, Sue Wallman . . .

And V for Singularity, which has inspired some of my most memorable kitchen dancing. Apparently.